QUEENS OF THE FAE BOOK EIGHT

Fae's Refuge

Melissa A. Craven

M. Lynn

Edited by Caitlin Haines

MYRKUR KINGDOM
NORTHERN VATLANDS
FARGELSI KINGDOM
LOCH VILLANDI
SOUTHERN VATLANDS
ELDUR KIN
DRAGUR FOREST
VINDUR CITY
ELDUR I
LOCH LANGT

NORTH EASTERN KATELANDS
KINGDOM
HUNTING LODGE
VALE OF STORMS
FIRE PLAINS
ELDFAL
LENYA
GRIMA KINGDOM
MINES
THE BURNING SEA
VONDUR KINGDOM
R CITY
THE ROCKY SEAS OF LENYA
THE GRIMA SHOALS

CHAPTER ONE
SIOBHAN

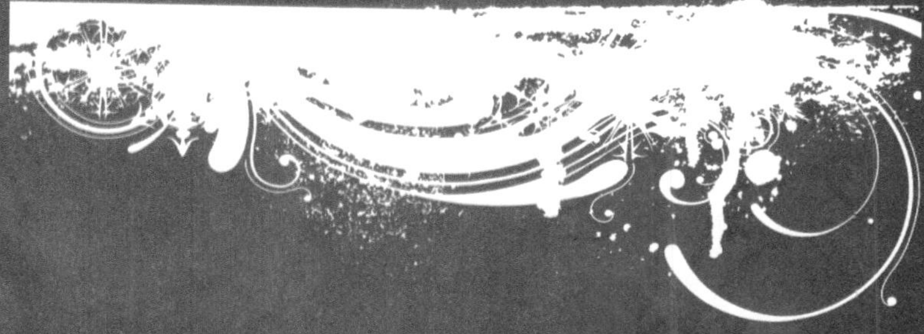

She couldn't stop moving.

Siobhan McGowan had never been in the human realm before. Not until a few weeks ago, when she entered a portal unwillingly. Princess Tierney hadn't meant to do it, she was certain of that. They'd known each other since they were little girls running around the palace together. Her friend would never intentionally hurt anyone.

But her magic was a different matter. The princess was powerful and sometimes she didn't know her own strength.

Exhaustion warred with her need to get home as she let herself take a brief break on the grassy hilltop of the Irish countryside. That was what a human had told her this place was called. Ireland. It was beautiful, with lush rolling hills, grazing sheep, and steep cliffs that dropped off into turbulent seas. Yet, there was also a starkness to the landscape, one that soothed her. It reminded Siobhan of her home among the rocky mountains of Iskalt.

In her weary state, she wasn't sure she could have handled brilliant blue skies or a blazing sun. The gray day suited her.

She lay back in the grass, wishing she could close her eyes for just a moment, but now was not the time. She'd come so far, and she was almost there. She could rest when she was home. After she'd delivered her message to the king and queen.

In the human lands, there was only one place to enter the fae realm without portal magic.

The rift.

That was what the people of Myrkur called the delicate tear in the veil between their lands and the human realm. Ten years ago, during the war for the prison realm, the Dark Fae king tried to conquer the human world, spilling the darkness of Myrkur through the rift. Now, all that remained to remind them of that time was something Siobhan wasn't even sure she could find.

But she wouldn't give up. She had to get home, had to find out what happened to Tierney, Gulliver, and Veren.

With a deep sigh, she heaved her tired limbs up to continue toward the clearing where the invisible fae village of Aghadoon once stood. At least, that was what she'd heard in the years since the war. She hadn't known that was where she was headed at first. She only knew she could sense the tear, like her home was calling to her. Not with words. She hadn't gone completely insane. But the air buzzed with an energy that pulled at her. It dared her to search the queen's old farmhouse until she found a collection of what humans used for money. It then tugged her across the sea, using all modes of human transportation. At first, it was overwhelming. Then, exhilarating.

She'd always had a secret interest in all things human. She'd even studied the basics of the human world with their flying contraptions and fast ships, but it was so different than she'd expected.

Siobhan would pay Queen Brea back if she ever managed to return to Iskalt. For all she knew, she was wandering into the middle of an unfamiliar land with no hope of finding the passage between the worlds, one that wasn't supposed to be visible on this side. But the pull was stronger here. She could feel it pulsing in her veins, calling her home. She didn't want to think about what would happen if she couldn't find it.

Every night, she replayed what happened in the portal in her mind. One moment, she'd gripped Tierney so tightly she swore they'd never part, and the next, an unseen power slammed into Siobhan's chest, forcing her back out of the portal.

The impact when she'd landed in front of the farmhouse had stolen her breath, but it took her a few moments to realize something had gone very wrong, that she wasn't home in Iskalt.

And that she was alone.

She only hoped she would find Tierney the moment she arrived in Iskalt and everything would be all right again. It was what kept her going.

"My father will be happy with these new revelations," she mumbled to herself, thinking of how much he hoped she and Tierney would find their way to each other. Talking to herself was a new hobby. It gave her something to hear other than the wind in her ears.

It wasn't until the reality of her situation sank in that she realized she truly had hoped the princess would choose her, that they could be happy together. Tierney O'Shea was special, at least Siobhan thought so. The princess cared about other fae, and she showed it in her every action. There was no one braver

… or more reckless. If the king truly forced her to marry an Iskaltian noble, Siobhan vowed she would make herself the best candidate for her hand.

"Who are you kidding, Siobhan?" she muttered as she trudged up the next hillside. She would prove no match for the likes of Veren Rhatigan, with his courtly charm and handsome face. Not when she was so utterly … rough around the edges. That was what most thought of her. She'd been raised to be her father's heir. The keeper of the mountain boundary between Iskalt and the Northern Vatlands—a wild country few could navigate. She would be the Marchioness of Belmore Keep one day. A noble title, but she would always be more comfortable in the saddle than as a lady, curtsying at the right times and saying all the right things. Most fae her age never tried to see past her well-worn leathers or the sword she was rarely without. She might be more warrior than lady, but she was still a prominent member of the noble class, and that alone made her suitable for their future queen's hand in marriage.

"I'll just have to try harder," she vowed. "One more hill." She clenched her fists as she gave herself a pep talk. Her legs ached, and a sheen of sweat and grime coated her normally matte brown skin.

Thankful for the strange human clothes instead of the dress she'd worn to Tierney's ball, she pushed through the burn. Her trousers were made from some kind of black fabric that stretched and moved with each step, and the large shirt hung off one shoulder and let air move underneath it to cool her.

Loose dark curls escaped her bun, sticking to the back of her neck, and she pushed them off to get some relief.

And then, she reached it—the top of the hill, where she could see over the land to the sea. A vast plain stretched across the valley. The rift was close, she could feel her homeland, like an old friend calling to her. She wasn't sure what she'd expected to see, but it certainly wasn't this.

It wasn't nothing.

Yet, there was no sign of the always moving village that once inhabited these lands, no sign in the sky directing her where she needed to go.

It was a blank canvas of green grass, waiting to be filled with color and hope. But she had no more hope to give.

Siobhan dropped to the ground, exhaustion finally winning out. The impact reverberated up her spine. She'd been so sure it was here, that this was the way home. She could still feel it tingling under her skin, that overwhelming sensation that home was just within reach. But maybe she'd put too much hope into a feeling when she had too little to go on.

If she'd been smart, she would have stayed at the farmhouse and waited for someone to come find her. They would have eventually. But Queen Brea was said to only visit her old home once or twice a year—that the people knew of. She'd tried to be patient, but after a few days the inactivity drove her mad. Siobhan needed to know if Tierney and Gulliver were okay. Veren too, she supposed.

She curled her legs up, hugging her knees to her chest. Tears fell from her eyes, tracking through the sweat and dirt on her face. "Tierney, please be okay."

Anger swept through her. Anger at this realm, at the magic that got her here, at the stupid rift between worlds that had given her so much hope. How had she thought she could find an invisible tear in the sky? Something no one in the human realm was supposed to be able to spot.

Her heart ached, but it was the familiar ache that led her here, the one she'd taken as a lead rope guiding her to where she needed to be.

"No. I'm done listening to invisible forces." Done listening to magic.

The ache grew, squeezing her heart until she gasped and clutched her chest. She bent over, trying to breathe. Pain seared through her chest, and she got to her knees. "Please." Whatever it was had to stop. It had to let her go.

Lifting her eyes to the horizon, she noticed the sky growing dimmer. The clouds blocked out the brilliant colors she'd seen so many times on her journey, but there was no mistaking the setting sun. Was the moon already above her, hidden by the clouds?

A drop of rain hit her cheek, and the rope around her heart pulled tighter. A scream ripped from her lips. It was like her magic was trying to shred her from the inside out, drag her heart right through her chest.

Siobhan managed to get to her feet. She started down the hill, her steps faltering as she stumbled and righted herself. The pain eased up the slightest bit, and she picked up the pace.

More rain broke free of the clouds, washing the human realm from her skin, cleansing her of everything these last weeks had put her through. Physical and emotional.

By the time she made it to the clearing, the pain was back to a dull ache and her clothes were drenched.

Her eyes darted around the open space, looking for anything, everything. Yet, it was empty, save for the rocks and sparse grass underneath her feet, the drops of water hitting her cheeks. An eerie silence surrounded her, only punctuated by the rain pounding into the ground.

"Why am I here if this won't get me home?" she screamed, knowing there was no one there to answer her.

She snatched a rock from the ground, wishing she had something to break. Instead, she threw it as hard as she could.

As it arced through the sky, she realized it hadn't made her feel any better.

She pivoted so she could look for shelter for the night and figure out what was next in the morning. Then, she stopped and looked back to where the rock she'd thrown should have hit the ground. It wasn't there.

Her legs too tired to run anymore, she stumbled toward where it had vanished, and that was when she noticed it. There was a space in the air the rain couldn't pass through. Instead, it looked as if someone held a bucket, collecting it before it could hit the ground.

"The rift," she whispered, inching closer.

Fear gripped her, and she hesitated, her heart kicking into high gear. It pounded so fast it drowned out the rain, drowned out the human world entirely. What if the rift sent her to some other unknown place? Like Tierney's magic, what if, somehow, it rejected her, spitting her back out?

What then?

Closing her eyes, she tilted her face to the rain as her magic grew stronger inside her. Full night would be upon her in no time, she could feel it. She asked herself what Tierney would do, but she knew the answer without thinking. She'd jump in with both feet, fear never even crossing her mind.

But Siobhan was not Tierney O'Shea.

She thought of her father, alone without her there at the too-large Bellmore Keep. He was most likely beside himself with worry. "I'm coming home, Father," she whispered, opening her eyes. She was a warrior. She knew what it meant to be brave in the face of danger.

With a deep breath, she reached a hand out, following the rain in its descent into the void. Her fingers disappeared from view, and the first thing she felt was warmth. It enveloped her hand, beckoning her closer, urging her to let herself disappear into another world.

Taking a step, she let more of her arm fade into the rift. The smell hit her, and she smiled. There was something distinctly sweet about the fae realm—a scent she couldn't attribute to anything else. The scent of magic, as comforting as freshly baked bread, as sweet as Gelsi berry pie, though she wouldn't dare eat that.

A smile curved her lips, and she took one last step. The drumming of the rain disappeared, and sunlight nearly blinded her as she fell the rest of the way, thudding into the hard earth between two giant boulders.

The ache in her heart disappeared completely, but now her back screamed in agony. The mountains of Myrkur did not soften the impact like the thick grass at the farmhouse or even the packed snow of Iskalt.

Rolling onto her side, she groaned.

But she'd made it. She knew it for certain the moment she was through. Maybe not home in Iskalt, but this was her world.

Water hit her face, and she realized the rain was still falling through the rift. She shifted out of the way, basking in the warmth of the sun. A shiver raced up her spine as the chill from her drenched clothes sank in. But they would dry, and everything would be okay.

A laugh bubbled out of her. And then another, until she couldn't stop. She wanted to kiss the ground, to dance in honor of the magic that showed her the way. But she would do neither of those things. Despite her current appearance, in this world, Siobhan was of noble birth.

So, she picked herself up, rubbing a sore spot on her back before straightening her shoulders. She just had to find someone in Myrkur who could help her, who'd sell her a horse in return for a great reward from her father.

The distinct flap of a Dark Fae's wings rent the air. Maybe she wouldn't have to search one out.

Siobhan looked to the skies, finally spotting the brilliant color of the fae's wings highlighted by the sun. She had tattoos stretching across dark skin and leather armor.

Siobhan had seen her before. Riona. Tierney's aunt. She heaved a sigh of relief.

Before she could call out to her, a line of guards rushed into the mountain gap, their heavy armor clanging together.

Griffin O'Shea marched forward and lifted his visor, revealing pale skin, a shock of auburn hair, and intense violet eyes, magic sparking in their depths.

Something wasn't right here.

She opened her mouth to speak, but she didn't get the chance.

Riona landed next to her husband, her wings folding in.

"As guardians of the rift, we do not allow passage here from the human realm." No recognition showed in his eyes, but why would it? She'd never actually met the fabled warrior. Griffin turned to his soldiers. "Arrest her."

CHAPTER TWO
TIERNEY

It was odd to see snow-capped mountains outside her bedroom window after so much time among the sweltering temperatures of Vondur. The Grima "palace" sat among the mountains near the rocky coast, far enough from the fire plains that they experienced the seasons.

The sight of snow never failed to send a pang of longing through Tierney O'Shea. Part of her wanted to hike up to the mountaintops just to feel something familiar, but Lord Cormac Agnew—the man who would have everyone believe he was regent over Queen Bronagh—assured her she would die before she ever reached the peaks of those mountains. Between the sheer altitude and freezing temperatures, the heights of Grima were a trial.

Tierney still struggled to think of this place as a palace. It was lovely, and comfortable in the extreme, but it reminded her of the hunting lodge her family owned in the farthest reaches of Iskalt. Grand enough, certainly, but it was an odd sort of kingdom here in Grima, where rolling green hills and valleys spanned jagged coastlines and rocky seas few ships could navigate stretched as far as the eye could see. The mountainous terrain to the north faded back into the fire plains and were nearly impassable, from what she'd learned.

The same fire plains that trapped Tierney from returning home from Vondur, trapped her here in Grima as well, and it seemed the mountains and treacherous seas were equally determined to keep her from finding safe passage home.

"Stop sighing, Tia." Gulliver brought her a cup of the rich, hot beverage that reminded her of hot chocolate from the human realm. Nowhere else in all the fae realms had she ever experienced anything as wonderful as chocolate. Her mother would be all too eager to trade powerful crystals for cartloads of this stuff.

"I miss home." Tierney moved to sit on the plush settee at the center of the common room she shared with Gulliver. A cheery fire burned in the massive fireplace, and stuffed heads of every kind of antlered creature in all of Grima hung on the walls, staring down at her in judgment.

"Me too, but I could get used to that view and this sweet milky heaven in a cup." He sipped his chocoah. "And the beds, Tia. The beds here are like sleeping on little fluffy clouds."

Tierney smiled. It was wonderful to be back with her best friend in a place of relative safety. But they were wasting time waiting for the queen to return from her survey of the army at the border between Grima and Vondur.

She still couldn't believe how welcoming the people of Grima were the moment she and Gulliver came to the palace asking to see Veren. Lord Cormac knew all about how they'd arrived in Lenya through the portal by mistake. He threw the doors open wide and welcomed them inside to await the queen's return.

It seemed Veren had ingratiated himself to the Grima general on the battlefield, and then later to the queen herself. Tierney had no doubt his charm had saved his life, though she knew firsthand how false that charm could be.

"I could love it here." Tierney sipped her chocoah, dipping a scone into the sweetness at the bottom. "If I could go home whenever I wanted, Grima would be the best vacation spot in all the fae kingdoms."

"And Vondur ranks dead last on that list." Gulliver flopped down beside her, putting his feet up on a fluffy footstool.

"We should probably clean up." Tierney set her empty cup aside. Their common room looked like a battle had come through. Discarded clothes and books lay everywhere.

"It's weird they don't have the usual servants here." Gulliver sighed. "That's the best part about being a guest in a palace; I don't have to see to my own laundry."

"We don't have to do our laundry now, Gullie." Tierney shook her head at her lazy friend. "We just have to send it down for laundering with the morning maids."

"This palace has weird rules," he grumbled, snatching up the suit coat he'd discarded after last night's formal dinner with the queen's uncle.

"It's not weird; it's just different." She folded up her stained overcoat, where she'd spilled wine on it at a luncheon picnic a few days prior. "I kind of like it." There were servants but none dedicated to a single royal or noble—not even the queen herself. Instead, there were maids, valets, pages, and any number of servant roles Tierney was accustomed to, but they served everyone in their small corners of the palace. The lady's maid who helped Tierney dress for formal functions also attended three other ladies staying in guest rooms along this corridor. It was efficient and left Tierney and Gulliver to care for themselves in most things they could easily manage on their own.

"Leave your dirty clothes in the closet at the front door, and the scullery maids will see to it in the morning." Tierney returned to her room to pick up a few more articles of clothing that needed washing.

They had been treated well upon their arrival at the Grima palace. Everything they could need to live as nobles had been provided. But Tierney liked how independent it felt to see to her own household chores. She drew her bath, washed and dried her hair, and even swept the floors herself. No one fussed over her or treated her like a helpless princess.

She liked the system here so much that if she ever made it home, she just might talk her father into making a similar arrangement in Iskalt.

"What do we do with books we've finished?" Gulliver peeked his head into her room, a stack of books in his hands. "Do I have to take them back to the library? Because I'm not sure I could find it again without a map." The lodge was a rambling structure, but it was an odd one. Where the palace in Iskalt was made up of many floors with grand staircases and towers, the Grima palace was all one level with vast rooms and hallways scattered across the rocky terrain. Endless corridors lined with windows overlooking cliffs, waterfalls, and cool mountain lakes provided some of the most beautiful scenery Tierney had ever seen. But it was easy to get lost without an escort.

"Leave the books in the hall by the door, and the page boy will return them for you." Tierney stripped the sheets off her bed and set them aside for the maids to take to the laundress.

She shook out a fresh set and went about making her bed. She found the task a fun novelty.

"You're such a weirdo, Tia."

"How very human of you." She glared at him. "Uncle Myles teach you that one?"

"Of course. He's where I get all the best human-isms." Gulliver stuffed half a pastry in his mouth.

An urgent knock sounded at the door to their suite. "Princess Tierney?"

The familiar voice nearly brought tears to her eyes.

"Veren?" She dropped her sheets and ran back to the common room at the sound of his Iskalt brogue.

"Your Highness." Veren crossed the room, taking a knee before her. "It is good to see you, though I wish it were under better circumstances. Lord Cormac has just told us of your arrival. You've been trapped in Vondur all this time?"

"I think you got the better deal." Gulliver clapped him on the back. "But we're glad to see you are well and not lost in a portal somewhere."

Tierney pulled Veren up from his formal bow and threw her arms around him. In the past, they had a complicated relationship, going from kind of liking each other to severe disdain, but she was overjoyed to see him now. "I'm so happy you're safe." She hugged him tightly, pulling back to look at him. "What have you heard of Siobhan? Is she here with you?"

"No. When I came through the portal, I was alone. I lost sight of you and Gulliver, as well as Siobhan, before I landed right in the center of a raging battle. There was no time to look for you. I barely managed to keep my head on my shoulders before I fell in with General Haggerty of the Grima forces."

"Hello?" A soft voice called their attention away from their bittersweet reunion. A small, young woman entered the room dressed in fine silks befitting the royal court here in Grima.

Tierney took her for another noblewoman at first, but she recognized the young man behind her. Prince Donal of Grima. The tiny girl must be the new queen.

"Your Majesty, please come meet my friends." Veren beamed at the unassuming queen.

The girl approached Tierney and took her hands. "It's a pleasure to meet a princess of another realm. An heir, no less. It's an oddity in Lenya for a woman to inherit the throne, yet here we are." Her clear blue eyes filled with sadness, and Tierney could imagine she was thinking of the mother and sister she had lost so recently. This morose girl had never expected to be a queen, yet she'd taken on the responsibility far beyond her years. She couldn't be more than eighteen years old.

"It's lovely to meet you, Bronagh." Tierney gave a nod to acknowledge the queen's higher ranking, but as Tierney was a Royal Highness herself, she didn't owe the young queen more than that.

Prince Donal joined them. "We welcome you to Grima. You may take refuge here for as long as you would like to stay."

The young royals struck Tierney as old souls, far more mature than they should have been at such an age. They reminded her of her younger brothers and sisters.

"I would like to hear of your trials in Vondur if you would be willing to share your experiences there." Bronagh gripped Tierney's hand. "I apologize on behalf of all of Lenya for your rough treatment at the hands of their barbarian king. I fear their newest king will be worse than his predecessor."

"Thank you." Tierney winced at the mention of Keir, but she accepted the queen's kindness.

"I must leave you for now, but please join us tonight for dinner. An informal affair. Just my brother and me and our uncle. We are eager to help you find your way home, though I remain uncertain how helpful we will be."

"Your kindness is much appreciated, Bronagh." Tierney followed the royals to the door. "We look forward to this evening and a chance to bring Grima and Iskalt together as loyal friends."

Tia closed the door behind the queen and her brother. She wasn't certain which way the wind would blow here in Grima, but it had to be better than Vondur.

CHAPTER THREE
TIERNEY

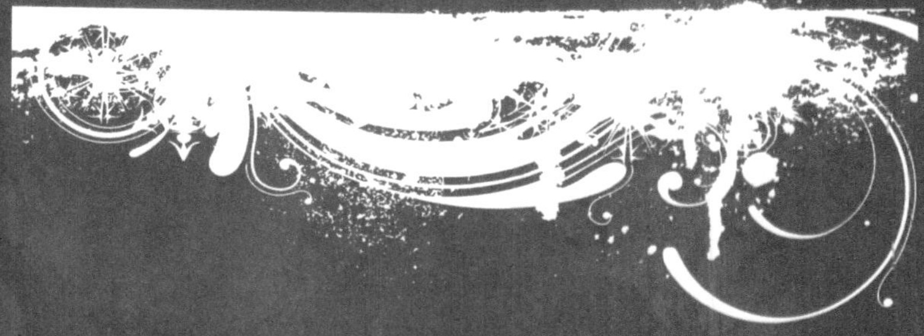

The moment they were alone, Veren turned to Tierney, panic in his eyes. "Do not tell Donal you fought Grima during the siege." He walked past her and threw himself on the plush settee, all the formal tones and niceties upon first seeing her gone.

"Yes." Tierney crossed her arms. "That was my first thought. I'd just go to the prince and tell him how many of his men I killed." She rolled her eyes. "Glad we're past that strange, you-being-nice-to-me thing."

"I'm always nice, Princess." He winked.

A snort sounded from behind her. "Oh, don't mind me," Gulliver said. "I'm sure you're relieved I'm alive as well, great and noble Veren. No need to say it."

Tierney bit back a smile. Gulliver had always hated Veren. He was even more protective of her than she was of herself. But Veren hardly knew Gullie, and he certainly didn't know the depths of the hatred born out of loyalty.

"Who are you again?" Veren asked. "Oh, right. The Dark Fae." The way he said it set Tierney's nerves on edge.

"I'm so glad we came all the way across this foreign kingdom to find you." She smiled sweetly, sarcasm dripping from every word.

Veren grinned, his brilliant white teeth flashing. "I've got to say, it was quite the shock to catch sight of you during the battle. The Grima soldiers have told me how Vondur views their women. Then again, maybe the Vondurians were just trying to get you killed."

Gulliver lowered himself to the settee, purposefully bumping Veren. Veren shoved him out of the way.

This wasn't going to help anyone. With a sigh, Tierney walked into the sitting area and faced them. "Okay, boys, this isn't going to get us anywhere. We need to make a plan."

"A plan?" Veren asked.

"To get home."

"Ah, yes, home. The place where both your parents and my own are bent on making their children marry."

Staring down at him, she narrowed her eyes. "I thought you *wanted* to marry me."

A harsh laugh burst out of him. "For my family, maybe. But do you really think I wanted to live the rest of my days with a wife who hates me?"

"I don't hate you. I ..." Her shoulders dropped. "Okay, maybe I did. But it was your fault."

"Here we go."

"I'm serious. You led me on just so you could be seen with the princess."

His brow creased, but he paused before responding. "I didn't have a choice."

She saw it then, the truth in his eyes. None of them had ever had a choice. His family played with his life just as her father had with hers. Making a quick decision she hoped she wouldn't regret, she stuck a hand out. "Truce?"

He didn't take it.

"Come on, Rhatigan. We're stuck here in this kingdom, separated from our own by deadly fire plains and raging seas. Siobhan is still missing. You, me, Gullie ... all we have is each other. Take my stupid hand."

One corner of his lips twitched before he reached out and slid his fingers into hers. "Fine, truce."

"Good." She pulled her arm back quickly and sat in the chair across from the two boys. A wooden table rested between them. Unlike the palace of Vondur, Grima's luxury wasn't built on crystals that had long ago lost their magic. It made her wonder what was different here. She hadn't seen anyone yet who even wore a totem.

"Okay." Gullie leaned forward, resting his elbows on his knees. "So, how do we get home?"

Veren looked from one to the other as if trying to make some decision. Tierney could practically see the wheels turning in his head. After what felt like an eternity, he stood. "Come with me."

Tierney ran to catch up with him as he pulled open the door. "Where are we going?"

"Do you have to know everything all the time?"

"Yes."

He pushed out a breath in exasperation. "The docks."

"Wait, this place has docks?" Tierney would never stop being amazed at the expansiveness of the Grima palace.

"Of course it does, we're on the sea."

She didn't miss the possessive "we're," but she ignored it. If Veren wanted to pretend he was one of these fae, she wouldn't stop him. "Iskalt is on the sea, and we don't have docks. It's more like one dock. And it's hidden so smugglers can pretend my father doesn't know what they're bringing into his kingdom."

"The king knows and doesn't stop them?" Gulliver looked sideways at her, his eyes wide.

"No. It's funny. Not all trade reaches the furthest villages in Iskalt, but smugglers have ways normal traders don't. So, he thinks it's good for the people to—"

"Will you two shut up?" Veren shook his head. "No one cares about Iskalt trade."

Tierney leaned closer to Gulliver and dropped her voice. "He's just salty because it cuts into his father's profits."

"Salty?" Gulliver asked.

"Yeah, isn't that a great word? Mom told me it means mad or—"

"Obnoxious," Veren cut in.

"No, actually, I was going to say vexed."

"I mean you're obnoxious."

She'd been called worse. With a shrug, she started whistling, the sound echoing off the stone walls.

Veren practically growled, but she didn't stop.

Gulliver joined her, the two whistling one of Iskalt's more famed drinking songs, one a princess like her had no business knowing. She could picture her dad's flushed cheeks now. And if she sang the bawdy words ... a giggle escaped her.

Veren, leading them through a series of halls where servants greeted him by name, gave her a skeptical look. "Has she gone mad?" he asked Gulliver.

Gulliver grinned. "Oh, dear Veren, Tierney has always been mad."

That brought another laugh out of her before she kept on whistling. It felt good to be with Gulliver, even Veren, to be free. There were no guards keeping tabs on her, no sneaking through tunnels. She got to go outside and feel the sun on her face. And a part of her believed maybe they could even find a way home.

Yet, she hadn't stopped thinking about the fae she left behind in Vondur. Was Keir wilting under the weight of the crown? Had Eavha found her voice? Would Declan recover from his king almost executing him?

Not to mention that Keir had to kill his own father.

She hadn't been able to get out of there fast enough when she was free, and she'd hardly said proper goodbyes, but something told her she'd see them all again.

Tierney hadn't been paying attention to the long and winding walk. Before she knew it, Veren led her through two heavy iron doors onto a wide landing at the top of a cliff. "I thought we were going to the docks."

He shot a grin back over his shoulder. "We are. They're down there." He pointed to the edge of the cliff. "Hope you're not scared of heights, Princess."

Gulliver gripped her hand, his fingers squeezing tight. She wasn't scared of heights. Her best friend, on the other hand ...

There was a steep wooden staircase built right into the face of the cliff, stretching far down below to where she presumed the docks were. Footsteps sounded, coming up the steps, and she slid out of the way to let a broad-shouldered man carrying a pile of broken wood pass.

"Morning, Lord Rhatigan." He nodded.

"Chasten." Veren returned the gesture. "How does our project proceed?"

"Very well. We should be ready within the month."

"Excellent. Tell Ania I wish her well in the last weeks of her pregnancy."

The man brightened. "I will. Thank you, my Lord." He hefted his load higher and continued down a path that skirted the palace, disappearing into a valley of boulders.

"Who are you and what have you done with the Veren we know and loathe?" Tierney had never known him to care about anyone but himself.

He pushed a hand through his hair and gave her one last look before beginning his descent.

Tierney had no choice but to follow him. Gullie came cautiously behind. The steps were slick, and they had to take each one slowly.

Tierney chanced a glance back at Gulliver to find his face had paled and he clutched the rock face.

None of them spoke until they made it safely to the bottom, where a series of docks spread out before them. Tierney had never seen anything like it. Wooden walkways stretched out over the water to bobbing fishing vessels, their sails billowing in the wind as they bobbed.

The creak of lines pulling tight, of wooden hulls scraping against the docks, filled the salt-laden air. Tierney lifted her eyes to the brilliant sun above. She inhaled deeply, drawing in the fresh, chilly air. This was what peace felt like.

The dark seas were calm save for the gentle rolling waves, much different from the stormy seas separating Iskalt from Eldur.

"I know," Veren said. "The ocean here is so different from the frozen seas along our shores."

For a moment, they really were in this together. "What have you become here, Veren?" she asked, her voice soft. It was more curiosity than anything that had her wanting, needing, to know.

He studied her for a moment. "When the Grima found me as they were retreating from battle, they were just desperate for soldiers. They'd lost a lot of men and women fighting the Vondurians. They asked few questions at first, but then the prince ..." He shook his head and turned to walk across the crisscrossing walkways.

"The prince what?" She gripped his arm.

"I saved his life. When we were running from battle. After that, he felt indebted to me. It earned me the respect of my fellow soldiers. Many of these servants, shipbuilders, fought side by side with me. Here in Grima, even those not in the army fight for their kingdom. When you face death with others, it brings you rather close."

Tierney had so many questions, but something caught her eye—a ship she didn't see until a fishing vessel pushed away from the docks to sail out. Sitting at the far end was the most beautiful boat she'd ever set eyes on.

Her feet took her that way without direction. When she reached it, her eyes skated up the smooth, dark hull, painted with the golden Grima crest. This was no mere fishing trolley.

Veren stepped up beside her. "This is what I wanted to show you. It's my project."

Tierney didn't take her eyes off it. "Why are you building a ship?"

"He wants to sail home across the sea." Gulliver's voice was low, quiet. "Don't you?"

Veren swallowed. "Think about it. There is no way across the fire plains. They are more dangerous than any of the other vatlands. The only way to Iskalt is around them."

But he didn't know. He couldn't. If he did, he'd certainly never imagine such a journey.

Tearing her eyes from the ship, she turned and shook her head. "It can't be done." There was no use hoping for the impossible. She started back toward the stairs she never wanted to traverse again.

Veren ran after her. "You can't just come here and tear down what I've been working on since I arrived and then leave with no explanation."

"You need to show him the map." Gulliver huffed, trying to keep up with their fast pace.

He was right.

"What map?" Veren asked.

Tierney climbed the stairs with slightly less caution than she'd descended them, just wanting to get back to her rooms and find the map. She yanked open the door, still marveling at how she could do it herself. In Iskalt, doors were opened by guards.

She stopped in the middle of the hall, and Gullie crashed into her, sending them both stumbling forward. A maid swerved out of their way to avoid the collision, and Veren mumbled something under his breath.

Righting herself, Tierney turned hard eyes on him. "I will never find my way back to our rooms. You lead."

He did so without argument. The palace twisted in so many different directions it made her head spin.

The moment she stepped into her rooms, she hurried toward the table beside the bed, where she'd put her few belongings, including a folded parchment.

"I got this in Vondur." She unfolded it and pressed it flat, revealing a map of Lenya that included the fire plains and the seas on both sides. "Honestly, I didn't think it would be too useful since we had no way to sail the seas anyway. But now ..."

"What am I seeing?" Veren leaned closer.

Tierney pointed to a spot on the map. "The southern seas are shallow and rocky. The Vondurians have limited coastline and even more limited seas for fishing. The way through is treacherous, and few have ventured beyond sight of the mainland. I was told no ship can navigate the rocky shoals. Countless vessels have crashed and broken apart against the rocks."

"I get it. What about the northern sea?" He pointed north, presumably where Iskalt's shores should be.

"That's more of an unknown, but what is known is right there in the center." She pointed to the swirling mass on the map. "The maelstrom lies beyond the Vale of Storms, a dangerous corridor, where no one dares to sail. No one survives the Vale long enough to reach the maelstrom."

"That's the thing, Tierney," Veren said. "This ship we're building, it's made to withstand anything. There has never been one like it. It will be a rough journey, but it's our only way home."

"We don't even know for certain if Iskalt is on the other side of those seas." Tierney let out an anxious breath. "We don't know how far it is. Even if we made it past such dangerous obstacles, we'd be sailing blind with no way to navigate whatever lies beyond the farthest reaches of this map."

He backed up, scrubbing a hand over his face. "We have to try."

"We'll find another way. Maybe my magic will return, and ..."

"No, the people of Grima don't have that kind of time."

Tierney froze. Something in his voice was very wrong.

Gulliver came to her rescue. "What do you mean?"

"The fire plains." Desperation leaked into his voice. "They're expanding."

"Ex—"

He cut her off. "They're encroaching on Grima, and we don't know how to stop it."

CHAPTER FOUR
KEIR

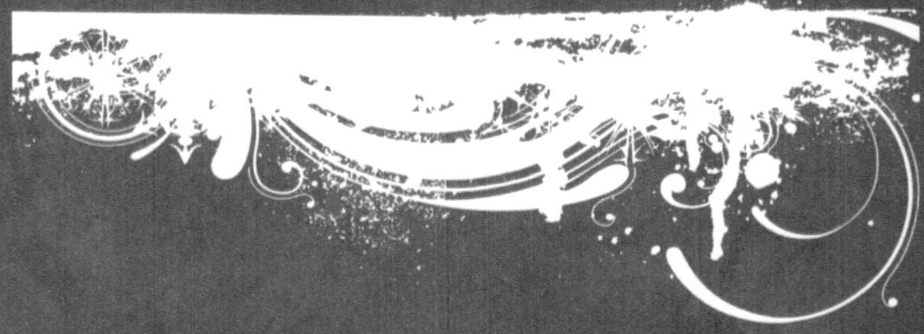

She left without saying goodbye. Keir lifted his sword, using the hilt to shield his face and deflect his opponent's blade. Steel crashed, and Keir's temper flared as he surged forward, putting all his strength into the downward arc of his weapon.

He couldn't get her off his mind. A woman traveling alone—well, with a Dark Fae man who probably wouldn't offer her the best protection—it just wasn't safe. Though, Tierney O'Shea wasn't just any woman.

Keir lunged forward, his knee bent as he leaned into the formations he could do in his sleep. Lifting his shield to block, he let his sword drop down toward his rival, grazing his arm with the sharp bite of the blade. The man howled and hobbled back, but Keir barely heard him over the din of his thoughts.

She'd left weeks ago, but he still couldn't sleep, worrying if Tierney had made it to the Grima palace. Had they welcomed her as a guest or as an enemy? Keir didn't trust them.

Yet, he understood her need to find her friends. To leave the place that had imprisoned her and nearly executed her and her closest friend in the world. In her shoes, he would have fled Vondur as soon as possible.

Still, the thought of her in enemy territory plagued his mind. More than anything, he wanted to see the end of this war. An end to the devastation, hunger, and bloodshed his people suffered. He wasn't sure he would ever see those of Grima as anything other than the enemy, but for Tierney, Vondur was the enemy. At least until he'd done the unthinkable to protect her. To give her the chance to find her friends and a way home.

His opponent was weakening. Keir took a step back to brace his footing, letting the stupid man come to him.

"I grow weary of this." Keir met the man's charge, springing forward at the last moment. Hot blood rushed down Keir's leg, but it was just a scratch; he had his opponent right where he wanted him. He ran his sword into the man's shoulder where it met his thick neck, but he didn't stop there. With the force of his momentum, Keir's blade sank into the man's torso, through his heart and lungs, and down into his bowels, until hilt met cold, dead skin.

The man sank to his knees, blood gurgling from his mouth. Keir braced his foot against the dead man's chest, pulling his sword free and letting him fall to the floor. Again.

Barely sweating this time, Keir turned to the silent onlookers. "Would anyone else care to challenge their king to the

Comhrac today?" He wiped his blade against his leathers, returning it to the scabbard at his hip.

With a deep breath, he stepped up onto the dais, returning to his throne. A throne he never wanted, though he would not change anything even if he could.

Keir still remembered long ago when his father had first challenged his predecessor and won the crown of Vondur for himself. Keir was just a boy then, but in the early days of his rule, King Turlach received many challenges. Yet, Keir could not remember there being quite so many.

It was nearly every day now. One nobleman or another stepped forward, speaking the binding words of the King's Comhrac that inevitably ended with their deaths at Keir's hands.

He was so tired of killing his own men, but his court was restless. Murmurings of his perceived weakness still spread. It wasn't that Keir himself was weak. There was a growing pile of bodies to prove that was not the case. It was his desire to feed and care for the common folk of Vondur that led his court to believing he was weak.

Some thought him a fool for taking surplus food from the army to feed the poor villagers who were starving. It wasn't a permanent solution, but it was a necessary one. He had every intention of caring for both the army and the common folk with long-term solutions that would make everyone happy. If his noblemen would stop challenging him long enough to allow him the time to make such changes.

The Vondurian court knew what was coming though. It was only a matter of time before they would be taxed to make up the difference. In Keir's mind, it shouldn't be a tax at all but a gift of common decency to see their kinsmen well cared for.

Such a gift would trickle down from the wealthiest noble house to the poorest of souls eking out a living along the fire plains. Pride. Pride in their country and their fellow Vondurians. That was the future Keir wanted. One where soldiers earned a fair wage to care for their families. Where they joined the army as a viable career and a way to proudly serve their people. Where armies no longer marched to foreign lands to wage a war no one would ever win.

But Keir wasn't sure he was the right man to inspire such a future. Not when he couldn't even sway the court to his side. Right now, everyone wanted something from him and he couldn't seem to get his feet under him long enough to make his next move and secure his rule.

But he refused to die at the end of a sword in the King's Comhrac.

Even now, his court still stared at him, taking in the bloodstains on the carpets and the fresh blood still streaming from his leg.

"Your Majesty." One of the stewards bravely stepped forward. "We should get you to the healing pools."

"Bah." Keir waved him away. "I'll not waste the power on a scratch. I'll be fine." He stood, his head swimming for a moment before Declan stepped forward to offer his shoulder to lean on.

"I'll see the king to his rooms. Get this place cleaned up." He scowled at the familiar faces, probably wondering which one would challenge the king tomorrow.

Keir made it out of the throne room under his own steam but was grateful for Declan's presence the moment the door shut behind him.

"You've got to stop these fights."

"I do what I must." Keir leaned on Declan as they made their way along the corridors to Keir's quarters. The same ones he'd always occupied.

His sister insisted he move into the king's rooms, but it still felt strange to think of his father's domain as his now.

"I would say congratulations," Declan eased him down into a chair in front of the cold fireplace in his rooms, "but I don't want to get yelled at again." He leaned down and ripped open Keir's pant leg to reveal his injury.

"It is never cause for celebration to kill my own men." Keir winced at the sight of his leg.

"That is hardly a scratch, Keir." Eavha entered the room and rushed to his side, her giant cat trailing behind. "I'll fetch the healer."

Keir grabbed her and pulled her back. "Don't. The last thing I need is for anyone to think I've been injured enough to call the healer. There'll be ten challengers tomorrow. Just ... stitch it up and put a bandage on it if you must."

Sheba let out a low growl, telling Keir to unhand his mistress. He obeyed.

Eavha glared at Keir. "You want me to stitch your leg?" Her face grew pale in the dim afternoon light streaming in through the windows. The skies were smoke-filled today as the winds blew in from the fire plains.

"It can't be all that different from your endless embroidery."

"Listen to him." Eavha stood, sharing a look with Declan. "He's lost his mind."

Declan shrugged and glanced back at Keir. "We could do it. It's just a few stitches."

"Fetch your sewing, Eavha." Keir reached for a bottle on the table at his side.

"Oh, very well." She rushed to the secret door that had connected their rooms since childhood. "Find him something to bite down on. I'll be right back. And get those boots off him while I'm gone."

Keir took a long pull on the bottle, wishing for something much stronger than watered wine. "She's gotten bossy, hasn't she?"

"I blame Tierney." Declan crouched down beside him, tugging on his boots. "And that pet of hers. It's quite territorial, isn't it?" He sighed. "That's going to take at least twelve stitches, Keir. You have any whiskey?"

Keir shook his head. "Get my belt, would you?" He gestured toward the chest of drawers in the corner opposite his bed.

Eavha returned a moment later, this time alone. Her hands were full of bottles and her latest embroidery project.

"Let's get this over with." She moved to set her things on the table beside Keir's chair. "Move." She shoved his feet off the footstool and sat down.

"Ouch, I'm injured here." Keir scowled at her.

"Stop whining." Eavha poured wine on her hands and into a basin, sloshing some along the wound that ran from his knee down to his calf. Shoving the bottle into Keir's hands, she picked up a long, sharp needle. "Drink that, it's stronger."

Her hands trembled as she threaded a needle.

"Relax. I can handle it." Keir took another gulp of crisp wine from the wineskin she'd brought with her. He wouldn't ask how she got it. The wine was for the men. Women her age drank tea.

"The thread is blue." Declan snorted.

"It's all I have." Eavha bent over Keir's leg and stabbed the needle through his skin without warning.

He sucked in a breath, stuffing the leather strap of his belt between his teeth, and urged her to keep going. Better to get it done quickly.

"Neat stitch work," Declan murmured over her. "She's pretty good at this."

Keir gripped the arms of his chair until he thought he might crush it under his hands, his teeth grinding into the leather strap.

"You can breathe now." Eavha tied off the thread and cut it. And then, she balled up her fist and punched his arm.

"Ouch, what was that for?" Keir clutched his arm.

"For making me do that. It was gross." She rinsed her hands in warm water and reached for a small jar she'd brought with her. "I don't know how much this will help, but I asked Ariella for something to aid with pain and infection. I told her it was for a hangnail for me."

"She'll know who it's really for," Declan said in a worried tone.

"She won't say anything. I trust her." Eavha dabbed the poultice mixture over Keir's leg.

"That feels good." Keir took a steady breath. "It's numbing the pain."

"Thank the heavens." She blew a sweaty strand of hair from her face and slathered a thick layer of the stuff over the wound and then wrapped it with a strip of fabric from one of Keir's old shirts.

"We have got to stop these challenges." Eavha patted her brother's shoulder, letting him find solace in the wineskin. She looked to Declan, worry creasing her brow. "He can't keep this up much longer."

"I don't know how to stop it. It's not unusual for a new king to receive the challenge of the Comhrac." Declan ran a hand through his unruly hair. "But the court always settles down in the end."

"Except, my court isn't settling down." Keir turned to the only two people he could trust, a smile tugging at his mouth. "At this rate, I won't be king much longer."

CHAPTER FIVE
TIERNEY

Tierney would never get enough of this palace with its winding halls, friendly servants, and even guards who smiled. There was a love for their kingdom in their eyes, but through it all, she could sense a weariness. They'd been through a lot. Losing their palace and hiding in the woods before taking it back. Fighting many battles for their lives.

And they didn't believe they'd find relief any time soon.

This morning, Tierney woke before Gulliver, avoiding him in favor of exploring on her own. She loved her friend, but he'd grown cautious since the war, despite growing up a thief. Now, he never wanted to do anything to disappoint Griff or others protecting him. Never wanted to go where they weren't supposed to or ask intrusive questions. She had no such qualms.

The freedom of movement here reminded her of her palace. Her mother insisted the guards always remain at an unobtrusive distance. She didn't want to feel watched and wanted the fae of Iskalt to access her should they need to. It was one of the many reasons she was such a beloved queen.

Tierney wanted to be just like her when it came time to take the throne. Respected, but most of all loved. Not only by simpering nobles seeking position but by the average fae who had nothing to gain from an immense loyalty.

She had long lost any sort of direction and found herself in a colder part of the palace. It didn't take much for her to realize why. A lengthy corridor stretched in front of her with doors lining both sides. They were open, allowing the wind to tunnel through the small space.

A blast of that wind struck Tierney, and she closed her eyes, savoring the feel. It wasn't nearly as cold as Iskalt, but the departure from the heat of Vondur still felt like it brought her closer to home.

A slow rain drizzled down, making a steady rhythm as it hit the stones. She walked forward, stopping in one of the open arched doorways, her breath stuttering. Enclosed on all sides by the walls of the palace was a garden, beautiful in its vastness. A winding path was framed with twisted bushes that looked like they were reaching toward the palace. Yellow and white flowering buds hung from their branches.

Color stretched in every direction. Pinks and blues and purples. It was like someone had captured a rainbow and managed to harness its power. Tierney had never seen anything quite like it.

Unable to resist, she stepped outside, ignoring the raindrops hitting her softly curled hair. The air smelled of fresh rain and roses, a heady scent that had her stopping to inhale deeper.

Before she could go farther, a man stepped into her path. It took her a moment to see his uniform and realize he was a guard. "No one is allowed into the queen's gardens."

Oh! She'd wandered into the royal quarters. Her cheeks heated. If anyone did that in Iskalt, her father would throw them from the balcony. Only, there were no balconies here.

"I'm sorry; I must have gotten lost." She smiled, trying to keep the royal tone from her voice. "It's such a large palace, and I'm a new maid. Can you direct me to the kitchens?"

His face softened. "Just don't find yourself this way again. The kitchens are—"

"Tarrow," a subdued feminine voice called from behind him. "Let her pass."

The guard, Tarrow, she presumed, gave Tierney a skeptical look, but he stepped aside. Behind him on the path was Queen Bronagh, her hands clasped together in front of her waist.

"Your Majesty." Tierney knew the best way to get home was to ingratiate herself with this family.

The queen seemed not to notice the rain dampening her pale blue gown. She had no expression on her face as she studied Tierney. Tierney's first impression of Bronagh had been that she was a sweet, but quiet girl, and she was starting to wonder if it was more than that.

Finally, the queen nodded. "Would you sit with me, Princess?" She gestured across the garden, where a small white gazebo sat perched among vining plants that crawled up the pillars. It would be a shield from the rain, at least, and Tierney wasn't ready to leave the garden behind.

Silently, she followed Bronagh toward the wooden benches in the gazebo and then sat facing her. Neither girl spoke for a long moment. Tierney drummed her fingers on the edge of the bench. She wasn't someone who got nervous or anxious, but there was something ethereal about this girl.

She was younger than Tierney, but there was no youth to her. Instead, she looked like she'd lived a hundred years, with wise eyes and a contemplative nature.

"I am told you fought my brother in the siege of Vondur."

Those words stopped Tierney's lungs from expanding. Her pulse pounded in her head, and a response popped out before she could stop it. "Veren wasn't supposed to mention that."

For the first time, the queen smiled, her lips barely moving. "In his short time here, Veren has become a trusted friend. He thought I deserved the facts and knew I would not hold it against you."

"You don't?"

"Tierney." She dropped her eyes, the first crack to her confidence showing. "We all do what we must to survive. If you had not joined the fight, you wouldn't be sitting here with me now."

"And that's a good thing?" She hadn't been sure. In a way, it felt like she had nothing to offer these fae who'd been so good to her.

"I believe it is." Bonagh pressed her hands into the skirt of her dress. "Tell me of Iskalt." She paused. "Please."

"Iskalt? Veren can tell you everything."

"I want to hear about it from you."

Tierney had avoided the topic of Iskalt in Vondur. Any talk of her home could have led to secrets she hadn't been ready to reveal. Not to Keir, nor anyone else there. Not while she was a prisoner. The king had hurt her for her silence.

But that king is dead, she reminded herself. And something about Bronagh made Tierney want to trust her, to have faith that she could truly help.

Tierney closed her eyes, picturing home. "We have fields of

snow, icy winds colder than you've experienced in your life. There's a vast lake that rages and seethes. Life in Iskalt is hard." For so long, she'd wanted out. A smile curved her lips. "But the fae are wonderful. My family ... I would live in the coldest reaches of the kingdom just to see them again."

She opened her eyes and tears hung in her lashes.

Bronagh leaned forward, looking like she had absorbed every word. "You miss them very much ... your family."

Tierney nodded.

"I do too."

For just a moment, they were the same, both separated from those they loved. Tierney by the fire plains, and Bronagh by death. "I'm sorry about your mother and your sister."

"Me too. But they were ..." She sighed. "They wanted us to continue this war. Donal and I tried to convince them to stop advancing their forces; we tried to put an end to all of this. And now, it is just us two and our uncle."

"You can still end it."

"I'm afraid it's not as simple as that anymore. The Vondurians ... they're a bloodthirsty lot. They will not stop until they have destroyed what is left of us and united Lenya under one crown. I will not let my fae become part of that barbaric culture. They deserve better." Anger flashed in her eyes, the first deep emotion Tierney had seen out of her.

"They do," Tierney agreed. "But I think you underestimate the new king. Keir is a good man."

"Vondur does not breed good men."

She thought of Keir, of Declan. And then of those like Torrin. "You're wrong. I have seen it firsthand. Keir is not like his father. He can be reasoned with, bargained with. You have to—"

"Enough." Bronagh didn't raise her voice, but she didn't have to. The word held command. "I did not invite you to sit with me to defend our enemy. We will deal with the Vondurian king when we must. For now, I need you to tell me about the crystals."

"Crystals?"

"In Iskalt. Veren tells me the crystals we so desperately seek are abundant in your kingdom."

Tierney had guessed as much when she first held a Vondurian totem. It was made from crystals similar to the fire opals Myrkurians used for trade. In Iskalt, they had no use for the crystals except as exquisite decoration. There was a table in her father's study made entirely of fire opal that probably could have powered half the people in the palace of Grima for a long while.

But what would it mean for Iskalt if she revealed the truth?

Bronagh sighed. "I understand your hesitation. You have to protect your fae just as I have to protect mine. But my kingdom will die if we can no longer gain access to our power. We must keep the fire plains from engulfing us."

Tierney looked into her clear eyes, sensing a sincerity in their depths. She didn't know if this was the right thing, but she drew in a deep breath. "Yes, we have crystals. The opals ... they are in most areas of Iskalt, hidden beneath layers of ice and snow. Most of what is accessible has been gifted to us from the other three kingdoms. My father and his allies have access to enough crystal for every man, woman, and child in all of Lenya."

The rain came heavier than before, drumming on the roof of the gazebo and momentarily distracting Tierney from her thoughts. This made little sense. How could the key to saving Lenya exist in Iskalt? A land they once believed was a myth.

Was that why she was here? Did something pull her where she was needed? Did her magic bring her here for a purpose? She'd always had a deep need to save people like when her brother was kidnapped or when the poor souls in the prison realm needed a way out.

But those were her people. Here, she was in a land that wasn't supposed to exist. Yet, something had happened in that portal to land her right in the middle of a dispute tearing two kingdoms apart.

"So," Tierney rubbed her hands up her arms, wishing she could call on her power to warm her, "you're telling me the key to saving Grima may lie in my kingdom, but I have to ask, what does that mean for Vondur?"

Bronagh slumped, letting her queenly façade fade, and she suddenly looked years younger, almost her age. "I can only think of my people right now. We have no more options, and we're running out of time."

And then, it hit her. "So, the boat Veren is building ... you aren't allowing it just to get us home. You—"

"Plan to come with you, yes."

They expected her to take them to Iskalt with nothing but the stars to guide them. With the roiling, rocky seas in one direction and an impassable maelstrom in the other, it was a death sentence.

Setting foot on that ship would likely mean never returning. "This is why you welcomed us into the palace."

The queen shook her head. "We welcomed you because an enemy of Vondur is a friend of ours. Yes, we ask for your help, but you are also welcome to stay here whether you agree or not."

But she wasn't an enemy of Vondur. At least, she didn't think she was. Keir was king now. She might not know what that meant for her or for the Vondurian fae, but it had to be better than before.

She wished she could ask his advice now, ask him what he knew of this Grima queen. Reality hit her a few days ago. She missed him. The man who'd kept her prisoner and then fought to free her. She missed their arguments, the way his eyes blazed when she annoyed him.

And yet, she sat here with his enemy, discussing a deal to provide them with magic ... if it was even possible.

Even if it was dangerous, shouldn't she try any means to get home? She rubbed the back of her neck and gazed up into the rafters of the gazebo. A spider web caught her attention, and she watched a tiny fly try to free itself. That was her. She was the fly caught in a web. No matter what choice she made, she would always be stuck, trapped.

She was no longer a prisoner, but this was not her home. Not her war. But was it her responsibility to intervene?

A breath pushed past her lips, and she let her eyes drift down to the queen's. "I will try to help you save Grima, but you have to make me a promise."

"I will do anything within my capabilities."

"It can't just be Grima. You must try to save all of Lenya."

A lightness entered her eyes, and she straightened her spine, sitting once again like the prim woman she was. "Veren was right about you."

"What did he say?"

"That you could be my greatest ally because you will always do what is right."

She thought of Keir and how she'd left after everything he'd done for her.

Not always. Sometimes, I do what is easiest.

Chapter Six
Keir

Keir slid the kerchief off his face, wiping the sweat from his brow. This close to the burning lands, the smoke nearly obscured the sky. His men were weary from marching in this heat, choking on the smoke they weren't used to breathing.

"It's a wonder anything can live here." Declan coughed, pulling his mount up beside Keir's. "That people choose this place as their home astounds me."

"I don't think there's much choice involved." Keir sipped cool water from a waterskin. "But when you don't have anything, you do the best you can with what you've got."

"I wonder if your court came on campaign with you, if they could witness these conditions for themselves, they'd understand why you've made the choices you have since taking the throne."

"They would still see what they want to see." Keir dismounted on the outskirts of the village, where his army camped. He couldn't stand another day among his court. He was a soldier and would never be comfortable among the nobility. A campaign to review his army was exactly what he needed. Maybe he could get things done away from all the simpering of court nobles trying to win his favor and the endless challenges from those who thought they could do a better job.

And if the reports could be trusted, his troops were growing by leaps and bounds in the last weeks. Keir would like to know where these magical new soldiers had appeared. His generals wanted him to believe the influx of recruits was due to the loyalty the new king inspired among his people. That kind of ego boost might have worked for his father, but not for Keir. Soldiers didn't appear out of thin air just when he needed them most.

"Identify yourselves!" Sentries swarmed the dusty plain, riding out to stop Keir from entering camp.

"Your king need not identify himself," Declan shouted back, stepping in front of Keir and waving several of his guards forward.

"Step aside soldiers." Keir moved through the crowd. "I am here to speak with your general." The sentry glanced at the standard his guard carried, clearly uncertain of who their king was. "I am Keir Dagnan, son of Turlach Dagnan. Your new king." He glared at the soldiers, weary from his travels and the pressure of ruling a kingdom. "Surely you've heard of the King's Comhrac even way out here?"

"Of course, your Majesty." The sentry stepped aside. "Right this way. I apologize for the hesitation, sire. It's only that

I didn't recognize you." The other sentries trotted ahead to clear the way. They were an eager lot, young and likely untested in battle.

Keir marched through the camp with his guard, trying to act like a king, but he didn't know what that entailed. So, he did the only thing he could do and acted like his father.

Ignoring the sea of unfamiliar faces, he stood tall, keeping a blank expression on his face. Kings didn't speak to lowly soldiers. But for all of his indifference, Keir didn't miss anything. The camp was poorly equipped. It reeked, and there wasn't a soldier in sight who was more than sixteen years old.

Not waiting for his escort to the general's headquarters, Keir stopped at a tent where several boys worked to start a fire. They bickered among themselves while another attempted to put together a meal of thin stew with root vegetables, wild onions, and a few unidentifiable chunks of meat. Three others sat by, sharpening their swords.

"Where is your totem?" Keir asked, crouching down beside the cold fire pit.

"Bugger off." One of the boys swiped at his forehead, not bothering to look up.

Declan stepped forward to chastise him, but Keir lifted a hand to stall him.

"You haven't been taught to start fires with your totem?"

"Don't have one." Another shrugged, trying to strike two rocks together to create a spark. "Lieutenant Briggs won't let us get an ember from a different fire till we prove we can make one with nothing."

"All soldiers have to learn to make fire this way. I take it you lot haven't earned a totem yet?"

"Wouldn't know how to use one if we did," another offered. He was the youngest of them all.

"How old are you, soldier?" Keir asked.

"Old enough, sir." He squared his shoulders and lifted his chin.

"Humor me." Keir hid his smile.

"Eleven, but I'm a good shot. At least, with a slingshot." He glanced down at the sword that was too long for his height.

"Of course you are." Keir reached into his bag, retrieving a pair of rough stones he probably didn't need anymore. "Try these." He handed the quartz to the slightly older boys still trying to start a fire. "You'll always get a better spark with quartz."

He spent a few more minutes asking the boys some questions about how they came to be in the army and teaching them a few tricks to get their camp squared away for the night. They were more than just green; they'd had no training at all.

"Why join the army at such a young age? Where are your parents?" Keir asked the most talkative of the bunch, the one adding small branches to the fire they'd finally coaxed to life.

"No parents, most of us. Our fathers and brothers died in the war, and our mothers and sisters are starving. Nothing left to do but join up and send half our wages home to feed the little ones."

"Aren't you afraid of dying in battle?" Keir moved to stir the pot of stew, adding a few herbs from his stores to bring some flavor to the meal. He frowned at the dry brown bread the boys passed around. It was full of weevils they picked out. Keir was no stranger to roughing it when times were bad, but these boys had no place fighting a war when they weren't yet grown.

The youngest shrugged, stuffing a piece of bread in his mouth. "Dying in battle's better than dying with an empty belly. Nowhere else to go."

As the days passed since he'd killed his father, Keir wanted the throne less and less. But the responsibility had fallen to him. He refused to lead an army of starving children when there was enough food in Vondur to feed everyone. It was the least he owed those families who had sacrificed their fathers and brothers in a war for power they would never grasp for themselves.

Keir stood, anger leaving his chest tight and his fists clenched. "Where is your general?" He turned to the sentry who had escorted him into camp.

"We've sent a messenger, sire. He's busy carrying out a punishment." The sentry trembled at the look on Keir's face.

"Take me to him, soldier." He left the boys with his own supplies. Things he'd carried from one battle to the next for more years than he cared to think about. He wouldn't need them now.

As they walked along a dusty path through the tents, the familiar sounds of camp life set him at ease. This felt more like home than the palace ever had. But the unmistakable sound of a strap against flesh stoked Keir's anger. The strap was part of being a soldier. Even Keir had received his fair share of lashes and had the scars to prove it.

"This is what we do to deserters." The gruff voice reminded Keir of his father. As the lash struck the boy's back, Keir winced. The boy couldn't have been more than fourteen. Just a skinny runt with his ribs showing, but he took his punishment, sucking back his tears.

The general reared back to strike again, landing the blow with the force used to whip a full-grown, seasoned soldier. "Your duty is to serve your king!" The general's face flushed red with rage. As he moved to strike again, Keir stepped in, yanking the whip from the man's grasp.

"How dare you!" The general turned his anger on Keir. "I am a general in his Majesty's army; who do you think you are to defy me?"

Keir ignored him, throwing the whip to the ground. "Release this boy." He turned to the sentry, who rushed forward to remove the restraints tethering the young man to the whipping post. "Take him to the healer."

"I give the orders around here." The general blustered.

"And I am your king." Keir turned his cold gaze on the stupid man who wasn't fit to lead a flock of sheep, let alone an army.

The general sputtered for a moment before he collected himself. "I see the news is true then. We have a new king. I beg your pardon, your Majesty." He attempted a courtly bow. "I was just punishing a deserter."

"All I see is a young, frightened boy who shouldn't even be here." Keir glowered, dangerously close to drawing his sword.

"Perhaps your Majesty would accompany me to my tent, where we may speak in private?" He gestured toward the grand tent at the center of the camp. No doubt it was fit for a king.

"No need. Why have you inflated your numbers, reporting an influx of recruits who aren't fit to wield their father's pitchforks, much less a sword?"

"They still need some proper training."

"They are children. How many ten and eleven year olds here do you expect to make it through their first battle against Grima?" Keir's voice rang out around the silent camp. "Or do you wish to throw them at the front line, hoping your seasoned soldiers can win this war?"

The general's face turned a darker shade of red, his mustache trembling as he spoke. "With all due respect, sire, I have only followed orders."

"Whose orders?"

"Your father's. I beg your pardon if I've missed any orders that have come directly from you since your rise to the throne."

"My father gave orders to recruit orphaned children?" Not even Turlach was that despicable.

"With most Vondurian soldiers already dead, sire, where do you expect your new soldiers to come from?"

"You have new orders, General. Send the boys home." Keir turned to leave before he did something he would regret.

"If I'm to do that, I'll not have an army to lead, your Majesty."

Keir whirled around, closing the distance between himself and the battle-scarred man who stood head and shoulders beneath him. "You are relieved of your command. You will gather your belongings and leave my camp immediately."

"You can't do that. Who will train these men?" The man blustered, and his face grew so red Keir thought his head might explode right off his shoulders.

"Declan Connel, you've been promoted to Commander. Please have your men escort this man to his tent to clear his belongings."

"What, now, your Majesty? Me?" Declan lunged forward. "Commander?"

"Yes. I need someone I can trust to make sure this isn't happening anywhere else. You have command of all the Vondurian troops. See to it these boys are sent somewhere safe. Somewhere that isn't here."

Keir ignored the outraged ranting of the former general, leaving Declan to clean up this mess while he continued surveying his troops.

"You three, you heard the king. Get this disgrace out of my sight," Declan barked orders to those standing around, sending half those present scrambling to get back to work.

Keir walked slowly along the path, relieved to see a company of seasoned soldiers sitting around their fires along the perimeter of the camp. The young ones didn't yet realize the worst part of camp life was the center.

"Have you taken leave of your senses?" Declan charged down the path to catch up with him. "Me, Commander of your entire army?"

"You're the best man for the job."

"I'm just a soldier in the king's guard. I never even thought about becoming an officer."

"You don't want it?" Keir turned to face his best friend. "Commander pays a lot better than the king's guard."

"It's also a nobleman's position. And in case you forgot, I'm a commoner. You expect your other generals to defer to me?" Declan's eyes were wild with uncertainty, flashing from one corner of the camp to the next, as if their conversation was somehow taboo.

"I do. Lesser men have risen to greater rank with minimal effort. No one deserves this more than you, Deck."

"I don't know what to say." He raked a hand through his sweaty hair.

Keir shrugged. "The job comes with a lot of responsibility. I expect loyalty and your best efforts. You will lead my army, but you will also take your place among my court. And when the time comes, you'll marry some nobleman's daughter ... or sister. And you'll be happy." Keir clapped his stunned friend on the back.

"*Marry*?" Declan shook his head. "I can't process what you just said right now. We need to talk about these boys. They need their pay, Keir. If you send them away, half of them have nowhere to go and no prospects for paid work. They'll starve on the streets of this poor village. These kids need what little pay they get to feed their families."

"You're not suggesting we let them fight?"

"Of course not. I don't know what the answer is, but sending them home isn't it."

Keir nodded. "Get me an accurate count of how many actual soldiers there are here. And a count of all the boys under the age of sixteen. We'll figure out what to do with them once we know how many we're dealing with. Maybe we can train them to be squires and stable boys. And if that doesn't work, we'll take them with us and place them in the king's guard.

"And after I deal with that piece of garbage calling himself a general, you and I need to have a long talk about what comes next."

Declan nodded. "I'll have orders ready to send out by first light."

Chapter Seven
Tierney

"May I escort you to dinner?" Gulliver offered Tierney his arm.

"Almost ready." Tierney smoothed a hand over the dark blue skirt of her dress. It reminded her of the elaborate gown she'd worn for her birthday ball. A much simpler version. Rather than the wide, cumbersome skirts Iskaltian and Gelsi nobles preferred, Tierney's simple dress fell to the floor without the hassle of layers and layers of petticoats and dress forms that weighed more than she did.

"You look fine." Gulliver held the door open for her so they could join the other nobles making their way to the great hall for the evening meal. "I'm starving."

"You're always starving, yet you never die." She adjusted

the silver belt at her hips, studying her appearance in the mirror. It was to be a formal affair tonight. But formal attire in Grima seemed more like everyday wear to Tierney. Even some of her day dresses at home would be considered too fancy and frivolous among the Grima court.

"I like the fashion here." She tugged on the long sleeve of her dress, clipping a silver broach at her throat. "Their clothes are lovely, with beautiful fabrics, but so comfortable." She tucked her strawberry blond hair behind her pointed ears and retrieved her clutch.

"They do seem to value comfort and economy in all things." Gulliver took her hand as they left their suite. His attire was nothing more than trousers, a dress shirt, and a soft suede waistcoat.

Several other nobles who called the palace home already filled the corridors, heading to the great hall and the queen's summons for a celebratory dinner.

Tierney expected a large crowd of guests, but the great hall was much smaller than the dining hall they normally attended for their meals.

"Princess Tierney O'Shea and Lord Gulliver O'Shea," the herald announced their arrival. A footman escorted them to the high table to dine with the queen and her brother. Their uncle, Lord Cormac, was absent.

Tierney was surprised to find herself seated next to the queen in a place of honor. Gulliver sat beside Prince Donal, who immediately captured his attention with questions about Myrkur. Tierney vaguely wondered if there was a bit of a divide-and-conquer maneuver happening at the formal dining table.

Like most things in Grima, the table was simple yet elegant. Fine linens covered the long table, with sleek goblets filled with the strange pale wine favored by the court. It was delicious, crisp, and fruity, and nothing like the rich dark wines of Iskalt.

Simple white china dishes trimmed in silver adorned the table, along with fresh-cut flowers from the queen's gardens. In Iskalt, the tables at such gatherings were so elaborate Tierney often struggled to see over the flower arrangements to the person seated opposite her.

There was something non-threatening about the way the Grima court operated. It was refreshing. Yet, Tierney had trouble trusting it. The queen might be young, but she was cunning. Odd for a girl who'd grown up with an older sister meant to inherit the throne had she survived the day their mother was murdered by the Vondurian soldiers.

"Good evening, Queen Bronagh." Tierney dipped her head toward the monarch. "I trust you are in fine spirits this evening. The court seems delighted with the impromptu dinner."

"It is good for the morale of the people to see their queen carrying on in the wake of so much tragedy."

"It's a shame our young queen hasn't had time to properly mourn her family." An older gentleman lifted his glass. Tierney recognized him as the swordmaster who had accompanied the prince at the siege.

At Tierney's look of confusion, Bronagh explained, "In Grima, royals do not mourn during a time of war. I will grieve for my sister and mother once Vondur has been defeated."

"Here, here." The swordmaster raised his cup to the queen. "To the defeat of our enemies."

Cries of agreement rang out around the table.

"What news of the front, Daniel?" another gentleman of the court asked.

Tierney supposed the topic of any conversation among the court would center on the war with Vondur, but she was torn.

She was a guest here, yet she didn't think of Keir, now the King of Vondur, as an enemy. He was a good man. The only reason she sat here now, drawing breath, was due to his actions at the King's Comhrac.

"The front has been quiet since the murder of their king," the swordmaster answered.

"Such a barbaric custom they have." The man, Lord Fitzgerald, if she remembered correctly, shook his head in disgust. "What is known of this new king?"

"He is King Turlach's son, Keir Dagnan," Tierney replied. "He is an honorable man."

"There is no such thing as an honorable Vondurian." Queen Bronagh patted Tierney's hand, as if she was a child speaking out of turn at the dinner table.

"I'll remind you, King Keir challenged your own Prince Donal to the Comhrac. Yet, when he won the fight, Keir allowed Donal to live, going against the traditions of your people and theirs. The siege at the Vondur palace could have lasted months before it turned into a full-fledged battle. But Keir, acting as he did that day, saved hundreds of lives."

"Pardon me, Princess Tierney," Donal turned a curious gaze on her, "but it sounds as if you would defend the Vondurians at our table. A table where you sit as an honored guest of our queen."

"I am a royal of Iskalt. I hold no sway in the disputes of Lenya. I am but an impartial observer. And as that observer, I can't help but think that if both sides of this war could set aside generations of hate and betrayal, you might be surprised to see that you both want the same things."

"And what is that, Princess?" Donal's cold gaze sent a shiver down her spine. The boy might be young, but he was intimidating—at least, in his palace.

"Peace." Tierney turned to the queen to give her reply. "A

thriving, united Lenya, where all have access to the power, and more importantly, all have full bellies when they go to sleep at night, not worrying about what fresh terrors the morning might bring."

"You speak of fantasies, Princess." Lord Fitzgerald sipped his wine. "None here shall fall under the rule of the barbarians across the border."

Tierney tilted her cup against her lips, taking a cool sip to fortify herself. With a smile, she ignored the lords and ladies around the table, focusing her attention on the silent little queen, who was still trying to find her voice among her court.

"I grew up in Iskalt. Our neighbors were the kingdoms of Eldur and Fargelsi. Each vastly different from the other. In generations past, Fargelsi was our enemy. My mother and father fought a long, brutal war to bring peace to our three kingdoms.

"When I was a young girl, we fought another war against the kingdom of Myrkur, which was unknown to us, much like those of Lenya here beyond the fire plains." Tierney dropped her gaze to her lap. "It was a difficult time. I was a small child, but I fought. My twin brother and I were pawns the Dark King of Myrkur thought to use to gain power." She took another sip of wine. "He is dead now, and his people are free."

Tierney turned her gaze to settle on each member of the court seated around the long table. "It took four kingdoms and two wars to find peace, but we did it. Our people are happy. They have access to power, knowledge of how to use that power, food is plentiful, and every single Iskaltian, Eldurian, Fargelsian, and Myrkurian, down to the last child, has a voice in our world. I would wish the same for all of Lenya. It breaks my heart to see good fae, on both sides, suffer when they don't have to."

A hushed silence fell as each fae present looked at their queen for her reaction to Tierney's words.

"Ah." A smile erupted across the queen's face. "The duck has arrived."

At her signal, servants flooded the dining room with platters of roasted duck and dishes Tierney couldn't identify.

"Prince Donal has provided our feast tonight." She smiled at her brother. "I am happy to see your hunting has been plentiful, brother."

"It is my pleasure, your Majesty." Donal sat back to allow the servers to fill his plate. "I hope all will enjoy the bounties of Grima this evening." He lifted his glass to the queen, and the others followed his lead.

"You might want to keep your thoughts to yourself, Tia." Gulliver flopped onto the settee back in their common room. "I like my neck where it is, thank you." Rubbing his full belly, he shot her a deeply satisfied smile. "They do have great food here. Far better than the Vondurian dungeons."

"So, you're saying I shouldn't think of Vondur as anything but the enemy?" Tierney shed her intricate silvery belt and broach, her temper flaring at the absolute farce that dinner was.

"Didn't say that." Gulliver patted his belly again. "Just remarking on the tasty food and the ... chilly reception your speech got from the queen. Maybe we should just stay out of it and focus on getting home."

"They're all just so stubborn." She tossed her jewelry onto the table and sat beside Gulliver. "That duck was delicious, wasn't it?"

"Pretty sure I took down a whole bird myself."

"How are we ever going to get out of here, Gullie?" Frustration brought tears to her eyes. Part of her just wanted to go home. And the other part wanted to help these warring kingdoms find peace.

"Did you mean it?" The gentle voice sounded behind them, and they both jumped to turn in their seats, peeking over the back of the settee to find the queen in their rooms.

"Um, hello, Queen Bronagh." Tierney leaped to her feet. "What, um, brings you to our rooms?" Tierney patted her hair, making sure it wasn't a mess.

"Did you mean it?" Bronagh lifted her chin, meeting Tierney's bewildered look with a fierce one of her own.

"Mean what?"

"The words you didn't say between the pretty words you did. You think this new king of Vondur can be trusted? Do you truly believe he wants the same things I do?"

"Without a doubt." Tierney didn't pause to consider her answer. She didn't know Keir well, but she'd witnessed his actions often enough to understand what kind of man he was and what he wanted for his people.

"The young Dagnan's reputation in battle is worse than his father's." Bronagh crossed to the sitting area and collapsed onto a chair with a weary sigh.

Tierney returned to her seat, leaning toward the queen. She always seemed so poised and collected, if a little too quiet. Tierney suspected the girl's silence was more about her shrewdly listening and watching than being intimidated by her position. She might never have expected to be queen, but she'd been trained for the role.

Tierney knew what that was like. She also knew what it was like to have a thousand opinions thrown at her, never knowing which she could trust.

"Did you know I was charged as a Grima spy you sent to infiltrate the Vondurian court?"

Bronagh lifted a brow in surprise. "I did not."

"Turlach used me to turn his court's attention away from his recent failures in battle and on to something juicier for them to gossip about. I found myself standing on the gallows beside my best friend and a brave Vondurian soldier—an innocent man. The executioner's hood was placed over my head, the rope around my neck."

"He would dare execute a foreign royal without the benefit of a trial? With a common hanging, no less?" Bronagh leaned forward, her elbows resting on her knees.

Tierney mimicked her posture. "He claimed there was no such land as Iskalt; therefore, I was nothing but a common spy."

"And he believed I was some kind of abomination." Gulliver grimaced.

"Ignorant beasts, all of them." Bronagh shook her head. "How did you escape?"

"We didn't. That was the moment Keir Dagnan challenged his father to the Comhrac. He is king now simply because he was trying to save our lives."

CHAPTER EIGHT
KEIR

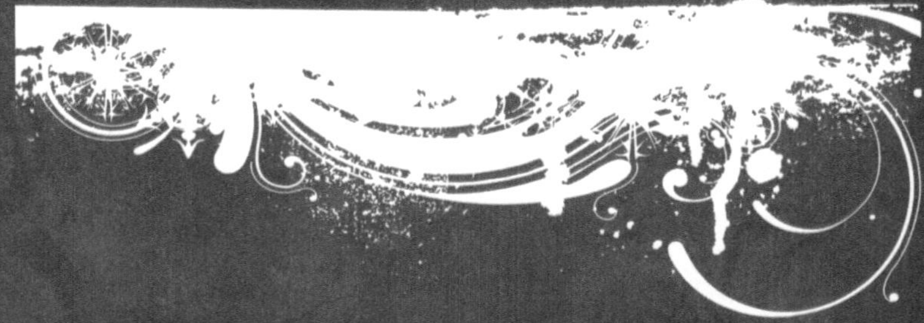

Keir lost track of his days. All he knew was they were long and longer. Provisioning troops, dealing with petty squabbles at court, preparing for whatever Grima sent for them next.

At least the constant onslaught of Comhrac challenges had ceased, his nobles finally realizing they would not win. Not when their king was determined to help his people. He couldn't do that if he was dead.

But how did one help the people of a war-torn kingdom? As the prince, he'd led armies to battle, but he'd never considered the true toll the war took on the villages, on the children of those he'd served with.

Lowering himself into a seat at the table in the informal

dining room, he rested his head in his hands and let his body relax for just a moment. He'd carried so much tension since the moment he realized what he'd have to do to stop his father.

He could still see it. That fight, the way betrayal shone in the man's eyes when he breathed his last breath. But he'd saved her. Tierney. He'd saved Declan. It had been the right thing to do, but right was never easy.

"Your Majesty?" Lord Robert entered the room, and Keir looked up into his kind face, relieved the aged man was the first to arrive.

He stood. "Lord Robert, I wasn't sure you would attend my summons." He held out a hand, but the man didn't take it. Instead, he bowed, as was fitting.

"I wasn't sure I would either, to be honest. When I left this palace, I vowed never to return." Lord Robert had been a trusted ally of Keir's father when he became king, but the relationship turned when he refused to send the young men from the village on his lands to fight for the crown.

"I'm glad you did. Please have a seat." Keir returned to his chair, his posture no longer relaxed. As a child, Lord Robert was like an uncle to him. Now, he was another fae who had to be convinced of Keir's sincerity.

A silence stretched between them before Keir spoke. "I am forming a council."

"In the small hall?" The man lifted one brow.

Keir's lips twitched. "When my father abolished the council years ago, he had the council chambers turned into a library. I will find a better place, but I prefer to look into a fae's eyes when I'm speaking to determine his motives. This table suits that endeavor."

Lord Robert nodded. "Sensible. And what are my motives, your Majesty?"

"I do not need to look at you to know that. Not unless you have changed in the last many years."

"Change is for the winds."

"Then, your motives are clear. You do not approve of our war with Grima."

Lord Robert folded his hands on the table. "You say *our* as if it belongs to all in Vondur. I make no claim on the blood your men shed."

"Ah, but it still belongs to you," Keir said. "You cannot escape what is happening. This kingdom suffers, and no speck of dirt will be unaffected."

A long sigh left Lord Robert, and he seemed to age right there in his seat. "What of you, your Majesty? I did not come here to learn that those I've protected will suffer. I want to know what you plan to do to stop it."

That was the question, wasn't it? Keir let loose a smile. "I plan to end the war, of course."

Lord Robert looked like he wanted to respond, but they were interrupted when the door opened and a guard allowed a handful of other nobles into the room. Keir invited many of his father's allies to join this council meeting, as well as those who'd opposed him. But that wasn't going to be the most difficult part.

"Lord Garnet." Keir smiled at the rotund man who'd never had a kind word for him. Yet, now that Keir was king, the fae had to keep his mouth shut.

"Your Majesty," he muttered with a stiff bow.

"Did we hear you say you plan to end the war?" Lord Osterian asked, his face bright. "Music to my ears, sire."

"It's preposterous is what it is." Lord Garnet's face went red. "With all due respect, sire, do you really think Grima will agree to end to war while the remaining crystals are in our possession?"

He didn't have an answer for that. Grima was an unknown, but they couldn't go on letting the men of this kingdom die. It would destroy Vondur faster than Grima could.

What would Tierney do? She was a strong-willed princess. He couldn't imagine her not involving herself in matters of the kingdom, and she'd been to war. How would she deal with unruly nobles? An enemy kingdom who kept coming?

Shouting ensued, one side of the table bickering with the other, and Keir had no interest in being the arbitrator.

When the door opened once more, they stopped.

Declan walked in, each step rigid like that of a soldier marching to war. He bowed. "Sorry I'm late, your Majesty."

Lord Garnet shot from his chair, one finger pointed at Declan. "Absolutely not. Your Majesty, this man is a commoner. The king's council has always been seated with noblemen. It's bad enough you have made him commander of your army, but I will not stand for this council's work to be tainted by a simple mind."

Declan looked ready to bolt, but Keir shot him a look that made him stay put. After a stunned silence, Keir fixed his eyes on the blustering lord. "The only mind that is simple is one that cannot see value in a diversity of voices. Declan, sit down. If I'm not getting out of this, neither are you."

No one argued after that. Well, about Declan anyway. The truth was, Keir didn't only want him there for solidarity. He respected the tactical brilliance Declan had gained from years in the guard. None of these pompous fools would last five seconds in a battle with the golden warriors.

Just when he thought they'd gotten through the rough edges of this first meeting, the door opened again. He expected to see a servant bringing tea, but instead, Eavha stood in the doorway.

None of the nobles noticed her at first, but Declan's

alarmed gaze met Keir's. Keir valued his sister's council, he always had, and he realized how wrong so many of the Vondurian traditions regarding women were. After the war, he vowed to make changes. But he hadn't wanted his sister to face the cruelty these men would inflict upon her.

But she stepped into the room with a flinty gaze, looking as if she was ready for the fight, and he realized he was wrong. It shouldn't have been his decision at all.

For a moment, pride warmed him. Pride and gratitude. Because, in the rigid righteousness of her shoulders, he saw Tierney. In the newfound confidence his sister showed, he recognized the foreign princess' influence.

Sensing his distraction, the noblemen around the table followed the king's gaze, finding the same courageous woman he saw.

Lord Osterian blinked rapidly before turning to Keir. "I'm sorry, your Majesty. I kept my mouth shut when you invited a commoner to join us, but this is highly unusual. Women cannot advise a king."

"Your Highness," Lord Garnet grunted, eying Eavha like a leech. "Go fetch a servant and tell them we require refreshments, my dear."

Eavha's face tightened, but her voice was sugary sweet. "I am a princess, my Lord, not your errand girl. I'd be happy to point you in the direction of the kitchens, though. Some warm biscuits would make this meeting so much more pleasant, don't you think?" And then, she walked right to the empty chair beside Lord Garnet and sat down.

Keir stared at her in awe, wondering how he hadn't seen this side of her all these years. He thought that was the end of it, but then Sheba strolled in, her teeth flashing with a growl. Just what he needed. He gave his sister an irritated glance. No one could quite control the cat except for Eavha, but she chose not to. Sheba prowled around the table, getting too close to a few of the nobles who seemed to be holding their breath, before settling behind Eavha. She laid down and began licking her giant paws.

Keir cleared his throat, needing to get this meeting back on track. "I meant what I said before. It is past time we value all Vondurians and the talents they possess." He looked from Declan to Eavha to a smiling Lord Robert.

Only Lord Garnet still seemed to be struggling, the others silenced by Sheba's presence. "But—"

Keir had to put an end to this. He stood, slamming his hands down on the wooden table and leaning over it. "My sister fought in the siege. When the Grimian warriors were at our gates, she and Tierney O'Shea stood alongside my men atop the walls as arrows rained down on them. Let me ask, Lord Garnet, where were you?" Not a single nobleman had ridden to the palace with their personal guard to fight. Not. One. But Eavha was there.

"Colluding with a prisoner, a Grima spy no less, is not exactly a point in her favor."

A low growl ripped from Keir's throat before he calmed himself, replacing the anger with the cool mask of a king and sliding back into his seat. "As this is our first meeting of the council, I must make a few things clear. First, the prisoner was no spy. Tia—Tierney, that is—is a friend of Vondur. Should she return, she is to be treated as such."

He didn't expect to see Tierney again, but a king could hope.

"Second, the commander and the princess are my two closest advisors. I trust them above all others. If you want influence with the crown, you must heed them." He searched each face, looking into their eyes for any sign of dissension. But even Lord Garnet looked thoroughly shamed.

"My father disbanded the council to consolidate power, but if we are to do right by our kingdom, I believe power must be shared. Not only among those seated here but with the villagers, the soldiers. I am not my father. You would do well to remember that."

He bit back the harsh words he wanted to say and instead settled for, "And last, I do not care about your bloodlines or the wealth of your lands. The only thing that matters to me is that you have Vondur's best interests at heart. I think you do. Despite your outdated notions of tradition, the men ...and woman ... gathered here can find a way to bring Lenya peace. And we won't stop until we do."

Keir realized the air in the room had changed. There were no more arguments, no more heated looks or seething tempers. Even the blasted cat seemed to stare at him in approval. It was a start.

Keir was the last to leave the council chamber, and he found Lord Robert waiting for him outside the door.

"Well," Keir started, "do you regret coming?"

Lord Robert put a hand on his shoulder, not something anyone typically did with a king. "Keir, your father would disapprove of everything that happened in that meeting."

He nodded. He'd be disappointed in a lot.

Lord Robert's weathered face stretched into a kind smile. "You are going to be a great king." He bowed. "I am here for whatever it is you need. Your vision is mine now."

Keir swallowed back a mountain of emotions. "Thank you, my Lord."

Lord Robert winked before turning and walking down the corridor.

His stomach grumbling, Keir headed toward the great hall in search of lunch. He'd almost reached it when Eavha accosted him, hugging him from behind.

"You were perfect," she squealed.

Keir glanced toward the guards, who were trying not to watch, and then into the great hall, where the nobles were sure to see them soon. With a groan, he pulled Eavha away from him and led her out of sight. "Are you trying to undo all the credibility I've just gained with my new council?"

She bit her lip, trying not to laugh. "I was just so excited for you. I mean, you were all, 'me king, you stupid nobles,' and it was the coolest thing I've ever seen."

He scrubbed a hand across his face. "Well, can you contain your excitement a bit?"

"Not really. It's a flaw."

He couldn't help the laugh that escaped. "You're incorrigible."

"Most of the time, yes." Her smile fell the smallest bit. "She'd have been proud of you too."

"Eavha, Mom has been gone since you were—"

"I'm not talking about Mom. I didn't know her enough to know what would make her proud. But Tierney, I think if she saw you in that council meeting, she'd have kissed you."

Warmth crept up his neck. "Honestly, I don't know where you get such notions."

"Aw, your cheeks are red. That's adorable."

"Eavha, stop." He searched the hall. "Where is Sheba? Don't tell me she's skulking around the kitchens again."

"Oh, no. I had her follow Lord Garnet out to the stables." She dropped her voice. "Has there been any news?"

He shook his head. They'd had no word of Tierney since

she left, and he tried to forget about her, about the moment he learned the fate his father handed her. She was strange, with her constant babble and sarcasm. He hadn't realized how much he enjoyed her company until she was gone.

Even though most of their time together had been spent fighting.

Eavha watched him too closely, and he looked away.

"She's gone."

"I know." Her shoulders dropped. "It's just ... she was my friend, the first woman who made me believe ... I don't know. She just made me believe."

"Are you two coming to eat?" Declan joined them, eyes flicking from brother to sister.

Eavha stared at Keir for a moment longer before sliding an arm through Declan's. "Come on, Deck. From one unwanted council member to another, let's go make them uncomfortable by sitting at the high table." A table reserved for the king and his closest noblemen. No commoners. No women.

Declan gave Keir a helpless look before Eavha dragged him off.

But Keir was no longer hungry. He turned, walking back the way he'd come, knowing there was work to do. He'd decided to become king when he challenged his father to the Comhrac. Now, he had to prove he was worthy.

CHAPTER NINE
TIERNEY

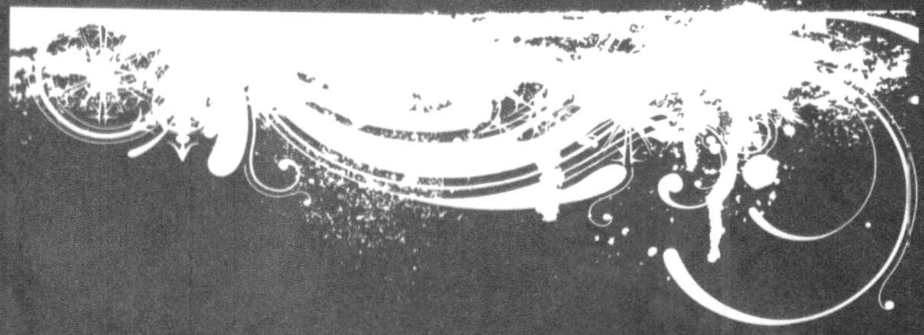

"Still abed, are we?" Some unknown—soon to be murdered—person zoomed around Tierney's bedroom.

"Wa's happening?" Tierney rolled over. "'M 'sleep. Come back later."

"Princesses don't lie in like spoiled courtiers. Not when there's work to be done." The curtains parted and blazing sunshine streamed across Tierney's bed. The bed she was still trying to figure out how to take home with her.

"This princess is on vacation." She ducked her head under the covers. "Be gone. Before I put the guard on you."

"You say the funniest things." The servant ripped the covers off the bed, and Tierney contemplated a beheading.

That would teach this idiot not to interrupt her sleep. Not when she hadn't had more than a few hours' rest.

"Come on." The girl clapped her hands, her voice too bright and chipper for such an ungodly hour.

Tierney sat up, her normally smooth, silky hair a pile of tangles hanging in her face. "Go." She swiped at her brow. "Away. Now." She lifted her gaze, rubbing her eyes to clear the cobwebs away.

"Queen Bronagh?" She gaped at the girl, blinking her bleary eyes. "What's happening? Why are you in my room in the middle of the night?"

"It's morning, and we have much to do. Come, come. Get out of bed. We have a plan to devise."

"We do?" Tierney slid her feet to the floor, still confused. "What plan?" She reached for her dressing robe, contemplating regicide.

"I've been awake all night thinking, and I'll need your help to make it happen."

Tierney stood, shrugging into her robe as she crossed the room. Without a word, she opened the door, gesturing for the queen to exit ahead of her.

"We don't have a lot of time—"

Tierney held up her hand to stall the queen's next words. "Make me some tea. Strong, black tea. I will join you in five minutes." She slammed the door in Bronagh's face.

Shuffling to her vanity, she sat, running a brush through her hair. It was morning, all right. The sun shone just over the horizon, but she'd wager the entire court was still in bed at this hour after the long evening of celebration.

Smoothing her hair back in a simple bun and straightening her dressing gown, Tierney couldn't fathom what the queen wanted from her.

Splashing some water on her face from the basin, she shook

the last vestiges of sleep from her fuzzy mind and went to join the Grima queen.

"And she'd better have that tea." Tierney yanked on the door to the common room, not in the mood for a meeting in diplomacy.

"Not a morning person, are you?" Bronagh sat on the settee. Tierney could have sworn they'd just left it an hour ago, but the queen brought tea and pastries, so she overlooked it.

"Nope." Tierney went for the steaming teapot, eager to get something warm in her belly. After a snack and a chat with the queen, she was going right back to bed.

Tierney took a big bite of a crusty lemon scone.

"I need you to teach me how to be a lady's maid," the queen blurted ... and Tierney promptly choked on her laughter.

She pounded on her chest, coughing. "You need me to do what?"

"Teach me to be a maid." Bronagh lifted a dainty pastry to her mouth.

"You're going to need to use more words. If you expect *me* to teach *you* to be a maid, we are in trouble."

"I would meet this Keir Dagnan for myself."

"And ... you want to be his maid?" Tierney took a deep sip of the scalding hot tea, hoping it would clear her head so the queen's words might make some actual sense.

"I would like to return to the Vondurian court with you. Not as Queen Bronagh, but as a member of your household. Someone who would go unnoticed."

"Okay. Why?" She set her scone and teacup on the edge of the table.

"I have great respect for everything you said last night. I want a united Lenya. I want all people of our two kingdoms to have the things they need." Bronagh stood up, twisting her hands as she paced. "This war needs to end. You say King Keir wants peace. I would like to observe him for myself before I attempt negotiations with him—negotiations my court would never approve."

"You want to infiltrate the palace so you can observe the king for yourself?" Tierney's mind chugged along, trying to keep up. "I can ... sort of get that."

"My uncle wishes to rule as regent." She whirled around. "He thinks I am too young and need further training before I can rule on my own."

"You have more strength of will than you would have your court believe." Tierney sat back, studying the shrewd young woman before her.

"I do not make big decisions. I keep my council small, with only those I trust implicitly, while I continue to establish my authority. But make no mistake, Princess Tierney, I am queen here, and I will rule Grima until the day I die."

"How would you explain your absence?" Tierney asked. For a girl with a tenuous grasp on her throne, leaving seemed like a bad idea.

"I will go on campaign, visiting the villages and my troops. I'll leave Donal and my uncle in charge. My brother is young, but I trust him to keep the nobles in line."

"You would risk leaving at such a precarious time in your reign?"

Bronagh stopped her pacing. "To finally bring an end to this war, I would risk far more."

"You want to make the right decisions for your people." Tierney nodded. "I can respect that."

"Then, you will help me?"

"I will do what I can." Tierney didn't want to think about returning to the place where she was almost executed. She didn't want to think about seeing Keir again. "But if you want to masquerade as a maid, then we're going to need help. And possibly a miracle or two."

"She wants to do what?" Veren blinked rapidly in the bright sunshine.

It was ungodly hot for the Grima region, yet they were traveling down the mountain roads to the sea.

"You heard me." Tierney patted her horse's vibrant red mane. "She wants to see for herself what the Vondurian king is like."

"It's out of the question." Veren trotted his mount up to her side, nudging between Tierney and Gulliver.

"That's what I said." Gulliver munched on a bright red fruit filled with succulent seeds. "She's got a few too many bats in the belfry, that one. I'd rather stay here for the rest of my life than go back to Vondur, but nobody ever asks me."

"We're going," Tierney said. "And who are you two to be making decisions for a queen?" She nudged her horse forward along the road. "The queen has a mind to make decisions for her people based on her own experiences with the new king. We're going to support that."

"But ... how? How does she expect to slip into the enemy's palace undetected?" Veren scoffed. "She's a queen. That's like expecting you to suddenly become a milkmaid among the Gelsi villagers. They'd know you for a royal without ever having seen your face before."

"She's going as a maid of my household." Tierney lifted her face into the slight breeze, searching for some relief from this oppressive heat. She hadn't experienced such temperatures since leaving Vondur.

"A maid?" Veren pulled his horse to a stop. "Have you both lost your minds?"

"I'd go with yes." Gulliver tossed the remains of his fruit down before the horses, letting them search for the plump seeds.

"The queen's lady's maid is her best friend. They grew up together, so Bronagh trusts her. She's working with the queen as we speak, training her to pass as a maid."

"The woman has never placed a cube of sugar into her own teacup, but you think she'll be able to make and serve tea to others?" Veren's face clouded with worry. He seemed to care for the young queen's welfare. "She's going to get herself killed."

"That's why you're coming with us."

"Us?" Gulliver snorted. "I'm staying right here, thanks. Those people put me in a dungeon and starved me to within an inch of my life. I won't give them a second chance."

"Keir wouldn't let anything happen to you, Gullie. And Veren won't let anything happen to Bronagh."

"And who's going to watch out for you?" Gulliver's tail swished behind him in agitation. "Don't say you can take care of yourself; we all know that. But you're going to need someone watching your back."

"Which is why you will brave the Vondurian palace at my side." Tierney turned her bright smile on her best friend.

"I swear, Tia O'Shea, if I find myself at the end of a rope for a second time, I'm never speaking to you again."

"So, we're in agreement then? We will return to Vondur on some pretense or another, bringing Bronagh with us to see for herself what kind of man Keir Dagnan is."

"Just one question, Tia." Gulliver turned in his saddle to meet her gaze. "How does this help us get home? How does it help us find Siobhan?"

Tierney sighed, looking at the dusty fields ahead of them. "I don't know, Gullie. First, I need to see how the fire plains are encroaching on Grima. I think that's the key to our next steps."

"See for yourself." Veren pointed across the dry, lifeless field as he nudged his mount forward, leaving the main road.

"This close to the palace already?" Tierney shielded her eyes from the bright sun glaring off the packed earth.

"When I first arrived in Grima, I rode with Prince Donal past these fields." Veren dismounted his horse, moving to stand beside Tierney, who remained mounted. "Just a few short months ago, that was a verdant green expanse, full of life. And over there." He pointed to a spot where the air shimmered and swayed as the heat rose from the ground. "That was a village. And not your average poor farming community either. It was a thriving village with a strong economy. Shops lined the streets and fields of every color spread into the distance. It's gone now."

"Where did it all go?" Gulliver squinted, trying to see the remnants of the village that once stood here.

"It's been swallowed up by the fire plains."

"It doesn't look like the plains." Tierney turned her horse in a circle, looking for the scorched earth, the lava pools, and the billowing smoke she associated with the burning lands.

"It started with the rising temperatures," Veren explained. "Then, a season of poor crops, lack of rain. Small things at first —or so I'm told. Then, the residents complained their water supplies had gone foul. Ponds and streams turned warm and then hot with the taste of sulfur. When the fires started, homes and businesses closest to the rising temperatures began to smolder, bursting into flames before anything could be done to salvage the buildings. Within a matter of weeks, there was nothing left. The families lost everything. Their livelihood. Their crops, livestock. Everything."

Veren pointed to a post in the ground just a few yards from the road. "Last week, the ground was green up to that post. Now, everything from there to the road is dying. It won't be long before the spread takes out the next village. Grima is in danger, Tierney." Veren settled wide eyes on her. "And I don't know how to stop it."

"All of Lenya is in danger." Tierney steered her horse back to the road. "And with both kingdoms at each other's throats, it might be up to us to find a solution."

"Just perfect." Gulliver groaned. "Why is it always us?"

CHAPTER TEN
SIOBHAN

"What did you do to her?" Prince Tobias ran past the guards stationed near the front of the Iskalt palace before Siobhan could even dismount.

Siobhan's relief at seeing the familiar face almost overcame her grief at still not knowing where his sister was. Almost.

Griffin slid from his horse. "Good to see you too, nephew."

Tobias crossed his arms, and he looked so much like Tierney in that moment Siobhan had to blink back tears. "It would have been good to see you before you took an Iskaltian noblewoman as prisoner."

"We didn't hold her prisoner." Griffin sounded tired from the journey, tired and sad. He hadn't asked for specifics of what happened in the portal once she told him she didn't know where Tierney was. He said Lochlan should be the first to know the full story.

"But you did arrest her."

Riona jumped down, landing with grace on the snow-packed ground. "Does it always have to be so blasted cold here?"

"Yes," Tobias and Siobhan said simultaneously.

From the moment they entered the ice kingdom, Siobhan knew she was home. As the gooseflesh rose on her arms and a shiver raced down her spine, she looked away. It wouldn't do to have any of them see her tears.

Two boys ran toward them and bowed to Tobias. "We've come to take care of the horses. The king sent us." Another young man followed behind, and Siobhan recognized him as the prince of Eldur, Tobias' suitor.

Tobias eyed the younger boys. "You're not needed. My uncle can care for his own horses after the trouble he caused."

The Eldurian prince snorted. "That was what your mother said."

Stepping to the side of her horse, Tobias looked up at Siobhan like she held all the answers he so desperately needed. "Come, let me help you down."

She slid a leg over the saddle and let her feet drop to the ground with Tobias' hands at her waist. He wasn't the twin she wanted to see, but he had Tierney's smile as he gave her a soft look.

"Let's get you inside." He wrapped a protective arm around her shoulders and led her away from a grumbling Griffin and a stoic Riona. They'd refused to bring guards with them, saying this was a family affair. But Siobhan was not part of that family, and she just wanted to go home to see her father.

"Give her some room to breathe, Tobes," Logan said. "You're suffocating her."

Siobhan had never been so grateful for a simple request before. The moment Tobias released her, she drew in a long breath and listened to the rapid pounding of her heart.

It wasn't her first time in the Iskaltian palace. There were royal balls and dinners, plays and musicals. But Tobias wasn't leading her to the grand hall or any of the other public places. This corridor wound up to the royal family's wing.

"So ..." Tobias didn't sound like he was sure he should speak. "Griff didn't hurt you, did he? He's not so bad, but really, he can be quite pigheaded sometimes."

"Pigheaded, your Highness?" The momentary confusion was a welcome distraction. "Like, a fae who has a pig's head? Is that a type of Dark Fae in Myrkur?"

He stifled a laugh. "No, um, my mom says it to my father quite often. It's like ... well, actually I'm not sure what it means. I just know she says it when he's being particularly insufferable."

"Well, then I guess Griffin and Riona both had pig heads at first. Then, I explained who I was and they immediately began preparations for our journey to Iskalt."

Tobias nodded. "We received word days ago and have been awaiting your arrival. Griffin explained everything in the letter. You came through the rift after my sister left you in the human world?"

"I'm not sure that is quite accurate." Tierney leaving her implied choice, and she got the feeling Tierney didn't have control over anything that happened.

"Oh, of course. I didn't mean it like that. But Tia shouldn't have taken you to the human realm."

"Toby," Logan warned.

"What?" Tobias looked back at his prince. "I love my sister, but she was reckless, and now she's across the fire plains in a land we know little about. I'm allowed to be angry. I'm allowed to hate her just a bit for being gone." His chest heaved with anger, and his eyes grew wild with frustration.

In his calm greeting, Siobhan hadn't realized how much the prince was hurting, but she could see it now in the tension he carried in his shoulders, the way his eyes wouldn't focus.

What he'd said didn't register until that moment. "Wait, across the fire plains? How do you know this?" Her heart swelled at hearing Tierney was alive.

"Maybe we should save explanations for when we've all gathered." Queen Brea stood in the doorway of the royal suites, looking as regal as Siobhan had always found her. The pale blue dress was embroidered with what looked like icicles. Her long hair was swept up into an unusual hairstyle, pulled back from her face with some kind of lace holding it in a high tail at the back of her head.

"Siobhan." She gave her a kind smile. "We are so glad you've returned, dear. Come, let's get you warm. Your father is on his way, and he will be brought up as soon as he arrives."

Siobhan's shoulders sagged in relief, and a soft sob escaped her lips. It was over. All this time alone, traveling through a world she didn't know, her arrest in Myrkur, the journey here upon learning Tierney hadn't returned ... it all came crashing down around her.

"Oh, honey." The queen pulled her into a tight hug. "You're safe now."

Siobhan's body shook. Under normal circumstances, she'd never let the royal family see her in such a state, but right now, she just needed a mother. Even if said mother was the queen.

"Come near the fire." She led Siobhan into a grand sitting room with plush velvet carpeting and soft white drapes. Two settees faced each other in front of the black opal hearth. They were the toughest gems in the fae realm, and it was a welcome sight seeing the familiarity in Iskalt.

Siobhan sat before the queen, something that was considered poor manners, but all she could think of was thawing her frozen limbs. She held them toward the warmth, and it snaked over her skin, coiling in her belly.

"Here." Queen Brea handed her a cup of tea before turning to her son. "Where is your uncle?"

"I made him take the horses to the stables." He shrugged.

"I knew you were my son." Brea ruffled his hair. "Your siblings?"

"Kayleigh is keeping everyone occupied in the nursery, so we won't be interrupted."

"Good, good. Now, we must wait for—"

"I'm here." King Lochlan walked in, his steps heavy and firm.

"Us too." Griffin followed him, looking like he'd gone a few rounds with a bull.

"What happened to you?" Lochlan asked.

Griffin sent Toby a pointed look. "Horse kicked me, and I landed in the hay."

Lochlan looked from his brother to his son with a sigh. "Tia isn't here so you become her?"

Toby's satisfied smile dropped. "If I do, will you make me marry an Iskaltian noble too?"

Siobhan winced at the vitriol in his tone, and she noticed both Griffin and Riona do the same. She'd never truly considered what this marriage arrangement would mean for Tierney. When Siobhan's father broached the topic of making her an eligible choice for the princess, Siobhan agreed, but she'd been half in love with Tierney already.

And if she'd said no? Her father would have accepted that.

The queen sat beside Siobhan and reached for her hand. "It's best not to get involved." There was sadness in her voice.

Lochlan walked to the tea cart and poured himself a cup. Then, he pulled out a flask and tipped it against the cup.

Griffin snatched the flask from him and didn't bother with the tea, drinking whatever was inside it straight. He grimaced, but he didn't stop.

"Okay." Brea brought everyone to attention. "Here's what will happen. I want to know every tiny detail about what happened to my girl. So, you boys will not get in the way. Toby, you'll stop blaming your father for the next hour. Griffin, you will listen to someone other than yourself. And Loch, you will not take whatever is said and go running into danger." Her eyes fell on Riona. "You just ... do you, Ri."

Riona nodded. "I don't know how to do anything else."

"Siobhan, start at the beginning." She patted Siobhan's hand. "Please."

"Well, none of us planned on going with Tia to the human realm. At least, Veren and I didn't. Gulliver jumped into the portal after her, but it sort of just pulled us in."

Tobias pursed his lips. "It must have been too powerful. Tierney has never been good at holding back, and with portals, everything needs to be precise."

"The human realm was ... different. But we were enjoying ourselves, eating odd food and watching a box with strange portraits that moved."

"A television," both Brea and Lochlan said at once.

Lochlan smiled. "Tierney loves the television. When she was younger, she wanted me to figure out how to make one work in our world, but that is magic we do not possess."

Siobhan went on to tell them about the rest of their time in the human realm, the party they'd thrown Tierney, how they'd planned to come home.

"We knew staying there wasn't right when fae would worry about us here."

Brea covered her mouth with her hand. "We checked the farmhouse, but it wasn't until a few days after she'd disappeared, when we figured out she hadn't just gone to Myrkur with Gulliver. It wouldn't have been the first time she left and didn't send word for days. When we saw the remnants of the party, we started to worry."

"Yeah," Tobias said. "No one ever feels good about Tierney opening portals. It's like the one thing she's terrible at."

"And what happened next?" Lochlan perched on the arm of a settee, tipping his teacup against his lips.

Siobhan twisted her hands together and stared at her lap. "She opened the portal. We all held on to each other, not wanting to be separated, but something pulled us apart. I lost consciousness, and when I woke, I was back in the human realm. Alone. From there, I made my way to the rift. It was this pull I couldn't ignore. I considered waiting for someone to find me, but the magic... I'd never felt anything like it."

Lochlan rubbed the back of his neck and met his brother's gaze. "Is it possible?"

"I don't know." Griffin shook his head. "It shouldn't be, but the O'Shea magic still has so many unknowns."

"Care to share with the class?" Brea nudged her husband.

Lochlan was quiet for a moment, thinking. "A portal is like a road. It goes from one point to another. In our case, from our world to the human world and back, depending on where you direct it to. It should not let anyone off that road until they've reached the final destination."

"I still don't understand."

"Siobhan began journeying down that road with Tierney and the others," Griffin explained. "But the portal let her off.

Whatever Tierney did, however she crafted the portal, it seems she created one with ... branches."

"Branches?" Brea scrubbed a hand over her face. "You're saying my daughter created a portal and led four people in, but something went wrong and the portal spit them all out in different places?"

"I wouldn't say spit ..." Lochlan muttered. "But essentially, yes. Her magic is strong, Brea. We've always known this. Strong and sometimes erratic. This time, it may have been too strong even for the portal."

A stunned silence filled the room. Too strong for a portal.

"So, Tierney, Gulliver, and Veren could all be in different places?" Tobias asked, reaching for Logan's hand.

"Toby ..." Siobhan couldn't wrap her head around any of this. "You said she's across the fire plains. How do you know?"

"I can feel her. Just enough to know she's alive. She's too far for me to feel her magic, to amplify it, but something in me just knows that she's okay and she's trying to get home to us."

There was a knock on the door, and Riona went to open it. After a moment, Siobhan heard her father's voice. "Where's my daughter?"

She jumped from the settee and sprinted across the ornate sitting room, caring nothing for propriety. Not now. Her father caught her as she crashed against him and folded her into his arms.

"My girl," he whispered. "My girl."

Her tears dampened his shirt as his familiar smell of cherry pipe tobacco invaded her senses.

He brushed her hair away from her face and looked down at her. "You're really here."

She nodded. "I'm home, Father. I made it home."

"Yes, you did." He smiled before his expression hardened

and he looked over her head. "I'm taking my daughter to our estate. She's done here."

"Lord Belmore." Brea stood. "We were speaking to her about Tierney, and—"

"No, it has been enough for today. She is exhausted, and this ordeal has been long and drawn out. I must leave this palace before I say what I wish to say."

"Father—"

"No, Siobhan, you do not owe them more."

Didn't he get that she wanted to help? "Father!" Her brusque tone had his surprised eyes finding hers. "You have a pig's head."

"Excuse me?"

"What happened to me is not his Majesty's fault, nor is it even the princess'. It was a mistake—sure, a large one—but there was no ill intent. We must work together to find the others."

"But you—"

"No. They're my friends, Father." Friends. She'd never truly used that word before. "And I will do anything in my power to bring them home." She turned to the royals seated before the roaring flames. Respect shone in their eyes. "What do we know about the fire plains?"

"Only that it is impossible to survive a journey across them," Lochlan said.

Brea nodded. "Impossible is a state of mind. I want to hear solutions, not problems."

Siobhan met Tobias' gaze and gave him a small nod, a promise. They would bring his sister home.

CHAPTER ELEVEN
TIERNEY

"I still think this is the worst idea you've ever had." Gulliver trotted his horse up between Tierney and Queen Bronagh. He tugged his hood down low over his eyes as they traveled the long dusty road that would soon take them into Vondurian territory.

"It wasn't my idea," Tierney said, chewing on her bottom lip.

"I know. I'm just saying there is no way either of you could ever pass for a credible maid. Not without weeks of training. A few days learning how to make tea isn't going to fool anyone who's ever had an actual maid. Not even Keir."

"We couldn't waste any more time, Gullie." Tierney cast a wary glance around them, looking for danger around every corner. "We'll keep working on Bronagh's training as we travel. See." Tierney nodded toward the Grima Queen. "She's working on her slouching right now."

"It will be fine, Gulliver." Bronagh made an effort to shrug off her queenly posture. "I only need a few days to observe the king from the shadows.

"She looks like a maid." Tierney admired the effort of the queen's maid. In a borrowed dress and her hair in a simple bun with a white cap over her head, she did look the part. As long as she didn't speak, most wouldn't give her much notice.

"She sounds like a queen." Veren rode up beside them.

"We have time to teach her some slang."

"Yeah, and what kind of slang do you know?" Gulliver asked.

"Human slang." Tierney's shoulders drooped.

"Exactly. And when Keir finds out we've brought the enemy into his court, we're all going to hang." Gulliver rubbed his throat absently.

Tierney balled her hand into a fist to keep herself from doing the same. The feel of the hangman's noose around her neck was not something she would ever forget.

"How close are we to the border?" Bronagh asked.

"We will reach Vondur lands by late afternoon." Veren studied his map with a frown. "I believe this road leads to a lesser traveled route that will allow us to slip past the border guards undetected. I studied all possible routes with Prince Donal before we left." He returned the map to his saddle bags. "He assures me this is the best way to reach the palace without risking the king's guard."

Tierney's stomach twisted into knots at the thought of facing the king's soldiers. Though King Keir had released her, the general assumption among Vondurian soldiers was that she was the hated Grima spy. She'd rather not run the risk of discovery out here on the road.

As they approached the border, Veren rode ahead to scout the way. A voice inside Tierney's mind screamed *Abort! Abort!* Her horse danced under her in response to her mounting tension.

"It will be okay, Tia." Bronagh's hand reached out to grasp hers. "You've assured me time and again that Keir is a different sort of king."

"And he is." Tierney nodded. "However, while there are several people I'd love to see again, I can't help but think of all the others who wished me dead."

"As much as I don't want to see anyone of Vondur ever again," Gulliver muttered, "it's been weeks since we left. Time enough for Keir to have established his rule. He won't let any harm come to you again."

"Let's hope." She let out a breath but still didn't feel any better about what they were doing.

"Ride!" Veren came charging back up the road, kicking up a storm of dust behind him.

"What's happening?" Bronagh turned toward him.

"I don't need to be told twice." Gulliver reached for the queen's reins and urged her mount to follow his away from the Vondurian border. "Come on, Tia!"

Just as they pulled into an all-out gallop the way they'd come, Tierney reared her horse back from the king's guard blocking their retreat.

"The bloody sneaks came up behind us!" Gulliver growled, his eyes scanning their surroundings looking for a way out.

"Get the mongrel!" The captain in charge barked out orders to his men. "The king has promised a high price for his head. And he'll pay handsomely for the Grima spy and her consorts too."

"Run, Gullie!" Tierney dug her heels into her horse's flanks and turned off the road, guiding her mount through the short, scrubby brush, heading for the cover of the forest. Casting a glance over her shoulder, she saw her friends following her lead. She had to find a way out. If Keir was searching for them, whatever awaited them at the palace wouldn't be good.

"This cannot happen again."

"Tia, watch out!" Veren shouted, and she turned a moment too late. Her horse skidded to a halt in front of a line of grubby, half-starved-looking soldiers. Circling back around, the other soldiers swarmed her.

"Gullie!" Tierney sobbed at the sight of her best friend lying on the ground with a soldier's foot on his back while another tied his hands behind him. "Stop! You can't treat him like that!"

"The king will decide what to do with the mongrel."

"Don't call him that." Veren struggled against the soldiers holding him. "Leave her alone!" He kicked out at the soldier pushing Bronagh to her knees beside Gulliver.

"Come on, *Princess*." The captain lunged toward Tierney, grabbing for her reins. "You might have escaped the hangman's noose once, but it won't happen again."

"The king released us," Tierney argued, kicking the captain's chin so his head snapped back, and he spit out a gob of blood.

"Get her off that horse."

Dirty hands and arms wrapped around her, dragging her off her horse and tossing her in a heap on the ground. She groaned and curled into a ball when the captain landed a brutal kick to her stomach.

"Tierney is the Crown Princess of Iskalt," Veren shouted, struggling anew against his captors. "You will treat her as such!"

"I know nothing of any land called Iskalt." The man spit on the ground. "You're in Vondur now, and we don't take kindly to Grima spies."

Tia tucked into a ball to avoid the kicks and bruising punches that raked across her torso and arms. Scrunching her face up, she closed her eyes and held her breath to avoid choking on the dust and grime.

"Welcome back, *Princess.*" A torrent of spit rained down on her.

Why did I think I could return here and it would be different this time?

CHAPTER TWELVE
KEIR

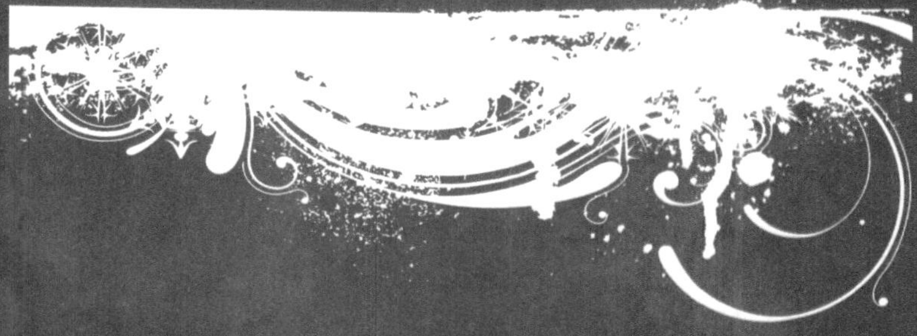

"We need to fortify the north wall of the palace." Keir glanced up at the crumbling stone damaged in the siege. His father hadn't bothered to do a survey of their defenses after everything that happened.

He really had to stop thinking about his father. None of this was about him.

"Sire?" The young builder who'd been tasked with recording the king's desires gave him a questioning look.

"Sorry, moving on. Let's go have a look at the battlements." He headed for the far tower and the spiral staircase within. In his mind, he saw Tierney and Eavha running up these steps to join the fight. He saw his men arguing with them, but the women winning.

With a sigh, he trudged up the stairs. Had he failed Eavha? She was on his council now, but something wasn't altogether right. This morning, he'd asked her to accompany him on this task, but she'd made up an excuse about needing to air out her rooms—a job Ariella should have done for her.

And then, when he stopped by her rooms to see how she was progressing, she wasn't there and the windows were firmly shut, leaving the space as closed in as ever.

She'd lied.

He reached the top of the walls, where a line of guards stood ready for any threat that could come from all directions. He'd had to bolster the palace guard with men from his troops, and not all of them were particularly good at the standing still part.

Keir took note of the few who squirmed and whispered amongst themselves while the others went rigid at the presence of the king, standing at attention. The chatterers were young, probably from a village unit that had never received a visit from the king.

"Your Majesty." The nearest guard turned and bowed. Keir recognized him as Colin, a man who'd worked in the palace for many years. "I think you'll find everything in order up here. Most of the damages during the siege occurred at the gates."

Keir nodded. "Those will be taken care of, and—" He stopped when he caught sight of movement near the tree line. He wasn't the only one.

"Guards!" Colin barked. "At the ready." Every third man raised a bow, preparing an assault on whomever traveled those woods.

Riders appeared, waving the king's standard high. As they neared in the blazing afternoon sun, Colin ordered, "Stand down; they're our scouts."

In the middle of the group rode two women, but Keir

couldn't make out their faces. If they brought prisoners, he had to know why. Why else would women ride with them? He hadn't yet allowed them to join the scouting parties in search of Grima troops.

"It's the Grima spy," a guard shouted.

Keir stepped forward, gripping the wall. Despite his own words, he knew there was only one person his men would call the Grima spy. Her blond hair came into view first. There was no mistaking it. The way she rode the horse like a Vondurian warrior, one leg to either side, the lithe movement of her body as the group trotted toward the castle.

"Open the gates," Keir yelled. He took off running down the stairs and out into the courtyard. The gates opened with an agonizing slowness, and he waited. The scouting party thundered through, pulling to a stop.

There was no doubt in his mind now. In the time since they'd been separated, he often wondered if she'd survived, if she'd made it to safety. With every decision he made as king, he asked himself what she would think. His entire life changed because he chose to save her, chose to believe she was who she claimed to be.

And now, she sat atop a horse just feet from him.

Keir lifted his gaze, skating it up the horse's flanks to Tierney's strong, trouser-clad legs. Up over her capable hands until he finally reached the scowl she directed his way. Her face was dirty and bruised. She looked like she'd been through war and back since he'd last seen her.

"Your Majesty." One of the scouts slid from his horse, but Keir paid him no mind.

Tierney jumped down with the grace of a seasoned fighter. She still wasn't smiling, but her eyes connected with his, anger swirling in their depths.

He'd missed that anger.

She strode forward to greet him, causing a stir behind her that she would dare approach the king without permission.

Keir opened his mouth to speak, but he didn't get a word out before Tierney's fist slammed into his jaw sending a sharp pain through him.

"Despicable," she growled and shoved him hard, forcing him to take several steps back. "Unconscionable."

"Tierney ..."

Guards gripped her arms, pulling her away. She didn't struggle, and her gaze remained burning into his. "You were supposed to be different, and yet here I am, once again taken captive by your men. My friends treated like animals."

"I didn't ..."

"Sire," Colin said. "Want us to escort her to a cell?"

"What? Absolutely not." He straightened. "Release her at once."

The guards looked at each other, as if not sure they should obey their own king. "Sire—"

"That was an order." Keir's voice took on a hard edge.

They released Tierney, and thankfully she didn't lunge forward again. Instead, she turned to check on one of her companions perched atop another mount. "Are you okay?" Her voice was low, soft.

The woman nodded but did not speak.

"Gullie? Veren?"

They both gave her an affirmative answer, so she turned back to Keir. "Why, Keir? You let me go. I came back for a reason, but I didn't get the chance to do it on my terms because you instructed your scouts to seize us."

"I didn't—"

"Tierney?" A shriek pierced the courtyard. Eavha sprinted toward the other princess, barreling into her. "I didn't think I'd ever see you again."

Tierney hugged her back just as tightly, something Keir couldn't help smiling at. The smile fell when he noticed what his sister was wearing. She was clad in leather armor not suitable for a day spent in the palace.

"I only wish I could have returned under my own volition." Tierney held her at arm's length.

"What do you mean?" Eavha asked. "What did Keir do now?"

He tried to object, but the girls ignored him.

"He had us arrested again."

Eavha gasped. "He wouldn't."

"Not if he was intelligent, no."

Eavha turned, her eyes narrowed. "I'm disappointed in you, brother. Just because Tierney chose to go to Grima does not make her the enemy."

"I—"

"You can't jump to conclusions just to suit your mood." She looked sideways at Tierney. "You would not believe it, but I think he's even more morose since becoming king."

"Not possible." Tierney shook her head.

"I wouldn't have thought so either."

"I'm right here, you know." Keir let loose a scowl that would've frightened the hardest of Grima's golden warriors. Neither girl reacted.

He couldn't help noticing the eyes on them from the guards and the travel weary scouts. "I will handle our visitors. Return to your posts." When none of them moved, he clapped his hands once to get their attention. "Now, soldiers."

Guards dispersed, and scouts led their horses toward the stables, leaving Keir standing face to face with two annoyed princesses, a woman he didn't recognize, a tall man, and Gulliver. They all stared at him with accusation in their eyes.

Keir rubbed the back of his neck. "No one is a prisoner, but maybe we should talk inside." He turned on his heel, knowing they'd follow him.

Eavha chattered incessantly through the halls, telling Tierney of all the palace gossip he didn't know existed. He tried not to listen, but the moment he caught his own name, he couldn't help it.

"Most people are okay with Keir being king and think he'll protect us," Eavha whispered. "But some of the women are still preparing."

Preparing how? He didn't get an answer because they arrived at the very same rooms Tierney inhabited before.

Pushing open the door, he gestured for them to enter.

When Tierney passed him, she looked up. "Will I be able to leave this time, your Majesty?" There was a bite to her tone, and he realized how much he'd missed that.

Very few fae challenged him. Most feared he might order their punishment if they spoke out of turn. It was how his father had ruled.

Once they were all inside, he closed the door. Before any of them could throw out further accusations, he spoke hard and firm. "Let me make one thing clear. I ordered no one to apprehend you. I will be questioning the captain who brought you in as soon as I leave here. He will be punished for acting in my name without orders to do so. I speak true, Tierney, when I say you and yours are always welcome in Vondur."

Tierney lowered herself to the settee, perching on the edge, and crossed her arms.

"Who are you?" Eavha asked. She was eying the tall man like he was a river running through the bone-dry desert.

The man smiled, clearly enjoying the princess' attention. "Lord Rhatigan." He lifted Eavha's hand, pressing a kiss to the back of it. "Heir to the Duchy of Rhatigan, at your service."

Tierney made a gagging sound. "The duke is his father.

This is just Veren." She stood and crossed the room, grabbing Eavha's arm and pulling her away. "Don't let the good looks fool you. He's a snake." She sent him a smile.

Veren winked. "We'll see if you still think so once I've won your hand."

Keir's throat tightened. "That friend you were seeking ... he is your betrothed?" He was glad she'd found him, but the idea of ...

A harsh laugh barked out of Tierney. "He wishes. If we ever find Siobhan, I'm choosing her. At least I can stand to be around her."

One of her friends was still missing? Keir studied the way she tried and failed to smile, the sadness in her eyes. His heart twisted at her pain.

Her expression returned to neutral, all traces of emotion gone. "This is Yvonne." She gestured to the small woman trying to make herself unobtrusive.

"She's a maid I took a liking to. I brought her with us to attend to me while we are here."

Keir nodded. "Eavha, please take Yvonne to Ariella. She'll show her where she will stay in the servants' quarters."

"But Keir—"

"Please just do as I say for once."

With a huff, she led Yvonne from the room, leaving Keir with Tierney, Veren, and Gulliver. Veren circled the room, picking up every item he could and examining them. "Wow, you really do build everything out of depleted crystals. Donal was right."

"Donal?" Keir's eyes snapped to the other man. "Just how close were you to the royal family of Grima?"

Tierney sent him a sharp look.

Veren shrugged. "I heard a few speeches. Vondurians are

evil, blah blah blah. Lenya isn't my kingdom, so I don't really care about your wars."

Keir didn't like Veren already, and he definitely didn't trust him. He'd have to assign a guard to keep an eye on him. For now, he turned away, intent on ignoring him and focusing on the woman he never thought he'd see again.

Tierney looked road-weary and a little worse for the wear but strong. Despite the tangles in her hair, the smudges of dirt on her face, she drew her shoulders back and held her head high. He wondered if she had a weapon hidden on her or if the scouts had completely disarmed her.

He had so many questions. Questions a king needed to ask a fae returning from an enemy court, but the words didn't come. Instead, he gave her a self-deprecating smile. "Eavha won't listen to a word I say since you left."

Tierney laughed and relaxed back onto the settee. "I don't think she ever really listened to you before that. She just didn't voice her disagreements." Her eyes slid shut.

"You're probably right." He sat on the other end of the settee, keeping a respectable distance between them. "I invited her to sit on my council."

Tierney opened one eye. "And how did that go?"

"She was pleased. Some of my nobles had issues with it. But in order for us to move forward, we must change. No good comes from remaining stuck in antiquated notions."

"I seem to remember a prince who believed in those antiquated notions."

"Just as the kingdom evolves, so do I."

Her lips twitched. "I yelled at you in front of your men."

He nodded. "I noticed that."

"I'm not sorry."

"I would not presume to believe you are." Keir felt her nearness, the way she seemed to radiate with life. "But, Tierney, this time is different. I promise you are my welcome guest and will be treated as such as long as I am king. What you endured before ... I cannot begin to express how—"

"Please don't apologize."

"But it is necessary."

A sigh breathed out of her. "Necessary is boring. Just tell me I deserved it because I probably did. Own your actions, your Majesty. I was a foreigner who arrived out of the sky in the middle of your battle. Don't be disingenuous and tell me you wish you'd reacted differently."

"What a strange world we live in."

"Especially when you consider we've now gone the last few minutes without yelling at one another."

Keir stared at her, at the way her face softened when she grew more tired, how sweet she could appear even when delivering the harshest of remarks. She lifted one brow, and he cleared his throat, getting to his feet. "I have some things I must attend to. I'll send Ariella to get you three something to eat. Feel free to leave this room. My castle is your castle, but please alert me to any trouble you encounter."

With one final glance at where Veren and Gullie lounged on the bed and then to Tierney, he turned on his heel and forced himself to walk away.

She was back. The woman who got him into this situation, the one that made him realize his fae deserved a better king.

He didn't know how long she would stay, or why she'd come at all, but at least he knew now what became of her. And that was enough. For the moment.

CHAPTER THIRTEEN
KEIR

Tell me I deserved it.

She'd wanted to believe Keir was justified in his actions, that the wrong he'd committed was for a reason. Yet, he knew the truth. What he'd done to her and her friend was unconscionable. He'd acted just as his father would have.

When Tierney first appeared at the end of the battle, Keir had only wanted to get home. He hadn't considered who she might really be, that maybe she wasn't the spy he'd assumed she was.

And even once he began to realize how wrong he was, he hadn't let her go. There had been so many opportunities, and still, he'd obeyed his father. Choosing the easy route over what was right.

Turning over in bed, Keir kicked the blanket tangled around his legs. Sleep was a fruitless pursuit tonight. His mind wouldn't quiet, not when he saw her every time he closed his eyes.

Tierney was a princess in her own right. Heir to her own kingdom. He didn't know how he'd ever questioned it. The way she held herself with authority, the fierceness in her eyes. She wasn't of Lenya, and soon, she would have to find a way home. But she'd changed him, changed his sister, changed Vondur.

And there was no going back to what they were before.

Rubbing his eyes, he sat up in the dark. It took a while to adjust and be able to see the table carved from totems that had long lost their magic, the walls glittering with fragments of crystals.

Even as a child, before his father became king, he'd thought the palace was a magical place. But now, he needed to get out of these walls. Sliding from the bed, he retrieved a tunic from his wardrobe and pulled it on over his chest—a chest that should have been crisscrossed with scars from all the wounds he'd suffered in battle. Most warriors of Vondur, who still lived, suffered from the remnants, the reminders of the war.

But not the king. For only he had access to the healing baths. It didn't feel right that so many should die while he hoarded such lifesaving magic for himself.

Stuffing his feet into his boots, he laced them up and pulled open the door. He'd hardly stepped into the hall before running into Declan, the commander giving him a formal bow.

"Stop that." Keir scowled.

Declan's voice was low to keep from being overheard. "We

must keep up appearances, your Majesty. I am your commander now."

"Yes, but you're still my friend, and I'll not have you bowing every time you see me."

"As you wish." The stubborn man lowered himself to one knee. "Is this better?"

Keir sighed. "Being king is hard enough without you making a mockery of it."

"I would never mock, your Majesty." His lips twitched.

"Just get up, Deck."

Declan rose to his feet. "I thought I'd have to wake you tonight."

"That would imply I ever went to sleep." Keir started down the corridor.

"You need your rest, Keir."

"Thanks for that. Why were you coming to see me in the middle of the night?" He stopped, realizing if it couldn't wait until morning, it must be serious.

"I just returned from the troops at the border. There have been no sightings of the golden warriors of late, but something is amiss in Grima."

"What do you mean?"

"We received intel that the queen has left the palace."

Keir froze. "And where would she go?" The palace was the safest place for her. She would know that as well as everyone else.

Declan shrugged. "No one seems to know. There are rumors she is on campaign, visiting some of the far reaches of Grima to solidify her reign, but no one has actually seen her."

A string of curses flew from Keir's lips. If the queen left the palace, she was preparing for something. "Keep the troops on high alert for anything out of the ordinary. I don't want us to be caught unawares."

Footsteps neared them, and Keir looked up to find the maid who'd arrived with Tierney. Her face reddened.

"I'm sorry, your Majesty," she stammered, dipping into an awkward curtsy. It looked like she'd done very few of them in her life. "I didn't mean to interrupt. My lady is up on the walls, and I was returning to fetch a cloak for her."

"That's quite all right, Yvonne." Keir stepped aside. "You can continue on your way."

She scurried off on her errand, and Declan chuckled. "Who was that?"

"Tierney's maid."

His eyes widened. "Tierney is back?"

Keir clapped him on the shoulder. "You missed a lot today. I'm sure you'll learn it all in the morning, but you need your rest and I need some air."

"That air wouldn't happen to be atop the walls, would it?"

Keir ignored him and changed direction, heading for the courtyard. Once outside, he searched the grounds, nodding to a few guards. When he tilted his head back, he caught sight of a lone figure sitting atop the wall silhouetted by the silver light of the moon.

His guards kept their distance from her, and he wondered if they were frightened. Honestly, she scared him a bit. Her lack of restraint, the way she did whatever it was she wanted to do. Even men in Vondur did not have those freedoms.

Before he knew what he was doing, he found himself climbing the spiral staircase and emerging onto the platform at the top of the wall. Tierney's eyes were fixed on the orchestra of stars above, and she didn't acknowledge him.

"Your maid said you were up here." He studied her, the way the light reflected off her dark eyes. How her lips curled into the smallest half-smile, like she found him slightly amusing.

Finally, she spoke. "I sent her away so I could be alone."

Alone. "I'll leave you to it then."

"Keir?" She dropped her chin, her eyes tearing from the sky overhead.

"Yes?"

"Stay."

That one word was all he needed to hear. Taking a seat beside her, he tried not to think of how improper this was for the king—to sit so casually on the wall, where anyone could see him. His father had taught him appearance was everything. He had to seem like he cared about everyone in his kingdom. But he truly did care, and he knew those attachments were dangerous.

A sigh echoed from Tierney. "I was just sitting here, wondering if my brother was looking up at the same stars."

"You miss him."

She lifted her eyes to the sky once more. "Of course I do. He's my other half. Without him, I am not whole."

"What makes you think you are not whole?"

She was quiet for a moment, her entire body still. "Can I trust you, Keir? I can't truly tell what kind of fae you are. Sometimes you're ruthless, but others, I think ..."

He lifted his hand, using his thumb to press her chin down so her eyes drifted to his. "You can trust me." They were some of the truest words he'd ever said. He wouldn't betray her, not again, not after all the harm he'd already caused.

Her lips parted, and a puff of air escaped. It wasn't until he withdrew his hand she spoke. "Toby, my twin, was born without magic. The only thing he can do is open portals. He's quite a bit better at that than me. But me ... I have the power of three kingdoms running through my veins. Yet, I'm at my strongest when Toby lets me channel the power through him.

My father and my uncle call him my amplifier. He makes me better, more focused."

"That's—"

"Kind of sad, I know. I can't reach my full potential without his help."

Keir shook his head. He hadn't been thinking it was sad at all. To have that kind of bond with another person, that they made one's magic stronger ... "It's amazing."

A small smile appeared on her face, and she looked away so he wouldn't see it. "I think that might be why my power barely works here. I'm too far from Toby, or maybe there's something about the fire plains that severs our connection. Without him, I'm nothing."

Didn't she see it? Even without her magic, she'd begun changing Vondur for the better. She stood strong atop these walls during a siege, inspired his sister to be more than tradition allowed. Taught Keir that being a good king was more important than winning battles that no longer mattered.

"Tierney," he whispered, his fingers flitting under her chin, turning her face. "You could never be nothing. Magic isn't all that you are." This time, he didn't pull his hand back. Instead, he let his fingers trace the curve of her neck, the shell of her ear. Yet, there was still one burning question she hadn't answered since her arrival. "Why have you returned to Vondur?" To the place that held her captive and almost killed her.

Tierney's breath stuttered, and she reached up, covering his hand with hers before pushing it away. She got to her feet and turned to look out across the lonely lands beyond the palace. "Vondur seems different from when I was here last."

He let her deflect his question for the moment and joined her at the parapet. "It is different. We're making progress. My council is working to feed the villages, and we're taking care of those who've lost their loved ones to this war. Eavha's example is making more women reach for their freedom. That one will be slow to change, but it's coming. I made Declan commander of my army."

"Good choice." She nodded.

"He's facing many problems, but I have faith our armies will be prepared for the next battle."

Tierney turned to him, her lips pursed. "Does there have to be another battle?"

"I'm afraid there does. We cannot let Grima take everything we have."

"But what if the Grima queen wanted peace? What if this fight belonged to her mother and your father, and those before them? You two could welcome in a new generation with a treaty."

Something about this wasn't right. His eyes narrowed. "Do you know where the queen has gone?"

Alarm flashed across her face before she hid it. "No. Of course not. I'm only saying what so many of your subjects are already thinking. Both Vondur and Grima. This war isn't theirs. Not anymore."

"For some reason, I don't believe you about the queen."

"Well, you can believe what you want. I don't care." She turned on her heel and marched toward the stairs.

He watched her for a moment before thundering after her, reaching her as she hit the last step inside the tower. He gripped her arm and turned her. She stumbled, falling against him.

"Let me go, Keir." There was no conviction in her words.

Hidden from view of the guards, he backed her up against the wall of the tower, hovering over her. In the shadows, her features grew dark, and he found he missed the light. "Why are you here, Tierney?"

"Please don't ask me that."

"Is it at the request of the enemy queen?" Was she truly a Grima spy now?

"No." The word echoed through the tower.

He bent closer, his face only inches from hers. "Then, tell me why."

Her breath warmed him, and he couldn't have moved if he tried. Her chest rose and fell rapidly against his, reminding him how close they were. It wasn't right, and still, neither of them pushed the other away. He knew what he wanted her to say. That she'd returned because he needed her, because she needed him.

But that was the thing about Tierney. She never needed anyone.

His forehead rested against hers. "Tell me to walk away. Tell me you returned to deliver a message from my enemy." He wasn't even sure that could have stopped him.

Her eyes met his, and she wet her lips. "I can't."

"Can't or won't?"

"Both."

He planted a hand on each side of her head, not letting his lips close that final remaining distance. If he did, nothing would be the same. Kissing Tierney O'Shea would only bring him to ruin.

Yet, he'd never wanted anything more.

"Say something to irritate me," she whispered. "Please."

He chuckled, the sound vibrating through them both. "I'm glad you trusted me tonight." Not with what he'd truly needed to know, what her presence meant. But he suspected the connection with her brother was something she guarded closely. It caused her immeasurable pain to be away from him.

"You're insufferable sometimes, Keir, but I do think you

want to be a good man. I knew it even when you had me tied to the back of your horse."

He cringed at the memory. "You had more faith in me than I did."

"Faith is easy." She smiled. "It's only a bit of magic."

"Here in Vondur, not even magic is easy."

Her smile fell. "I—"

"My lady?" Yvonne stopped in the doorway, her mouth dropping open. She had a cloak clutched in her hands.

Tierney pressed both palms to Keir's chest and shoved him back before turning to her maid. "Thank you, Yvonne. I think I will return to my rooms now. His Majesty and I were just discussing Grima."

Keir didn't know why she felt the need to tell her maid this, but he nodded along.

Yvonne pursed her lips. "I'm sure."

To his surprise, Tierney didn't chastise her for her insolence. Instead, she hurried to her side and put an arm around her shoulders. "Come, we can talk in my rooms."

Keir watched them cross the courtyard and enter the palace before scrubbing a hand over his face. Nothing about that woman ever made any sense.

CHAPTER FOURTEEN
TIERNEY

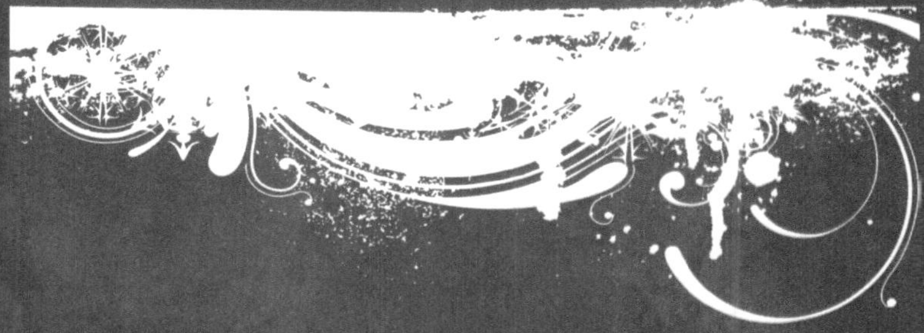

Bronagh had to be around here somewhere. Tierney had barely slept all night after the conversation with Keir, but now he wasn't the royal on her mind.

"Wake up." She kicked the edge of Veren's bed in the identical room next to hers.

He grumbled something unintelligible and rolled over.

"Veren."

Nothing.

Gulliver pushed open Veren's door and poked his head in. "She's not in the hall eating breakfast."

Tierney let out an exasperated huff. "I checked her room in the servants' quarters, and she wasn't there either."

Bronagh hadn't shown up with her usual morning tea—

something she was horribly bad at, but she had to do it to keep up appearances.

"Stop tickling me," Veren muttered with a small giggle. He still hadn't opened his eyes. "Oh yes, please keep doing that."

Tierney's eyes widened and met Gulliver's before they both broke down in laughter. It seemed Veren was a flirt even in his sleep. Lenya hadn't changed everything about him.

"Is his tea tray from last night still on the table?"

Gulliver crossed the room. "Yes, but it's cold now. If you're that desperate for tea, I can go and—"

"Just bring me whatever remains in the pot."

Gulliver did as she asked, and Tierney was pleased when she took the pot and it was still mostly full. Not hesitating, she dumped it on Veren's head.

He woke up, sputtering and spitting stale tea from his mouth.

"What in Iskalt's name is wrong with you?" he roared, wiping his eyes.

Tierney handed the pot back to Gulliver. "Bronagh is hiding from me. Get out of bed, Sir Ticklish."

He gave her a confused look as Gulliver folded in on himself in laughter, his tail flicking behind him.

With a roll of her eyes, Tierney grabbed Gulliver's arm and dragged him into the corridor.

Veren threw on a shirt and scrambled after them. "Why exactly is Bron hiding from you?"

Tierney ignored his question, not ready to face what had almost happened. The kiss. She'd come very close to kissing Keir, a man who had held her captive not so long ago, one who did nothing but infuriate her.

Bronagh's enemy.

Tierney had become sort of friends with the Grima queen, definitely allies at least. She could only imagine what went through her mind when she caught Tierney in such a position with her rival. Even if the reason Bronagh was here was to ascertain if she could trust Keir to help save Lenya, it didn't mean he wasn't her enemy.

Gulliver looked sideways at Tierney. He'd always been able to read her, to tell when she was hiding something.

They were passing near the great hall when she heard her name. "Tierney."

"Just keep walking," she said to the others, "and see if he gets amnesia and forgets he saw us."

No such luck. Keir stepped out of the hall, stopping them in their tracks. He looked freshly bathed, with slightly damp hair pushed back away from his face and a pressed red jacket bearing his family crest. Sometimes, it was easy to forget how imposing he could be.

No emotion showed on his face as he pulled his shoulders back and stood ramrod straight. He showed no indication that anything had happened the night before, or almost happened.

"Can I help you, your Majesty?" Tierney lifted her eyes to his. For a long moment, they remained in a silent standoff.

Finally, Keir cleared his throat. "We need to talk."

They did. She still hadn't told Keir about the danger facing all of Lenya, and it was time. Turning to Veren, she sent him a pleading look. "Find B—Yvonne. Tell her I wish to see her."

Veren took off, eager to get out of Keir's presence.

Keir turned on his heel and marched away, probably expecting Tierney just to follow his every move.

Gulliver slid his hand into hers and held her back for a moment. "Please tell me you didn't."

"I don't know what you're talking about." She pulled away from him and started after Keir.

He fell in step beside her, his voice low. "That's why Bron is upset, isn't it?" He scrubbed a hand over his face. "You and

Keir, seriously? Tia, you're the Iskaltian princess. Every noble son and daughter of Iskalt is dying to be chosen as your consort. Keir is not one of us."

"I know that." She sighed. Lying to Gulliver always made her feel sick. "Fine, we almost kissed and Bron got a front-row seat."

Gulliver didn't react at first, but she hadn't expected him to. If it was Veren beside her, he'd probably curse and lecture her. Most fae would have, but not her friend.

Instead, he brushed his hand against her arm, a gesture of kindness. "Do you have feelings for him?"

"What?" She reeled back. "Don't be ridiculous."

"You sort of enjoy doing stupid things."

"Falling for that man would be beyond stupid, Gulliver. It was a moment of weakness, okay? Nothing you need to worry about. It's definitely never happening again." As she said the words, she realized Keir had stopped in the doorway of the throne room and heard every one of them.

Face flaming, she walked past him, surprised that for once it wasn't filled with courtiers and servants.

Keir pulled the door shut after them and flipped the latch. "Now," he turned, "it's time you tell me the truth. There's no getting out of it now."

He was right. She couldn't avoid this conversation any longer. "I don't know where to start." She dropped into his throne, throwing one leg over the ornate wooden arm.

A dark scowl crossed Keir's face, but he didn't tell her to move. "I'm listening."

Gulliver hung back by the door, his eyes flicking from Tierney to Keir and back. "Tell him about the fire plains."

Keir's eyes blazed as they focused on her. "What about the fire plains?"

A throbbing started in the front of Tierney's head, but she

pushed the pain away, trying not to let it distract her. Rubbing her temples, she sighed. "They're expanding."

Silence. It was so quiet Tierney could hear every intake of breath, every shifting foot.

"Explain." There was no longer any irritation in Keir's voice.

"The fire plains are encroaching on the Grima borders, and we don't think they can be stopped without more magic than what currently exists in Lenya."

By the time Tierney had finished telling Keir about the danger Lenya faced, the dull pain in her head had turned into a searing agony.

Keir had looked skeptical, but she could tell he wanted to believe her, to trust her. The one thing she hadn't told him was about the ship being built in Grima for the sole purpose of crossing the impossible seas. That wasn't her secret, and Bronagh hadn't yet decided to trust him.

When she finally returned to her rooms, Tierney wanted to bury her head under a pillow to block out all light, all noise, and sleep for the next year. But when she opened the door, she found Veren and Bronagh waiting for her.

The queen sat on the settee, her arms crossed over her chest. Her eyes narrowed as they settled on Tierney. "You."

"Me." Tierney closed her eyes against the sun streaming through her window. "Can you yell at me another time? I have a splitting headache."

Bronagh studied her for a moment. "Veren, go to the kitchens and fetch the princess lavender tea."

"Me?" Veren sat up where he'd been lounging on the bed.

Bronagh fixed him with a firm stare. "Yes, you. I have spent days acting as a servant to serve our purposes. The least you can do is fetch some tea. If you do not plan to be useful, why are you here?"

If it wasn't for the headache, Tierney would have laughed. Bronagh was younger than them, but she was every bit the queen, and Veren had never come up against the likes of her.

"They won't have lavender tea," Tierney said. "Ask for gentian tea. It's their specialty. It's pretty awful, but I'm desperate."

He stomped from the room.

Bronagh turned to Tierney. "Lie down. Gulliver, draw the curtains. We do not have time to waste on illness and must have a conversation, but we can make you more comfortable."

Tierney thanked the sweet mercies when the sunlight disappeared behind the thick fabric.

Bronagh fluffed up the pillows Veren had flattened. "Get in bed."

Having no energy to argue, Tierney did as she was told, sighing as her body relaxed into the feather mattress.

To her surprise, Bronagh took a seat on the end of the bed. "I think there is some vital information you failed to tell me before we embarked on this mission."

Tierney closed her eyes. "Last night ... it wasn't what it looked like. Keir and I, we're not ... he held me captive."

"Yes, I am aware."

"I don't belong here."

"That too is obvious. What is not obvious is what I walked in on. Tierney, I want us to work together to both save Lenya and get you home, but I cannot do that if I don't know everything."

Tierney pushed herself up. "There is nothing to worry about. I have told you everything. You have my word."

Bronagh studied her for a moment longer before issuing one short nod. "Well, then, we have a different conundrum to face. I do not trust this Vondurian king. But we need him, we need his crystals and his cooperation, if we are to make it across the sea."

Tierney nodded, regretting the movement immediately. "I understand, and I know my word is not enough. You must learn how Keir thinks for yourself."

The door opened, interrupting their conversation. Veren walked in, carrying a silver tray laden with teacups, flatbread and peppers, and a pot of tea.

Bronagh's brows drew together. "I only sent you for tea."

"I was hungry." He shrugged as he set the tray down. Both boys dug into the food like wild animals who hadn't been fed in months.

"Watch out for those peppers; the purple ones will rot your insides." Tierney nibbled on a piece of flatbread, not in the mood for the Vondurians' spicy food.

Sighing, Bronagh slid from the bed to pour a cup of heavily honeyed tea. She brought it to Tierney. "Drink this."

She sipped it slowly, cringing at the bitter taste despite the copious amounts of honey. Swallowing, she frowned as an idea formed in her mind. "For you to decide if Grima can trust Keir, you must spend time with him."

"Yes, that is our problem."

"A problem is only an opportunity to be creative. Don't worry, Bron. I've got this."

Gulliver froze with a yellow pepper roll halfway to his mouth. "Oh no. In Iskalt, when she says that, everyone knows to be very afraid."

Tierney drained her tea and sank back against the pillows. Her plan would have to wait until she rested and got rid of this blasted headache.

It was dark by the time she woke again, but Tierney's headache was gone. As were all her companions. Perfect. There was no time to waste if she was going to put her plan into motion.

She had to find a way to procure a certain herb that could make someone very sick. A last resort, for sure, but she wanted it on hand when or if the time came to use it.

Kicking off the blankets, she crawled from her bed, bracing herself for a moment as a wave of dizziness washed over her. It didn't last, and she hurried to find her boots and pulled them on. After lacing them, she used her fingers to tame her hair before giving up and pulling it back into a low tail, searching for anything that could secure it the way human girls did when they didn't want to bother.

A ribbon. That would have to do.

Once she was ready, Tierney rushed into the corridor. At this hour, the kitchens should be deserted, allowing her to search for what she needed.

The kitchens sat in the center of the complex behind the great hall, with the network of corridors and tunnels surrounding them. It wasn't easy to get there without being seen, so Tierney didn't try. She nodded to the few guards at their posts.

A sudden clanging noise reached her ears, faint but present. She turned, trying to find the source of the noise, but there was nothing there. Pausing, she listened again. She could have sworn she heard someone's voice issuing orders.

Her mission momentarily forgotten, she tried the door on her right and found that it led into an ornate sitting room. Red velvet carpets stretched to a wall of windows that looked out onto the palace grounds. Bookshelves towered overhead, full of dusty leather tomes.

To the left, a hearth stood cold in front of two settees with carved backs. But something wasn't right. Next to the hearth, a panel in the wall had been shifted, and it didn't look square.

The sound reached her again, louder this time.

Who would be making such noise in the middle of the night?

Tierney approached the tilted panel, pressing both palms against it. It shifted sideways, revealing an opening to the tunnels. Of course.

As Tierney stepped into the tunnel, she realized what she'd heard were the sounds of a sword fight.

She hurried through the dark tunnel, brushing her hand against the cool stone wall as a guide.

When she finally reached the end, it opened into the giant cavern that held the healing pool. But that wasn't all that was here.

A circle of women cheered and laughed, swords dangling from their fingers as they watched two fae dance around each other, their swords flying through the air.

She stepped closer until she recognized the two at battle. Eavha and Declan.

"Come on, Eavha." Declan grinned, an action Tierney wouldn't have associated with him. "You have more than that."

Eavha ran at him, leaping into the air.

He blocked her, and they went tumbling to the ground in a heap. Eavha didn't move off him, instead looking down at him with a smile stretching her lips. "Be careful what you wish for, Deck. There's always more to me."

He looked like he'd stopped breathing altogether. The other women didn't seem to have noticed as they continued to cheer.

Eavha lifted her gaze, her eyes widening when they landed on Tierney. She scrambled off Declan and got to her feet. "Tia." Pushing through the crowd, she ran toward Tierney. "What—how did you find us? Is Keir with you?" She looked behind Tierney, visibly relaxing when she didn't see anyone else.

"No, it's just me. What is this?"

The women eyed Tierney curiously, and Declan gave her a wary look.

But Eavha smiled. "Training."

"Training?"

She nodded. "You inspired the idea. For too long, the women of this palace, this kingdom, have had to rely on others to protect us. But no more. We deserve to fight for our homes too."

Pride welled within Tierney's soul. She'd inspired maids and cooks and wives to meet in the middle of the night to learn to fight. And it was all Eavha's doing. Tears sprang to her eyes. "Eavha, this is amazing."

"Oh gosh, don't cry." Eavha laughed, pulling her into a hug. "We're trying to be warriors here."

Tierney chuckled against her leather-clad shoulder. "And doing a good job of it, I see. You did very well."

"I have a good teacher." She released Tierney and looked to Declan. His face reddened.

"I'm proud of you."

Eavha gave her a shy smile. "Yeah, well, I'm proud of you too." Her voice dropped. "You did sneak a queen into this palace right under my brother's nose, after all."

Tierney stumbled back. How could she possibly know who Bronagh really was?

CHAPTER FIFTEEN
KEIR

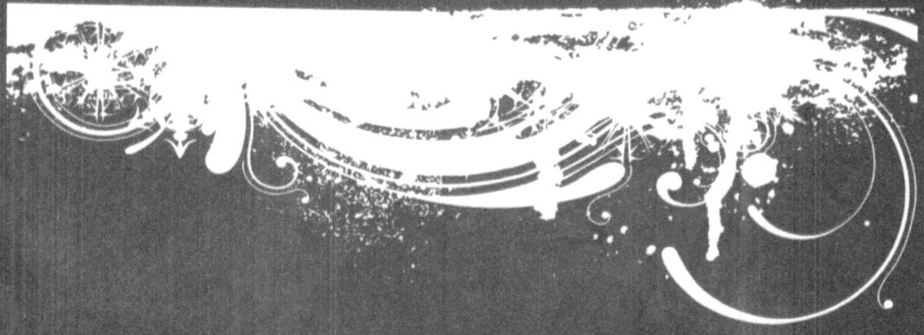

"Do you think she was telling the truth?" Declan asked from his seat at the council table. He and Eavha had arrived early for the meeting so Keir could tell them what he'd heard.

"I don't know." Keir rested his head in his hands and leaned forward in his seat. "I want to trust her."

"Then do." Eavha leaned back and crossed her arms. "It's not that hard. I didn't trust her once. I told her I wasn't sure I believed her story about Iskalt, and I have regretted it every day since. Tierney deserves our faith, brother."

"But why?" Declan asked, earning him a sharp look from Eavha. "Has she been with the Grima court since she left us? What kind of lies have they filled her head with?"

Eavha slammed a hand on the table. "If you think for one second Tia would fall for any of their lies, then you're even dumber than I thought."

"Eavha, be reasonable."

"Me? I'm the unreasonable one? Tia returned here to warn us, to help us. I don't see how you both can sit there and question that."

"Enough." Keir lifted his head. "My mind is already overwhelmed with questions without you two squabbling. Declan, I don't think we can dismiss everything she's told us. Eavha, we can't just believe it either. We must find out for ourselves."

"How?" The irritation faded from Eavha's face. "The fire plains are expanding, Keir. It might only be into Grima now, but eventually, they'll encroach on Vondur. You won't believe anyone from Grima, so how do you expect to verify Tia's intel?"

Declan met Keir's eyes, getting to the conclusion quicker than Eavha. "Someone will have to go into Grima."

Keir hated the idea of sending one of his fae into enemy territory without an army behind them. If they were found ...

"Oh, wow. You're serious." All energy faded from Eavha's voice, and Keir knew exactly how she felt. This wasn't what any of them wanted.

He'd thought of little else since Tierney's revelations. If she was right, if the fire plains were truly expanding, it put all of Lenya at risk. He'd fought for the crown to protect his people, and that meant more than simply fighting the golden warriors of Grima.

"I'll go."

Keir closed his eyes at Declan's declaration. He should have known his friend would volunteer. "Deck—"

"I know what you're going to say." Declan rubbed the back of his neck. "I'm commander of your army; I can't abandon my position. But there have been no battles since you became king, since we stopped seeking them out. Your generals can manage without me for a short while. And even if we were fighting for our lives, this is bigger than that. We must learn the truth of what is happening. For all of Vondur. This war won't mean anything if none of us survive the heat to celebrate the victory."

He was right. Keir knew he was. And if he was being honest with himself, Declan was the best fae to send. There was no one Keir trusted more, no one more capable.

"I don't ..." Keir heaved a sigh. The ball had started rolling down hill, and there was no stopping it. A king must make sacrifices, must send his fae into danger, knowing full well they may never come out. "You're right."

The three of them fell into a full silence, the air thick with things unsaid. It was a while before anyone spoke.

"I'm going with him," Eavha said, her voice unwavering.

"Absolutely not." Keir would not send his sister into enemy territory. Flashes of a familiar battle skipped through his mind as he recalled what his men had done to the Grima queen's sister. Would that be Eavha's fate if she were captured?

"You don't control me."

"Actually, I do. I am the only family you have, but more than that, I am your king. Declan doesn't need to take care of you while he's trying to protect himself." That wasn't the only reason, but he hoped it would be the one to get her to back down.

Eavha shot to her feet, her chair screeching against the floor. "Have you ever thought, your Majesty, that maybe I can take care of myself?" With that, she stomped from the room.

"She can, you know," Declan said, his eyes still on the door Eavha left through.

"I know she probably thinks she can, but this is Grima, Declan. You won't be able to take other soldiers with you for protection because of the attention it would draw. It won't be a simple jaunt across the border. If anything happened to her ..." He swallowed. "I have to keep her safe. You and Eavha are the only family I have left."

Declan reached out and put a hand on Keir's shoulder. "I will learn the truth of this and return. You have my word. We won't lose each other yet."

Keir tried to smile, but he couldn't seem to perform the act. "You need to leave immediately. Gather provisions in secret so the council doesn't learn of your mission. We will only involve them when we must."

Declan stood. "Keir—"

"Don't you dare say goodbye."

Declan's lips twitched as he bowed. "Whatever pleases your Majesty."

He was barely out the door before the first council members appeared.

The palace somehow seemed too large without Declan at Keir's side. He'd left the day before, and Eavha had also been avoiding the king. Tierney spent most of her days in the company of her own people, Veren and Gulliver. And that maid of hers from Grima. It made sense. He'd told himself she wasn't Vondurian, but seeing her with her friends made it crystal clear.

She didn't belong here.

Keir had just finished a long meeting that lasted most of the morning when he decided enough was enough. Eavha had to stop pouting. It wasn't right for a princess.

Stopping outside her door, he rapped his knuckles against

the solid wood, waiting for her to answer. No answer came, so he knocked again.

"What are you doing?" Tierney walked down the corridor, stopping at his side.

"I need to talk to my sister."

"Me too."

"In private."

"Me too."

He stared at Tierney for a moment, realizing she wasn't going to back down. "I could order you to leave."

"You could try." Her lips stretched into a smile. She was teasing him.

Before he could respond, Eavha's door opened, revealing a nervous-looking maid. "Your Majesty." She dipped into a curtsy.

Keir looked past her into the empty room. "Where's the princess?"

Ariella kept her eyes trained on the floor and bit her lip. "She's ... out."

"Out where?"

Tierney sighed. "Obviously somewhere she doesn't want her grumpy brother to know about." She turned to Ariella. "Don't mind his Majesty's mood today. He doesn't like when women don't jump to his every command."

"Not only women," he growled. "I am king. It is my duty to command those under my rule."

"Sure, okay." She rolled her eyes, and Keir wanted to yell at her, to make her realize his power.

And he also wanted to kiss the smirk off her face.

That thought was quickly replaced with another. He knew where his sister had gone. Panic built in his chest, and he released a curse. "Ariella, did your mistress leave the palace?"

"That's a stupid question," Tierney said. "There's nothing out there but trees and—"

"Yes." Ariella still wouldn't look at him. "Your Majesty, she rode out last night."

Keir whipped around so fast he almost knocked Tierney over. After holding her upright, he took off down the hall, heading for the stables. If he left now, he might be able to reach her before she crossed the border into Grima.

"What's going on?" Tierney ran to catch up with him.

"Eavha is in danger."

"What? How could you possibly know that from the conversation we just had with Ariella?"

"I just do."

She grabbed his arm, pulling him to a stop. "Talk to me, Keir." Her voice held none of the mockery it had before. Instead, there was something akin to understanding in the tone.

Keir turned to her, his eyes wild. "I sent Declan to verify your intel about the fire plains. He's crossing into Grima. I think Eavha went after him."

"And you're scared for her."

"Of course I am! She's headed for Grima."

Tierney pursed her lips. "It's not the barbarous place you imagine."

She knew nothing. Leaning toward her, he dropped his voice. "For Vondurians, it is. What do you think they'd do to the enemy princess if they caught her on their lands? Think, Tierney, for once in your life."

Anger rose in her cheeks, flushing them red. She shoved him backward. "And you should trust for once in yours."

"What's that supposed to mean?"

"If you'd trusted me, you wouldn't have had to send anyone to Grima, but no, I'm just a spy in your court."

"Aren't you?"

"Screw you, Keir. I've done nothing but try to save your blasted kingdom."

"I don't have time for this." He turned away, but Tierney's words called him back.

"Don't chase her. She'll only run faster. Trust me, I know from experience."

He stood still, his back to her. "This isn't the same. I am not your father, and Eavha is not you. Grima will kill her. They won't give her the courtesy of making her a prisoner instead."

"Courtesy." Tierney snorted. "Yes, Vondur was so courteous while I was being beaten and almost hanged. You can take your courtesy and shove it. Let your sister make her own decisions. She is not a child you can keep locked away. The harder you try, the more she will yearn for freedom."

Her words rang with truth. If he dragged Eavha back to the palace, he could still lose her. With a sigh, he turned to Tierney. "Like you?"

After a beat, she shook her head. "I was already free. I just didn't realize it until I lost that life."

"Your Majesty." A young boy sprinted across the courtyard, skidding to a halt and bowing. "You're needed in the throne room."

"Thank you." It felt natural when Tierney fell in step beside him, accompanying him on whatever urgent business this was.

They walked into the throne room to find Lord Robert standing near the throne with a bedraggled woman who looked like she might collapse at any moment. Two small children peeked around her legs, a boy and a girl. Each face was blistered red, their clothes singed and hands chapped with burn marks.

Relief flooded the mother's face when she took sight of

him. "Your Majesty." She curtsied as low as she could in her weakened state.

"Madam." Keir nodded. "Have you been offered food?"

"It's on its way," Lord Robert answered. "They've traveled a long way and need rest, but you must hear their news first."

Keir lowered himself onto his throne.

Tierney approached the woman, a kind smile on her face. "I'll get you a seat." No one sat in the throne room except the king, despite the chairs lined up against the back wall, but Keir didn't protest. Tierney had noticed the need before he had.

Grateful, the woman lowered herself into the chair Tierney brought and pulled her children close. "We've come from Brenandi, your Majesty."

Keir leaned forward. Brenandi was the closest Vondurian village to the fire plains. "Please, tell me your news."

"Those who were able to get out in time evacuated the village." She stifled a sob. "I'm sorry, sire, it's just ... we've lost everything."

An ache threatened to crack open Keir's heart. "Start at the beginning."

She nodded and wiped dirt from her son's cheek. "It started when the water turned bad. Our children grew sick, and we did not know why. Eventually, many of the adults fell ill as well. We lost over half the village to that first plague. And then, the heat came for us. We've always survived in high temperatures, but t-this was different. Worse. In some places, the air could scorch the breath in your lungs, leave your skin black."

The fire plains. Keir met Tierney's eyes. "Sulfur in the water?"

"Most likely. It happens from time to time for those who live along the borderlands. The expanding heat's just something we've grown to expect when the winds change. But the fires and putrid air." She shuddered at the memory. "By the time we realized what was happening, it was too late for most."

He should have known Tierney would never have lied about such a thing, but instead, his best friend and sister were headed into enemy territory to verify something he now knew to be fact.

The fire plains were coming for them.

And Lenya had so few functioning crystals that they were powerless to stop it.

Magic help them all.

Chapter Sixteen
Tierney

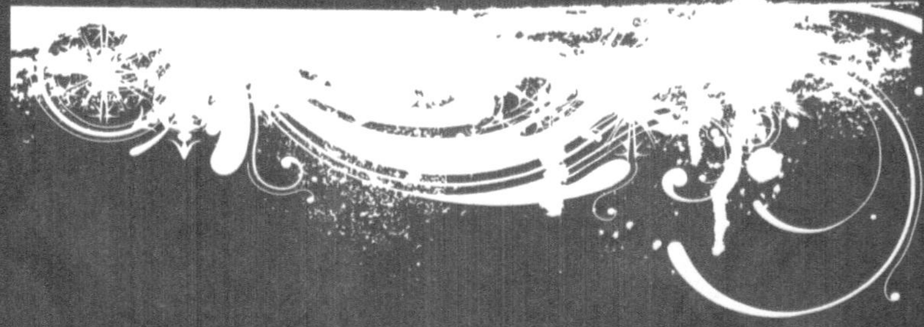

"We're twiddling our thumbs here, Tia." Veren threw himself onto the settee in her room.

"I hate to agree with this one, but I think he's right." Gulliver rummaged through the remains of their tea tray, looking for anything that hadn't been eaten. "We need to decide what's next for us. I, for one, would like to go home with my neck still intact." He stuffed a shriveled grape into his mouth and paced across the room. "Are we going to search for Siobhan or brave the voyage across the stormy seas and hope we find our way home?"

"The ship is ready. We just need to decide when we're leaving," Veren said. "Once Bron has a feel for the king, she will decide what is next for Grima, but for the moment, I feel our fate is tied with hers. She will sail all the way to Iskalt and back if that is the only way to save her kingdom from the spread of the fire. And that might be our only way home."

"I can't think of leaving until I know Lenya will be safe." Tierney twisted her hands in her lap. She desperately wanted to go home—was more than willing to risk the dangerous voyage on Bronagh's ship—but she wanted things settled with these two warring kingdoms before she left.

"The Vondurians will see to their own destruction. One doesn't need to stay here long to see they are a nation of brutes with a thirst for war."

"Veren, that's very narrow-minded of you." Tierney stared out the window at the shimmering horizon where the fire plains made their slow march toward the palace and the people here she cared about. What would happen to Eavha? Ariella? Even Keir and Bronagh?

The door crashed open and a disheveled, soot-covered Bronagh walked into the room. "That blasted king will not stay put long enough for me to observe him." She slammed the door behind her and dropped into the nearest chair. "Did you know when a noblewoman and her maid visit this palace, the castellan can order her maid around?" She dabbed her apron against her forehead. "Veren, please bring me a glass of water if you will. I cannot move another step."

"Of course, your Majesty." Veren shot from his seat to do her bidding.

"Oh, you poor thing." Tierney tried to hide her chuckle. "What did she make you do?"

"I had to clean the fireplaces in the princess' quarters. I don't know how to start a fire, much less clean up after one."

"What did you do with the ashes? Take a bath in them?" Gulliver snickered.

She turned a fierce glare on him. "I flung them out of the

window. And I hope they landed on Keir's head!" She snatched the glass of water from Veren and downed it in three gulps. "Is this place always so magic-forsaken hot?" She slumped back, wiping the wilted hair out of her face.

Gulliver and Veren were busy trying not to laugh and being entirely unhelpful. Why was it always up to Tierney to take care of everyone? She moved to the basin in the washroom, longing for her washroom at home with its hot, plentiful water and fluffy towels. Taking a clean face linen, she dipped it in the cool water and went to kneel beside Bronagh.

"Thank you, Tierney." Bronagh sighed as she wiped the cool cloth over her soot-stained face. Bronagh closed her eyes, letting Tierney bathe her face and hands. "We really have to rethink our plans. This isn't working."

"Our plans?" Gulliver mouthed, rolling his eyes at Tierney.

"We're not getting anywhere. I need more time with the king, but he's all over the palace and grounds from sunup to sundown. I don't think the man ever sleeps."

"I'm afraid Veren is right, we are twiddling our thumbs here." Tierney moved to sit on the settee between Gulliver and Veren. "We have to get her some time with Keir. I want to believe he is a good man. As much as he irritates me, I can't shake this feeling that we can trust him to do the right thing in the end. That he would work with us to save all of Lenya and end this stupid war."

"But I have to see these things for myself if I have any hope of gaining my court's support for an endeavor involving the enemy." Bronagh fanned her face with the hem of her apron. "I have to know if he can be trusted. I need to see for myself what kind of man he is. If we're going to deal with the encroaching fire plains, Vondur and Grima need to work together."

"I had hoped he would trust my word about the fire plains." Tierney rubbed her temples, where her head throbbed.

"But the first thing he did was send one of his men to verify the information."

"So, while we wait for the king to catch up to the rest of us, let's get Bronagh a front-row seat to a day in the life of King Keir." Gulliver leaned forward, his elbows resting on his knees.

"How?" Bronagh asked. "I'd have to chase him around the palace."

"Who serves the king? Does anyone know?" Gulliver asked, sharing a look with Tierney.

"He has a maid to keep his quarters clean, but he refuses a valet to help him dress. I think her name is Shannon. Why?" Bronagh asked. "You two look like you're contemplating something nefarious that might get you both locked up in the dungeons."

"We slip her something—and maybe a few of the other maids too just to make it look legitimate." Gulliver shrugged. "Tierney managed to get her hands on a potent herbal blend we can sprinkle over their morning porridge. It'll send them to bed for a day with a wicked upset stomach and lethargy." The corner of Gulliver's mouth turned up. "Then, Tierney can offer a certain stand-in maid for his Majesty's use, and whenever he has need of something—which we'll make sure is quite often—he'll send for Bron."

"That's a ridiculous—" Veren began, but Tierney cut him off.

"It's our last-resort, back-up plan. I think we're there, guys. We need to take action and get back to Grima soon."

"But how did you find this herbal blend?" Bronagh asked. "Are we certain it won't kill the poor maids?"

"I found it in the kitchens with all the medicinal herbs," Tierney said. "It's supposed to help sluggish and sour bowels."

"Do we even know how much to give them?" Veren asked.

"I tried it on a few guards in the dungeon," Gulliver

explained. "Turnabout is fair play and all that." He shrugged. "A healthy dose of the herbs in the porridge pot will send the maid staff to bed right away."

"But Bron's a dreadful maid. No offense, your Highness, but you'll likely set him on fire before the day is out, much less brew him a proper cup of tea." Veren wiped a hand across his sweaty brow.

"Surely one of you can teach me how to make a decent pot of tea." Bronagh turned pleading eyes on Tierney.

"Sure, I can brew tea ... from the tray my maid brings to my rooms in Iskalt." Tierney cringed. If she ever got out of this mess, she was going to learn to be more self-sufficient. "But she blends the tea and portions everything out. I wouldn't know where to start or even where those things come from."

"Good grief, you nobles are a helpless lot." Gulliver crossed the room to retrieve the tea tray Bronagh brought Tierney that morning. "Okay, first, let's look at the tea leaves here." He scattered some of the dry tea leaves they hadn't bothered brewing because Bronagh's tea always tasted like mud. "Tell me where you got this blend."

"I saw the other maids scooping tea from several jars, so I took some from each."

Gulliver sifted through the myriad of leaves on the tray. "Next time, use a small scoop of the pale green ones and another of these shriveled looking flowers, with some of this bark looking stuff. Leave the others where you found them. Less is more when it comes to tea blends. And you're serving the king, so bring him lots of honey. Any tea tastes better with honey. Load him up on the savory pastries they serve here, and the little round biscuits and cubes of cheese. Watch the other maids to see how they arrange their trays, and try to mimic what they do. If they use a small vase with flowers, then that's what you do. If they use a large plate, you do too. Several small plates, you get it."

Bronagh nodded. "Sounds easy enough, but when I'm faced with all those different plates and utensils in the kitchens, my mind goes blank. I don't know how the serving staff makes it look so easy."

"Are we really doing this?" Veren ran a hand through his hair. "It's risky. What if the king finds out who she is?"

"He won't even give her a second look." Gulliver seemed so certain of it.

"You're sure?" Tierney had a bad feeling about this. It was bound to turn into a circus act and reveal them all as Grima spies.

"Positive. Kings don't look at servants. Most nobles don't. Especially here. Vondurian men barely recognize the women of the nobility. They have no eyes for those who serve their tea."

"He's right," Bronagh said. "The men in this place have little regard for women beyond those who warm their beds. It's like they believe we are somehow inferior and it's our place to stay out of their way. Did you know I'm not allowed to speak to a man until he gives me permission? It's absurd."

"It's infuriating," Tierney agreed.

Veren groaned. "This is going to be a disaster."

"We have to do something." It was a risk, but if Bronagh was going to get what she came for, they needed to act sooner rather than later. Tierney was running out of time.

Tierney and Veren arrived at the throne room earlier than usual the following morning. Keir spent most mornings with his court, listening to his lord's reports and requests the way Tierney's mother and father would hear directly from their people—no matter their class. In Vondur, it seemed the common folk didn't matter much. At least, not in the eyes of the court. Though, she liked to think Keir would change all that.

Gulliver joined them a few minutes later, giving Tierney a flash of his mischievous smile to let her know he'd accomplished the task. The poor maids were probably already off to their beds.

"Easy as giving me a cupcake and asking me to eat it." Gulliver sidled up to her, offering her his arm. "Shall we take a turn around the room and see if we can run into a maid-less king?"

Tierney tucked her arm around his and nodded. "Let's do just that, though I will never understand this court's obsession with walking around the throne room when there's a perfectly good garden outside. Keep up, Veren; we're going to talk to the king."

"I don't know how you plan to get through the mob around him." Veren walked on her other side, his hands clasped behind him like a soldier.

As they joined other groups walking aimlessly around the room, Tierney kept her eyes on Keir. He seemed bored, like he would rather be anywhere else. She couldn't say she blamed him. Swarms of courtiers vied for Keir's attention, but to Tierney, he looked more like a caged lion than a man who actually wanted the attention he was receiving.

"This is stupid." Tierney tugged Gulliver and Veren along with her. "I'm a princess of Iskalt. If I want to talk to a king, I don't need to play these infernal court games."

"Just don't get us put on the executioner's block this time."

Gulliver walked uncertainly with them. "You know how this room makes me nervous."

It was just a few weeks ago she, Gulliver, and Declan stood on the gallows right outside this room. She shuddered to think about that day.

"Your Majesty." Tierney dipped her head into the graceful nod of a crown princess greeting another monarch. Several of the courtiers surrounding Keir gasped at her lack of butt-kissing, as her mother would call it. They still believed her a Grima spy and Gulliver some kind of abomination of dark magic.

"Princess Tierney and Lord Gulliver." Keir returned her nod, ignoring Veren altogether. "We don't usually see you here at court since your return. I'm delighted you've decided to join us." He didn't even sound like himself. She decided she preferred surly, grouchy soldier Keir over this pompous imposter.

Tierney ignored the lords and ladies who refused to move aside for them. She stepped around them, as if they were nothing more than statues. "Your throne room isn't our favorite place, you'll understand." Tierney lowered her gaze.

"Nor is it mine," he murmured under his breath, sounding more like himself. "As a matter of fact, I'd like to escape, and your arrival has given me an idea."

"We'll follow your lead then."

"I'm afraid duty calls, my lords and ladies." Keir beamed a benevolent smile to the crowd of sycophants. "I have an important meeting with the Princess of Iskalt and her noblemen." He offered Tierney his arm and led her to a private chamber where he now met with his council.

Not what she had expected, but they could definitely work with this.

Keir held the door open for her and the others. The room

was cozy with plush carpets and heavy oak furniture. Her mom would call it a king's man cave.

"Please have a seat." Keir gestured at the small sitting area under the windows just beyond a huge table.

"I don't suppose we could trouble you for some tea, sire?" Gulliver took a seat in one of the leather chairs.

"I'm sure we can find someone to serve us. I'm afraid a sudden sickness has sent all of our maids to their beds, so I'm fending for myself today. We have a shortage of servants these days, even when they are all well."

"Nonsense, your Majesty." Tierney suppressed a smile. "Please allow me to have my maid, Yvonne, serve you today."

"It's not necessary. I'm a soldier. I've been serving myself since I was a child, and I've never acclimated much to having servants."

"Please, I insist." Tierney stepped to the door to have a footman ring for Yvonne to bring them tea. It seemed like the show was about to start, and she had to make it a good one.

Chapter Seventeen
Keir

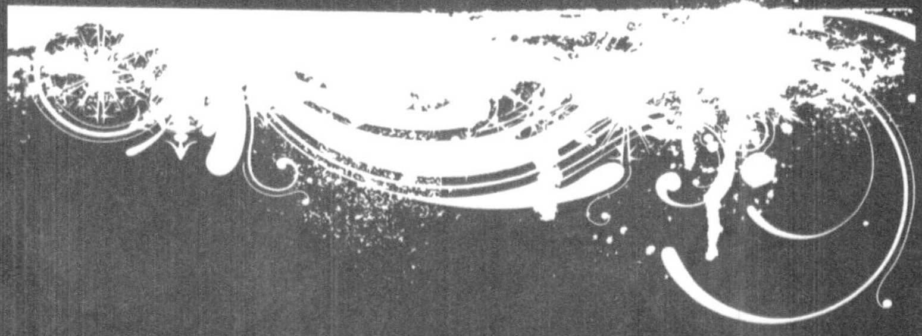

For a reason Keir couldn't begin to fathom, he hated Tierney thinking he couldn't get by for a single day while his maid had taken ill. He wasn't some pampered king who'd never done anything for himself. Life as a soldier was so very different from life among the shimmering, crystal-infused walls of the palace.

He preferred it.

Yet, he smoothed his features, not letting his irritation show. If he had to play the aloof royal with this princess to put distance between them, he would. She'd accused him of not trusting her, but she didn't understand.

Releasing her and letting her travel to Grima under her

own control was the ultimate trust. There were so many things she could have told the enemy, and yet, she'd returned.

Tierney's maid, Yvonne, bumped into the table with a curse. Her cheeks flamed in embarrassment. "Your Majesty, I didn't mean to speak with such vulgarity in your presence."

"It's fine." He waved her worry away and focused on looking like nothing bothered him. The truth was, he owed Tierney an apology. Declan and Eavha hadn't yet returned, but he already knew the story Tierney told was true.

The fire plains truly were expanding, and if they didn't stop it, none of this would matter any longer.

Lifting a hand to the carved winged totem hanging at his throat, he felt the weak magic thrum in his veins. What would it be like to have infinite amounts? To be able to use the power for mundane tasks like cleaning the dribbles of tea the maid had spilled on the table or sparring with a partner? He imagined the freedom of not dreading the moment he had to discard one totem and fashion another weaker one.

"So ..." Veren drummed his fingers on the table. "It's not that I don't appreciate all of this silence, Keir, but is there a point in you bringing us here?"

Keir's jaw clenched at the man's informality. Something about him had struck him the wrong way.

Before he could answer, Yvonne yelped and lunged toward the table as she fell, her tea tray hitting the edge. It was a disaster he couldn't look away from as tea whipped through the air. He glanced down in horror when it hit his jacket, creating an immediate stain.

No one spoke; no one moved.

And then, Tierney laughed, the sound so out of place in the moment he couldn't help but lift his eyes to hers, couldn't help studying the light on her face. She'd rarely been open around him, happy. She was always too busy arguing.

The corners of his lips turned up.

Yvonne scrambled from the floor. "I'm so sorry. I'm not used to carrying tea trays, and when I tripped, it slipped from my hands."

She kept rambling, but Keir was fixated on one thing. What kind of maid wasn't used to carrying tea trays?

Tierney cleared her throat. "What Yvonne means to say is, her normal duties at the Grima palace don't include serving tea. They do things a bit differently there. Yvonne kept my rooms clean, as well as all other rooms along the corridor. Someone else came along regularly to serve tea."

Something was off in her words. Keir thought he knew her well enough by now to know when she was hiding something. He shook his head, trying to clear it of the distrust that had been ingrained in him.

"Tierney," he said formally, "I owe you an apology."

"Excuse me?" She looked his way in shock. "The great King Keir is apologizing? For what? I mean, there's just so much."

"Do you ever shut up?"

"Not often," Gulliver put in.

Tierney shot him a grin, sticking her tongue out at him in the oddest gesture. Something was seriously strange about this woman.

"It's true," Veren said. "I mean, I've been trying to get her to stop talking since we first courted."

An irrational bolt of rage raced through Keir at that, but the others ignored him.

Tierney scowled at Veren. "Courted is a big word for what we did. I liked you, and you liked my future crown."

Veren frowned. "Not true."

"Sure, okay." Tierney snorted, which caused Gulliver to laugh.

Yvonne hung back by the wall, staying out of the way like the good maid Keir didn't believe she was. But he didn't have time to analyze his suspicions.

"Are all Iskaltians this infuriating?" Keir asked.

Tierney shrugged. "Most of us, yes. You should meet my parents. They're worse than me."

That wasn't possible.

Gulliver lifted a hand. "Um, I'm an infuriating Myrkurian, not an Iskaltian." He coughed. "Just for clarification."

Keir rubbed his face, wondering what he'd gotten himself into the moment he took Tierney captive. His calm king façade slipped, and his back shook in silent laughter.

"Your Majesty?" Yvonne placed a fresh, un-spilled cup of tea in front of him. "Are you okay?"

"Is he seizing?" Tierney yelled. "Someone do something."

Gulliver stood and rounded the table, looking ready to help him.

Keir leaned out of his reach. "Touch me, Gullie, and you'll lose that hand."

That made him back away and reclaim his seat.

Keir's laughter faded, and he shook his head. "I brought you all here so I could apologize. You asked what for, and at first, I thought it was only because I hadn't trusted you about the fire plains, but there is so much more. If it wasn't for me, you may have found each other sooner. You could be back home instead of involved in our fight for survival. For that, I am truly regretful."

Tierney opened her mouth before shutting it without uttering a word.

"Well," Veren said, "that was unexpected."

But it was Yvonne who moved into sight and seemed unable to take her eyes from him. She looked confused, like she was trying to put the pieces of some puzzle together and they didn't quite fit. Her brow furrowed, and she didn't try to hide her curiosity.

There was something about the woman Keir couldn't put his finger on, something that made him think she had a secret buried deep.

"Keir ..." Tierney's voice was soft, but she didn't get a chance to complete the thought. The door opened, and the council started filing in.

Lord Garnet took a seat and glanced at Tierney and the others. "Sire, it is time for us to begin. Maybe your friends should wait outside."

He shook his head. "No, they're a part of what I must tell you." It was time. This affected all of Vondur. In the time since Keir learned the truth of the fire plains, he'd contemplated their next moves many times and come up with nothing that would help stave off the coming danger.

"You are my council," he began, "and what I say to you must stay here. There has to be trust between us." He met Tierney's gaze at that.

In turn, each council member nodded their agreement.

"The time has come for us to acknowledge a new danger."

"Has Grima started marching, your Majesty?" Lord Osterian asked. They'd been waiting for Grima's next move, but it hadn't come.

"No, this danger is not Grima." He drew in a long breath. "The fire plains are encroaching on our lands."

A flurry of chatter broke out, but he silenced it with a raised hand. "The deathly heat is expanding. The fae of Brenandi have left their lands."

"We must send someone to find out what's happening." Lord Osterian stood, his eyes panicked. "Are you sure this is true, sire?"

"I have no doubts. The source is ..." He looked at Tierney.

"A reliable one. General Connel and Princess Eavha have been sent on a mission to gather more information." He wouldn't tell them Eavha disobeyed orders and went on her own. "We will know more when they return."

Talk turned to what actions they could take, but Keir knew only an infusion of magic could help them now—magic they didn't have enough of. He sank into his chair as his lords spoke.

"What if the general and the princess don't return?" one of them asked.

That thought had crossed Keir's mind too many times in the last day. What if he lost them both?

The council meeting lasted long into the night. By the time it was over, Keir was tired and hungry. Yet, he didn't move from his chair. Everyone else left to find their own meals, and still, he sat.

It wasn't until the chair beside him scraped against the floor as someone pulled it out that he realized he wasn't alone.

"Yvonne, would you mind fetching the king something to eat?" Tierney asked as she took the seat.

"Not at all." Yvonne's voice was softer than normal, and she dipped into a small curtsy before hurrying away, leaving Keir and Tierney alone.

"You're a good king."

He lifted his gaze, meeting hers, and a smirk came to his lips. "That wouldn't be a compliment, would it, Princess?"

She rolled her eyes. "You bring out the worst in me. It won't happen again."

His smirk fell, and he leaned back. "Sometimes, it feels as if I'm just guessing at what's best for my kingdom."

"That's because you are."

"I'm not sure if—"

"That wasn't an insult, I swear. For my entire life, I've been raised to one day rule my kingdom. Standing at my father's side, watching him handle the easy tasks and the hard ones. You can never really know what the right thing to do is, but I don't think that matters. What matters is that you try to see what's right."

"And you think I do?" He sighed. "Because there are times I feel too much of my father in me."

"No." Her single word held so much conviction. "Don't ever say that. Your father wanted power. He hoarded magic and executed dissenters. What is this really about, Keir?"

So few people used his name without a formal title in front of it. He was always the king, his Majesty. It was only in small moments with Tierney he was Keir.

"Declan and Eavha ..." He swallowed heavily, unable to voice the fears shadowing him.

Warmth enveloped his hand, and he looked down to see Tierney gripping it. "You're scared for them." She smiled sadly. "You can't protect everyone from all things."

"I used to think I could."

"As did I ... when I was ten. And then, I became the central figure in a war that nearly destroyed the four kingdoms of my home."

"I've been at war for so long I'm not sure I'd know what peace felt like."

She squeezed his hand, still not letting go. "It's better than you could ever imagine. In Iskalt, the lack of war keeps our fae fed and housed. We have no more destroyed villages. I can walk to the village from the palace without an armed escort."

"Truly?"

"Well, as long as my father doesn't find out. He's a bit ...

overprotective. But I've spent a lot of time in the village with my friends. Life without war is simpler. You should really try it some time."

He laughed. "Peace sounds so ..."

"Peaceful?" She raised a brow. "Just think ... Eavha and Declan could get married and have children without sending them off to war. You could—"

"Wait." He narrowed his eyes. "Declan and Eavha are not—"

"In love?" She grinned. "Well, probably not yet. But they will be. Eavha needs to get a bit older for him, but she's already there."

"No."

"Oh, absolutely." She lifted her hand off his and reached toward his face, trying to force his lips into a smile. "Might as well get over it now, Keir. You might think you have control over that girl, but control is an illusion."

"Like your father trying to force you into marriage?"

Her hand dropped, and the smile faded from her lips. "And you see how that turned out. He's in Iskalt, and I'm here."

"I'm glad you're here." The words slipped out before he could stop them.

Tierney was still for a long moment, and he inched closer, unable to resist the draw of her hopeful spirit, her rebellious gaze.

"Keir," she whispered, her breath warm against his lips.

"Yes, Tia?" He wanted nothing more than to close the remaining distance, to give in to whatever this pull was between them.

Her eyes fluttered shut. "We can't do this."

The words were a stream of icy river water showering down on him. Pulling back, the king's mask slipped into place.

"Yes, of course. That was wrong. I'm not sure what got into me. Will you accept my apology?"

"For magic's sake, Keir, you don't have to apologize."

The door opened, and Yvonne entered, carrying a tray laden with breads, cheeses, and fruits. She fumbled with it, finally getting it to the table after kicking the door shut behind her. "I'm sorry that took so long, your Majesty. I had to find someone to show me how to slice the bread."

Keir barely heard her because his eyes were still on Tierney, who'd stood and walked toward the door. Pulling back her shoulders, she yanked it open, not sparing a single glance behind her.

When she was gone, Keir buried his face in his hands.

"May I speak, sire?" Yvonne asked, shifting on her feet.

"Yes." Keir looked at her, seeing a glint of steel in her gaze. This woman had strength.

"Tierney O'Shea will find her way home. I don't believe anyone could stop her. They all will. It is best not to get attached." She dipped into a curtsy and left.

Keir stared after her, wondering what kind of maid had the audacity to speak to a king of such things. The problem was, her words rang with truth.

A truth Keir would force himself to remember.

CHAPTER EIGHTEEN
TIERNEY

"Keep your dagger up." Tierney tapped Margery's wrist until she held her dagger at the correct height. "Relax your hips, and square your shoulders. Be confident."

"Yes, my Lady." Margery gripped her weapon tighter, relaxing her stance.

When Eavha left to follow Declan, Margery—the wife of a minor nobleman—came to find Tierney, asking for her help with the ladies. They needed guidance, Margery claimed.

They needed a miracle. Tierney winced at the way Margery's opponent came at her, wrist limp, her silly jeweled knife clutched in her hand.

"Is that a fork or a knife, Lady Astrid?" Tierney observed the two women sparring.

"It's a breast dagger, Madam," Astrid said, affronted. "I assure you it is very valuable and perfect for a lady's hand."

"The rubies and sapphires certainly are valuable, but a three-inch blade will never cause more than a scratch in a real fight. I suggest you all dispense with the fashionable weapons and use the ones Declan provided for sparring."

"Those are for men, my Lady." Ines wrinkled her delicate nose. "They are far too heavy for us."

Tierney moved to the weapons' table, where Declan had laid out a variety of small swords and daggers, but they were soldiers' weapons. Serviceable. Old. But not pretty. "With practice, they won't be too heavy." She lifted a slim sword with a steel blade and lightweight pommel. She tested the weight of it in her hand.

Moving to another pair of sparring partners, Tierney corrected their stance, showing them how to move on the balls of their feet. "That's better. Yes, just like dancing, it will help tremendously to move on swift feet to avoid your partner's blade."

"Do women really serve in your father's army?" Lady Meghan asked from her seat on the sidelines. Several of the ladies came to watch but were not yet ready to join. Tierney suspected it gave them a thrill to watch the other women dally with swordplay.

"My father's army is made up of men and women in various roles. Some female warriors are officers and some are soldiers, but there is little difference between them on the battlefield. Where I come from, a woman is not limited by the confines of her gender."

"I still can't believe you will inherit your father's throne."

Lady Clodagh shook her head. "It just seems so surreal. A woman as king."

"I will rule someday, but I will be a queen. Both of my aunts are queens who rule as well. My mother is a queen who rules beside my father, the king. He includes her in every decision he makes because she is his most trusted advisor."

"What does one call a man who marries a ruling queen?" Lady Margery giggled at the very idea.

"A prince consort. My uncle Myles and uncle Finn are both prince consorts, but they take active roles within their kingdoms."

"Can you even imagine, ladies?" Lady Clodagh fanned her face with an intricately carved fan. Tierney thought it was made of ivory at first, but of course, it was made from a crystal that had long since lost its magic. "A world where we rule our lands and carry our titles while our husbands stand in the shadows? It seems like the stuff of myth, doesn't it?"

"Iskalt is the stuff of fiction, my dear girls." The dowager duchess of ... some vast holding or another had become the bane of Tierney's existence. She had a beautiful young granddaughter she intended to marry off to King Keir. She had decided Tierney was a dangerous distraction their king showed far too much interest in.

Even now, she rapped her cane against the stone floor of the chamber they had been using for their clandestine sparring sessions near the king's healing pool. "This is nonsense, and you should all be ashamed of yourselves. Females may rule in Grima, but this is Vondur, and our men are strong and capable. They don't need us getting in the way of a thousand years of tradition." The old crone fairly vibrated with fury. "Prince consorts, indeed," she scoffed. "What foolishness."

"Ah, but traditions are meant to evolve." Tierney lifted her sword and sank into a defensive crouch. Turning in a circle, balanced on one heel, she scanned the room for a sparring partner. "Yvonne is from Grima."

"Yvonne?" the girls whispered in confusion.

"My maid." Tierney beckoned Bronagh forward to choose a weapon from the table.

"I am." Bronagh lifted her chin, selecting a short sword with a wide blade. "And in Grima, if a woman wants to learn to protect herself, it is her right to do so." She gave the weapon a few practice swings. "From the queen right down to the lowliest maid. Women can inherit titles, land, and they can choose whether or not they wish to be married."

"Their fathers don't sell them off to the highest bidder?" Lady Meghan asked.

"She is free to choose her husband. A father provides a dowry for her to set up her household, but it is her money. It never passes on to the husband."

"My father allowed me to choose among a select few suitors he approved," Lady Meghan said. "It was kind of him to choose men close to my age. Years later, when I introduced my wonderful husband to our youngest child after her birth, he claimed she was so beautiful she would fetch the highest bride price in all of Vondur." Her smile faltered. "I know he meant well, but it has never sat well with me. She is a sweet, lovely child. Not a prized pig to be sold at market."

"It is tradition." The old duchess harrumphed, tapping her cane against the stones. "The husband and father know what is best."

"Yvonne, shall we show these ladies how it's done?" Tierney ignored the crotchety old woman, pacing around the center of the room.

"Yes, my Lady." Bronagh slipped off her apron and tossed her weapon from hand to hand to get a feel for it.

They circled each other for a moment, sizing one another

up. Tierney knew the Grima queen was skilled with a sword, but she was looking forward to sparring with her to see what she was really made of. Tierney had learned from the greatest sword masters in all the four kingdoms. Few could best her.

Tierney, with her feet firmly planted, made the first advance. Lunging toward Bronagh with her sword lifted high and at an angle to protect her torso, she flicked her wrist, her blade meeting Bronagh's in a crash of steel. Bronagh danced back a few steps, crouching low, her sword even with her shoulders.

The Grima queen was quick with a blade. Together, they danced in a circle around the room. Forward and back, their weapons slicing through the air to meet with a clang. Back and forth they went, but Tierney couldn't gain any ground on her. In one moment, she moved aggressively in an attack, only to find herself retreating again in the next.

Sweat beaded Tierney's brow, and it felt so good to have a real opponent. One who didn't let her win or refuse to fight with their full skill because of who she was.

"What is the meaning of this?"

"Your Majesty." The old duchess stepped forward. "I'm so glad you are here. "These young ladies have lost what little sense they had."

"Keir." Tierney grinned, pushing the sweaty hair back from her face. "Isn't it wonderful what your sister started while I was gone?" Her chest burned with the exertion, but it felt good to have her blood thrumming through her veins.

"This is Eavha's doing then?" Keir stepped into the room, his hands resting at his back with an unreadable expression on his face.

"Before you even ask, I didn't give her any ideas. She started this on her own. "

"And this is ...?" A dark brow lifted in question.

"Sparring practice. The young ladies of your court would like to know how to protect themselves." Tierney couldn't wipe the smile off her face. She was so proud of Eavha for doing this all on her own. "Princess Eavha asked Declan to teach them." She pointed to the weapons' table, still working to catch her breath. "Though, they could use smaller weapons sized for a female hand."

"And your maid has been trained well. As well as you have been."

"She's an excellent partner." Tierney gave Bronagh a nod of approval.

"Do they train all the maids in Grima to fight so fiercely?"

"They do, your Majesty," Bronagh replied. "All people of Grima are trained with the sword from an early age. Even women."

"What a strange concept." Keir shook his head.

"You never know when an invading army might arrive to overrun the palace." Bronagh's voice grew hard with scorn.

"That's enough, Yvonne." Tierney shot her a glare.

Bronagh's face flushed with the realization she'd spoken out of turn. "Beg your pardon." She gave the world's worst curtsy. It would be a miracle if they got out of Vondur before Keir figured out he held the Grima queen within his grasp.

"Terribly misguided." The Duchess shook her head, moving to stand beside the king. "I couldn't leave them down here unchaperoned, and I wasn't sure who I should tell, your Majesty. It is difficult to know how to handle such things now that my husband has departed this world."

Keir held up his hand to stop the duchess' dithering.

"A secret circle of Vondurian ladies." He moved around the room, eyeing each woman like an officer surveying his troops. "Ladies proficient with the sword."

"It's not as absurd as you make it sound, Keir." Tierney

couldn't stand the tension. This was such a small thing to give these women. Some confidence that if push came to shove, they could protect themselves and their families. Was that too much to ask of this strange kingdom? "I am as proficient with a blade as any soldier in your army. And with a little dedication, the right weapons, and lots of practice, these ladies can be too." Well, they could be better than they currently were.

"It's fun, your Majesty." Lady Margery dipped into a perfect curtsy. "It's good exercise, and if it helps us protect our children, what is the harm?"

"Is that something you ladies fear?" Keir turned to the others. "That there could come a time when there will be no one here to protect you and your children?"

A few heads nodded.

"Your Majesty." Margery stood by meekly with her head lowered, eyes downcast. "Many of our husbands are officers and minor noblemen. They are frequently away. Along with your soldiers. Some of us live in remote areas of the kingdom. We come to court for protection while our husbands are at war. But if I could take my children home, knowing I could protect them, I would much rather be there to see to the estate in my husband's absence."

"I see." Keir turned to Tierney. "You claim you can match any of my men?"

"I can."

Keir moved to the side of the room to inspect the weapons Declan had provided. "These are terribly old. Some are rusted." He shrugged out of his coat. "They will have to be replaced. With smaller weapons, as you said." He drew his sword from his hip.

"What did you say?" Tierney took a step forward. For a moment, it sounded like he would let them continue their practice.

"With Declan away, you'll need a new instructor." He moved to the middle of the room. "But perhaps today, I will be sufficient." He pointed his weapon at Tierney, his mouth tilting up in a wicked grin. "Let's see if you can match *me*, Princess."

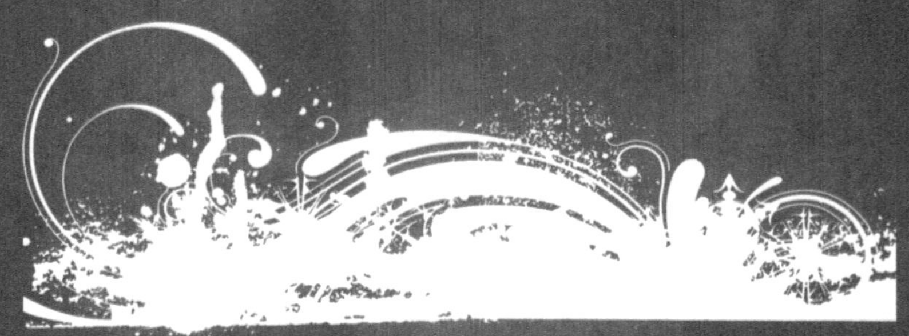

CHAPTER NINETEEN

KEIR

Tierney stared at Keir as if she hadn't heard a word he said. He knew it was a bad idea the moment it was out of his mouth, but he couldn't take it back now.

Most of the women wouldn't meet his eyes, and he supposed that was Vondur's fault for teaching women subservience was best. Yet, there were two women here who didn't seem to follow those rules.

Tierney stared at him, a wicked gleam entering her gaze.

And behind her, Yvonne, a mere maid, lifted her chin and matched his hard look. He'd suspected it before when she did every part of her job poorly, but this was no maid.

Tierney's voice snapped him back to the challenge at hand. "Are you sure you wish to challenge me, your Majesty?"

She stepped closer, her voice dropping. "I won't go easy on you."

Narrowing his eyes, he bent until his lips brushed her ear. "You don't stand a chance, Princess."

A laugh burst out of her, and she stepped back, examining the blade in her hand. With a shrug that seemed to say it was good enough but not perfect, she lifted it. "Let's make a deal, shall we?"

Keir raised his sword, taking up his stance. "What kind of deal?"

"When I win, you agree to train these women until Declan returns. No finding another instructor. It will be you."

"I am a king, Tia." He blew out a frustrated breath. "I do not have the time to train anyone who is not in my army."

"Then, you will let all Vondurian females who wish join your army."

"My men will never allow it."

"Then, I guess you better beat me." The flickering light from a nearby torch cast her face in an orange glow, giving her a deadly look that chilled Keir to the bone. If this was Tierney without magic, he couldn't imagine what kind of force she was with it.

But still, women joining the army would cause men to leave in droves. One day, he hoped Vondur could get there, but today was not that day.

"Fine, if you should best me, I will find the time to train them."

A triumphant gleam entered her eye. "And what do you want on the slim chance you win?"

There was only one thing he truly wanted that she could give. He stepped closer, dipping his head so his lips were only inches from hers. "You." The word was almost a growl.

"Me," she whispered, her mouth popping open in surprise.

His gaze flicked from her lips to her eyes and back again. "I want a taste, Tierney O'Shea. Just one."

The world seemed to still as her entire body went rigid. The only sign of her rapid thoughts was in the heaviness of her breathing. For once, Keir didn't regret letting her know how much he wanted her, how much he thought of closing the distance between them and claiming her in a single kiss. Just one, and then he could shake her from his mind.

Stepping back to give her space, he waited a few agonizing moments.

Finally, Tierney nodded. "I accept." The shock faded from her face, and one corner of her mouth curved up in a slow, delicious arc. "Don't be too nervous. You won't win."

Her words brought a smile to his face. "Big words. We'll see if you can live up to them."

Tierney shot him a wink before bending into a low crouch, her sword at the ready. It was an aggressive kind of stance he'd never seen before, but she looked so at ease with the weapon he realized she'd obviously been trained by a great sword master.

Just as he had. He bent his knees and readied himself the way Daniel taught him before abandoning Keir for the Grima court. That was a long time ago, but he'd never forgotten the lessons.

Never take your eye off the opponent, young prince.

Know where their weapon is at all times.

Do not underestimate a rival.

He'd already failed at that last one. He'd underestimated Tierney the moment she'd shown up during the battle against the golden warriors.

He wouldn't make that mistake again.

A slow murmur came from behind him, and he realized he'd forgotten they weren't alone. But it was no matter. This was between him and Tierney.

She made the first move, which was fine with him. He was a defensive fighter, not an attacker. Her sword crashed against his as she lunged. She pulled away with shocking speed and pivoted on one foot to turn and strike again.

Each blow was stronger than the one before, but Keir fended them off easily, matching her for both strength and speed. Yet, Tierney kept coming. "Nice footwork, Princess." He smirked as he stepped out of her way.

"Oh, just wait." She danced toward him, her sword arcing through the air. He blocked the blow and then turned to meet her next. "I was trained by the O'Shea brothers."

"Your father?" He ducked a blow, not letting her drive him back.

Her breath huffed out. "And my uncle Griff." She jumped so suddenly he didn't see her feet leave the ground and only had a moment to fend off her quick strike, pushing her onto her heels. "Along with the best sword masters of the four kingdoms."

She landed gracefully without missing a step. "My father taught me how to use my size to my advantage." She whirled around, her sword coming from the left and then the right, clashing with his. "He taught me how to make any weapon an extension of myself."

And he'd taught her well. Keir's arms ached as she forced him back a step, taking his ground. The women behind him scrambled out of the way, their eyes on the fight.

Breath burned in his lungs, and he tried to drive her in the other direction. But she didn't give an inch, jumping over his sword when he swept it low and then ducking the next blow.

The weapons weren't blunted, so they had to be conscious of each attack, able to stop before seriously injuring the other. If they had wooden swords, he knew Tierney would have already rapped him over the head with it.

She didn't want to kill him. At least, he didn't think so.

He stepped into her attack, thinking of what a bad idea it would be to win this fight. Nothing good would come from kissing this woman. Yet, he drove forward with all of his might, trying to take that victory.

"And your uncle?" he grunted, remembering she'd said two men taught her to fight. "What did he teach you?"

A grin slid across her face. "Oh, you'll see."

He wasn't sure if he found that answer intriguing or terrifying. Maybe both.

The women cheered, and it took him a moment to realize they wanted Tierney to win, to not only best a man but to beat their king. "It seems you've won over even more fae in my kingdom."

She shrugged. "Only because I challenge how they view their place in this world." She leaped forward, her sword barely missing his side as he jumped.

"You must be beloved in Iskalt."

Darkness crossed her features, and he wasn't sure if it was because she'd turned out of the torchlight or if it was something else. Her foot connected with his stomach, shoving him into the stone behind him. When had she forced him to the wall?

His totem burned against his neck, begging to be used in the fight. But he refused to draw on it against Tierney.

"Iskalt thinks I'm trouble." She admitted, holding the tip of her sword against his chest. "Do you concede?"

Here in the shadows, her eyes looked almost black. Blond hair had broken free of its braid, hanging in sweaty strands around the pale skin of her face. Red tinted her cheeks from the exertion. She looked like a forest wildling—a creature meant to live freely in the countryside instead of trapped in a castle in a role that was going to destroy the fire inside her.

"Trouble is sometimes what a kingdom needs." Vondur had certainly needed her brand of recklessness.

Her sword dipped the slightest bit, her grip loosening on the hilt. Keir batted it away and stepped around her to take up his stance once again.

Tierney scowled, her eyes narrowing. "You really want to know what Uncle Griff taught me?"

All he could do was nod.

"You asked for it." She walked toward him slowly, her eyelashes fluttering against her cheeks. "Why do you want to kiss me, Keir?"

"Um ..." He didn't have an answer for her.

A smirk appeared on her lips. "Is it because I challenge you?" Her tongue poked out to wet her lips. "Or because I make you challenge yourself?" She didn't stop moving until she was within reach of his sword, but he didn't raise it. "Imagine it. A moment just for us. One with no interruptions, no pressing duties." She smiled. "If you want me, your Majesty, come and take me."

There was a dare in her eyes, one Keir couldn't make himself resist as he shifted toward her, his sword still keeping them a few feet apart even though his fingers relaxed.

Tierney moved so quickly he couldn't track her as she ran to the right before turning and heading straight for him. He prepared for an attack, but his mind was no longer in it.

Tierney jumped, landing in a somersault and sweeping his legs out from under him. His back hit the ground with sharp pain, but he didn't have time to evaluate himself because Tierney was there, straddling his waist, her sword at his throat.

She stared at him for a long moment, her chest heaving, before leaning down and bringing her face close to his. "My uncle taught me how to fight dirty." Her lips curved up. "To use every advantage I have. Do you concede now, your Majesty?" The way she used his title sent a shiver through him.

"Yes," he breathed. "I concede."

With a satisfied nod, she climbed off him and stood. Extending a hand down, she grinned. "Maybe next time."

He didn't take her offered hand, and she drew it back seconds before some of the other women mobbed her, uttering soft congratulations and trying not to offend their king.

Smiling in spite of himself, Keir pushed to his feet, stretching to rid himself of the ache in his back.

"Tomorrow," he said to the gathered women. "Sundown." With that, he walked out, not sparing another glance for Tierney.

She was right, of course. One had to use every advantage in battle. He'd just never thought she'd have an advantage over him, that she could throw him off so easily.

He scrubbed a hand over his face as he headed toward the great hall in search of an ale. Finding the women training had been a shock, but he was proud of Eavha for helping them. He only wished she and Declan thought they could tell him about their secret club.

Footsteps sounded behind him, and he turned, expecting to find a guard heading to their evening post.

Instead, Tierney jogged to catch up with him. She stopped a few feet away, looking much less confident than she had during the fight. "Keir ..."

He was too tired for guessing games. "What is it?"

"Thank you."

That surprised him, and it must have shown on his face.

"For agreeing to train them. It was important to Eavha."

She didn't say it, but he suspected it was important to her too. Tierney acted as if she cared for little more than returning home, but he knew the truth. She wanted to help his fae.

"That was our deal."

She shrugged. "You're the king. No one would blame you for breaking a deal."

"I would never go back on a promise to my fae, Tierney." Or to her, but he didn't say that last part.

A small smile appeared on her lips. "I'm starting to see that."

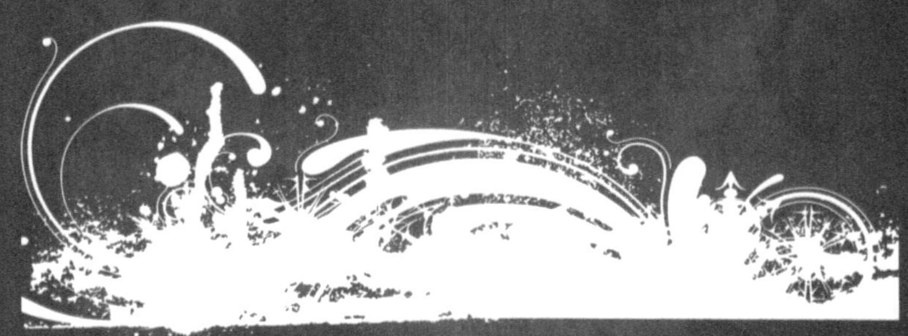

Chapter Twenty
Siobhan

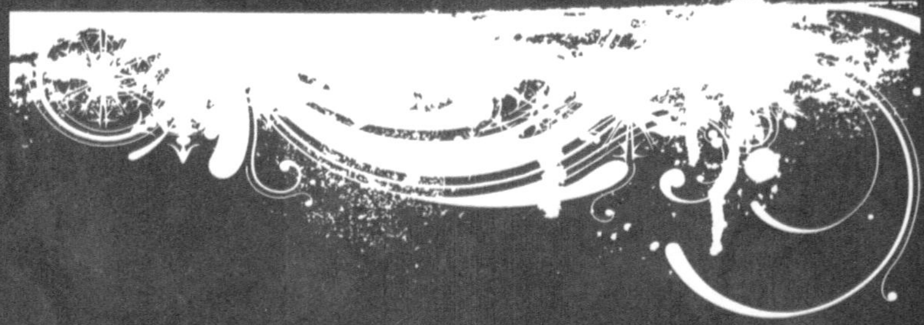

Siobhan followed Toby and Logan across the castle grounds and down to the lake where the special library was supposed to be located for the moment.

She squinted in the sunlight and saw nothing but snow-covered fields as usual.

"You can't see it yet, Siobhan." Toby laughed, his breath coming out in a white cloud. "My grandfather has to invite us inside." He pointed to two ancient-looking columns buried in the snow. "The village of Aghadoon is just through there. It used to be that only those with the blood of Gelsi royalty could see the village when they weren't inside, but Grandfather and Aunt Neeve found a way to change the magic. Now only those who have been invited may see it once they cross the threshold."

Toby stepped through the columns and disappeared.

"Whoa." Prince Logan stepped back. "Wasn't expecting that."

"Do we wait here?" Siobhan asked.

"I can't remember. It's been a long time since I visited Aghadoon. I was just a kid the last time it was in Eldur."

"You guys coming?" Toby stuck his head out through the columns. "I promise it's not weird. Well, it is weird, but it's safe." He reached for Logan's hand, pulling him through.

"Anything for Tia." Siobhan sucked in a breath and stepped through the columns. The first oddity she noticed was the absence of snow inside the village. Green grass grew in front of quaint little buildings and houses. It was still cold, but not Iskalt cold. Siobhan shed her gloves and hat, stuffing them into her coat pockets.

"Most of the houses are vacant these days. Just those traveling with the village live here. A few residents stay here while they're researching. And Grandfather Brandon, of course, along with a few of his Gelsi subjects who monitor the library."

Toby led them down a cobblestone street to the center of the village, where a lone building sat. It was larger than the others but still not what Siobhan would call a library.

"This is supposed to house all the histories of magic in the whole world?" She stepped up onto the wooden porch beside Toby and Logan. "It's a shack."

"Ah, but looks can be deceiving, my dear." Prince Brandon stood in the open door of the library, beckoning them to come inside. Siobhan's heart skittered to a stop as she stared at the once king of Fargelsi, father of the current queen.

"I beg your pardon, sire." She sank into a deep curtsy.

"Dispense with the formalities while you are in Aghadoon,

young Siobhan. Come inside, and let's see what we can learn of my granddaughter's fate."

"Have you found anything new, Grandfather?" Toby slipped off his coat and hung it on a peg by the door, turning to help Logan out of his coat. They were so cute the way they took care of each other.

"I have, but it's led to more questions than answers, I'm afraid." Brandon moved to the large table at the center of the room. "Make yourselves at home while I bring out my findings. Perhaps you can give Siobhan a quick lesson on how the library functions."

"Will do." Toby pulled a chair out for Logan and one for Siobhan like the perfect gentleman he was.

"Thank you." Siobhan sat down opposite the boys, staring around the musty old building filled with ancient books. "I expected it to be bigger."

"As Grandfather said, looks can be deceiving." Toby shifted through a stack of tomes scattered on the table. "What is physically on the shelves changes based on the researcher's needs. We've yet to catalog everything this library contains, and I doubt we ever will. As the library presents us with what it thinks we need, the contents of the shelves change from one moment to the next."

Siobhan shook her head. "Sometimes, magic is terrifying."

"How so?" Logan tilted his head in question.

"Just the idea that we have to rely on this unknown entity to present us with the knowledge we seek is kind of awful and scary—as a concept, I mean."

"Right you are." Brandon rejoined them, hidden behind a stack of books he carefully set on the table. "It's the unknown of Aghadoon that presents the first problem. Who made the library function this way? And what were they trying to hide within these fathomless walls?"

"Deep questions for another time, Grandfather." Toby lifted a book from the pile. "Tell us what you've discovered."

"These books contain all the references of Lenya that I can find. So far." Brandon moved to sit beside his grandson. "I found a passage here." He flipped to a marked page in a huge leather-bound book with a faded title. He ran his finger down the page. "Here it is; see what you make of it."

"A relic of the old world. From a time long before the four kingdoms formed, an ancient race of fae ruled a land rich and fertile. From their great cities, these fae achieved feats of magic those of the four kingdoms could never fathom. Before its destruction, this land was known as Lenya."

Toby looked up from the book. "Destruction?"

"Keep reading." Brandon gestured to the book.

"The kingdom of Lenya withered and died in a series of natural disasters that resulted in the formation of the Vatlands that encroached upon the land, consuming everything. Ages passed before the Vatlands began to recede and the four kingdoms rose to power, thriving in the lands between the blight that destroyed the once vast and fertile lands of Lenya."

"But if we're living in what once was Lenya, then where is Tierney?" Siobhan leaned forward. "Is there a map of the old Lenya?"

"That is an excellent question, Lady Siobhan." Brandon rose from his seat. "I haven't thought to look for ancient maps. I can't imagine any have survived, nor that they would look the least bit familiar to us, but let's see what we can find." He disappeared among the rows of bookshelves, his footsteps fading unnaturally in the small building.

Toby flipped through the pages of a different book, searching through the sections his grandfather marked for them to study.

"Listen to this." Toby reached for his suitor's hand, as if he drew strength from his presence.

Siobhan watched them wistfully. She wanted what they had. Someday. If they could bring the princess home, maybe she could have that with Tierney.

> *"Before the ancient civilization of Lenya faded into the ether, a blight spread across the lands. Vast fertile plains burned as temperatures rose, killing thousands who could not escape. Putrid swamps with noxious gasses engulfed villages. Cities and towns sank into the depths of marshlands and swamps, where none survived. The ground shook, breaking the land into deep canyons that flooded with vicious waters. Massive mountains rose so high there was little air left to breathe. Yet, legends have prevailed of a small band of Lenyans who survived."*

"If they survived, wouldn't they be among us?" Logan asked, leaning closer to peer over Toby's shoulder.

"No." Toby sat back, his face paling as he met Siobhan's eyes. "There's more.

> *"Legend claims this band of brave Lenyans found a way to stall the spread of the blight beyond the burning lands, preserving their way of life from ages past."*

Toby leaned against his chair, sliding the book forward.

"That's where my sister is. I can feel her pulling me toward the fire plains."

"But how can we find a way across?" Siobhan reached for the book, her eyes scanning the pages to read the histories for herself. "And how could we ever know what lies beyond?"

"We probably won't, but this could help." Brandon returned with another enormous book nearly the size of half the table but thin like a portfolio.

"An atlas?" Toby stood to help him with the giant book.

"It's the oldest one I could find on the fly, as your mother would say." Brandon carefully lifted the cover, and Siobhan held her breath. The book seemed so old it might disintegrate before their eyes.

"Lucky for us, the magic of the library keeps these records in whatever condition they were when added to the library. I'd say this one was on death's door when it arrived here."

"It's a map of the four kingdoms." Siobhan moved to stand behind Toby as they all crowded around the large map.

"It even shows Myrkur." Logan pointed to the dark corner on the northwestern side of the map.

"This map predates the Vatlands." Brandon ran a careful hand over the region of Fargelsi. "Before Lake Vilandi formed."

"Look at Eldur." Logan's voice was barely a whisper. "It's as green as Gelsi. And it's bigger."

"Good thinking, Siobhan." Brandon patted her on her shoulder. "You have a mind for problem-solving."

"And here I thought I was just a warrior along the wild borderlands." Her face flushed at the former king's praise.

"Not many fae trapped in the human realm would figure out how to find the rift and travel there all on their own." He gave her another pat on the shoulder.

"Now, if I could just find a way across the fire plains."

At her mention of the Eastern Vatlands, they all turned to the opposite corner of the map.

"That's different." Toby moved to get a closer look. "The fire plains start around here." He pointed to the northeastern corner of the current Eldur lands. "If we go off the size of the known vatlands between Gelsi and Eldur through the marsh-lands, and the mountains of the Northern Vatlands between Iskalt and Myrkur, then there is no way the Fire Plains could consume a third of this map." He ran a hand over an area the size of Iskalt far to the east.

"It's a plausible theory." Brandon studied the map. "If some portion of Lenyan civilization survived, then it's a safe assumption they were sealed off by the fire plains."

"So, we just need to figure out a way across or around them." Siobhan turned to Logan. "What lies beyond the seas to the east of Eldur?"

"Nothing, I'm afraid. At least nothing Eldurians have discovered. The seas off our coasts are plentiful and smooth sailing for leagues and leagues. But the seas become rocky and dangerous as they turn toward the fire plains. Some say it's as hot as the vatlands there, where the waters churn and bubble and blazing hot steam bursts from the rocks like geysers."

"And what of the Iskalt seas?" Siobhan asked, turning to Toby and Brandon for answers.

"The sea between Iskalt and Eldur is calm and easy sailing," Toby replied. "But the shorelines along the fire plains are impossible to navigate. It's too hot, and the smoke lies thick across the water. I'm not sure what lies beyond the eastern mountains. The frozen tundra in the east is a difficult journey, and then the mountains are as treacherous as the western Vatlands."

"Some have made the journey." Brandon ran a fingertip across Iskalt on the map. "But not much is known of the seas beyond eastern Iskalt. I imagine it is colder than we could fathom."

"So, what you're all saying is no one knows what lies east of Eldur and Iskalt. But if this map is even partially accurate, something is there, and based on Toby's connection with Tia, in all likelihood, she is where we cannot reach her."

"There is more." Brandon returned to his seat, dragging another book from his stack. "The ancient Lenyans were not like us. The histories here speak of them as a superior race of fae. Capable of great feats of magic."

"That does not sound good for Tia." Logan scooted closer to Toby.

"See here." Brandon placed the book on the table, pointing to a faded etching of a king and queen on their thrones. "See how they each clutch a crystal in their hands?"

"What does it mean?" Toby asked, staring at the image.

"Their magic is not like ours. Where the sun gives Logan his day magic and Siobhan receives her night magic from the moon, and I gain my magic from the land itself, Lenyans used carved totems made of a certain kind of crystal that allowed them to touch their magic."

"What kind of crystal?" Siobhan asked, though she couldn't fathom needing to use an object of power to access her magic. To her, reaching for her magic was as effortless as breathing.

"As near as I can tell, it seems like they used what the Myrkurians call fire opals. We have them here in Iskalt, and all across Gelsi and Eldur as well. They are pretty to look at, and they make lovely decorations, but for us, they contain no power." Brandon set a rough-cut stone on the table. A fire opal.

Siobhan picked it up, but it was just a rock like any other. It sparkled with a turquoise core that bled into an orange burst of color that looked like flames. Hence, the Myrkurian name for it.

"This gives them power?" She wrinkled her nose at the concept. "What strange magic."

"It only lasts for a time." Toby read from the book, "*Each totem provides Lenyans with power until it drains from the crystal and another is needed to replace it.* It is this power that allowed them to build cities as grand and populated as modern human cities. I made that last part up, judging by these images. This city here, with huge buildings, reminds me of New York in the human realm. Without the cars." He tapped a finger on a page with another etching.

"You're right. It's a lot like the human cities." Siobhan didn't care for those places when she traveled the human realm. "Too many people." She eyed the etching of busy streets filled with people and large buildings with huge columns and statues that towered above them.

"I think we are dealing with a very different kind of fae." Toby frowned. "If they are so powerful, even Tia might not be able to fend for herself." He gave a shudder, like he dreaded the thought of his powerful sister among such people.

"We have no choice. We have to find a way across the plains." Siobhan studied the map again. "How long does it take to walk across the Southern Vatlands?"

"When one knows the way, it can be done in a little more than a day's walk." Brandon sat back in his chair. "More if the person is uncertain."

"So, we need a way to survive the intense heat of the fire plains for two days. A shield might work to block the heat."

"One would have to sustain it day and night, though," Brandon said.

"A team of Iskaltians and Eldurians could manage it. And

maybe a Fargelsian to help along the way." Toby eyed his grandfather.

"Your mother would kill me for even letting you think about it." Brandon shook his head.

"What if we moved the library?" Logan asked. "We could try to move it to the other side, right?"

"We cannot risk the contents of this village." Brandon refused. "If we landed in the middle of the fire plains, all here would be lost."

"So, let's move to the border." Toby looked at the map again. "We can go to this side of the plains and search for a way across. We can use the library to help us find the right magic, and then we'll already be there to act on it. I feel like we're running out of time, Grandfather."

"I can't let you do it, Toby. It's too risky."

"You really think she's there?" A weary voice caught them by surprise.

"Mom." Toby hopped up from the table. "How long have you been listening?"

The queen stood in the open doorway, looking haggard, like she hadn't slept in all the time since her daughter went missing.

"Long enough. Answer my question, Tobias." She moved to sink into a chair at the table.

"She's there. I know it. I can't feel her every day, but when I do—when she feels a strong emotion—I know she's there. She's calling for me. I have to go."

Queen Brea nodded. "The connection you two share has always astounded me. It's like you have your own little language. Logan, dear, could you go fetch the king?"

Logan's throat bobbed as he swallowed. "You want me to go where now?"

"Loch is in with his council. Go tell him we're leaving for

the fire plains in an hour, and if he wants to come with us, he better get his butt down here."

"Y-yes, ma'am." Logan stood, and Toby walked with him to the door. "If I don't come back, send out a search party."

"He won't kill the messenger. Just be assertive. He respects that." Toby leaned in to kiss him on the cheek. "Good luck. And remember, he's really not that scary."

"To you maybe." Logan stepped outside, and Siobhan laughed when he took off running as fast as his legs would carry him.

"We're really going?" she asked the queen.

"Yes, and while we're waiting on Loch, catch me up with whatever this map is we're looking at."

CHAPTER TWENTY-ONE
TIERNEY

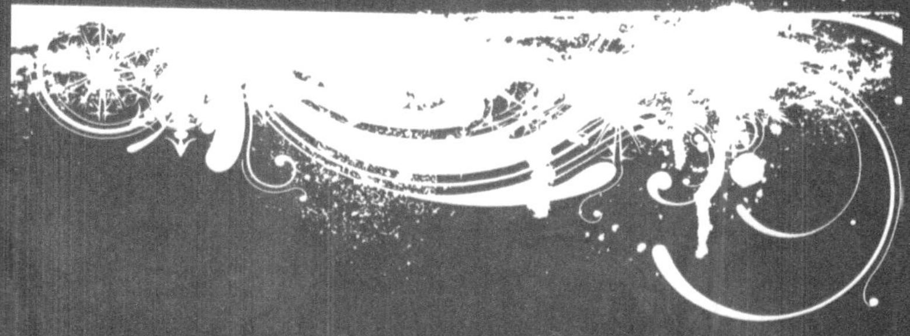

I would never go back on a promise to my fae, Tierney.

Those words had stuck in Tierney's head since the moment they dropped from Keir's lips. Because she believed them. Every moment she spent with him only proved one thing: he could be trusted to do what was right.

"How can you not be sure yet?" She paced from one end of her room to the other and back again. "He has shown you nothing that proves he will use the danger to all of Lenya as an excuse to destroy Grima."

Bronagh sat on the settee, bent over with her head in her hands. At that moment, she looked nothing like the queen she was. Each passing day posing as a maid wore on her, Tierney could see it. She needed to be back with her people, to lead them.

But the best way to lead them right now was to discover if they had an ally to stop the destruction.

"I wish I had a totem," Bronagh grumbled.

Tierney stopped moving and planted her hands on her hips. "How would magic help you make this decision?"

"It wouldn't, but feeling the power within me ... it makes me feel sane."

A breath puffed past Tierney's lips, and she dropped onto the settee beside Bronagh. "I understand that. I stopped counting how many days it's been since I last had use of my power, and sometimes I wonder if that was the only part of me that ever made sense."

Bronagh lifted her face, turning to eye Tierney. For the moment, they weren't a queen and future queen. Instead, they were very much the young women life hadn't allowed them to be. Unsure. Confused. Conflicted. But young women whose duties included more than raising their children, tending the fields, or even fighting for their kingdoms.

They would never be free from the burdens of the crowns that belonged to them.

"Lenya used to have great power." Bronagh smiled, a sad tilt to the action. Tierney waited, letting her speak, knowing she had to. "In Grima, our elders speak of ancient stories where crystals were in abundance. A Lenyan fae could draw massive amounts of power from their totem all at once because if they depleted it quickly, there were a hundred more to replace it in their possession."

Bronagh sighed, her entire body relaxing into the settee. "Those Lenyans, long ago, assumed the mines would never empty, that we would always have the magic we needed. But now ..."

"Now, you must be judicial in your use of the crystals," Tierney finished for her.

"They are only to be used in battle, and even then, one must draw slowly." She turned her entire body to face Tierney. "What I am saying is that we too once defined ourselves by how much power we possessed. And now, we know it is the wielder, not the magic itself that has the true power."

Tierney shook her head. "I have no real power."

"You forget, Tia, I've been forced into the company of the gossiping maids for weeks. I've heard of your accomplishments. Yesterday, I saw my enemy, one who has always seen women as weak and inconsequential, give deference to you."

"To be fair, it was his fae who had those views on women. I'm not so sure about Keir."

"And still, the Vondurian king agreed to take time to train the women of the kingdom." She touched Tierney's hand. "Not all power is magic."

Tierney turned the words over in her mind, knowing they were true but not feeling like it. She'd always defined her worth by what she could do. Took down the prison magic. Intimidated villagers who wronged her or Toby. Emulated anything her father accomplished. She wouldn't have been able to do any of that without magic.

There was a knock on the door, and Bronagh straightened, pulling her hand away moments before Gulliver walked in.

"Where's Veren?" he asked, glancing around the room.

Tierney's brow furrowed. "Since when do you want to be anywhere near Veren?"

"Since he promised to spar with me."

Her shock must have shown on her face because Gulliver scowled. "I can want to learn how to fight better."

"You can want to," Veren said, walking in behind him and

throwing an arm over his shoulders, "but it doesn't mean you will."

Tierney crossed her arms. "Why would you go to him instead of me?"

"I feel like I should take offense." Veren kicked off his dusty boots and lounged on the bed.

If the expanding fire plains didn't kill him first, Tierney would. "Off my bed." She stood, crossing her arms as she faced him. "And I don't want Gullie training with you because you'll let him down."

A look of hurt flashed across his face, and he rolled from the bed. "Whatever, Tierney." He stormed from the room, and she turned to the others.

Bronagh pursed her lips. "You're going to be a queen." She stood, smoothing the creases from her soft blue dress as she did. "You should try a little more kindness." She went after Veren, leaving Tierney alone with Gulliver.

He gave her a disappointed look.

"What?" she snapped. "It's Veren."

"Not the same Veren we knew in Iskalt. Come on, Tia, don't tell me you haven't noticed. Something changed in him during his time in Grima. I'm not sure if it was having to fight in battle or not being *the* Veren Rhatigan for the first time in his life, but he's not the guy who used you."

The sad truth was, Tierney had seen that. She knew Veren was trying to be different. But for so long, many of the noble children of Iskalt just wanted to be seen with the princess who destroyed the prison magic, to be associated with her. It made it nearly impossible to trust anyone. Especially someone who'd been vying for her hand in marriage only months ago.

"I suck."

A smile curved his lips. "It's very appropriate to use a human word when you just acted like a human."

"You take that back."

He leaned forward, dropping his voice, a hint of mischief in his gaze. "Human."

That was it. Tierney launched herself at him, and they fell sideways onto the bed in a heap of kicking legs and struggling arms. Managing to pin him, she dug a knee into his stomach. "Tell me I'm not a human."

"But all the human words," he wheezed. "The entitlement, the attitude. Oh, and not to mention your obsession with human things."

"You're the one who wants to court a hamburger. It's odd how in love with an item of food you are."

"Who got us into this mess with their little trip to the human realm?" The teasing note in his voice was the only reason she didn't kill him right then.

Her knee dug in hard. "Call me a fae."

A throat cleared behind them, and they both froze. Tierney looked over her shoulder, not letting Gulliver free. "Oh, it's the king. Look, Gulliver. He probably thinks we're being intimate."

"Fine," he yelled. "You're a fae!" He shoved her off in disgust. "Don't ever say the word intimate in regard to us again."

A giggle burst out of her, and she was glad there'd never been anything more than a sibling relationship between them.

Keir cleared his throat again. "I'm glad we're clear that you are, in fact, fae." He muttered something under his breath.

"Oh." Gulliver sat up. "I was supposed to tell you the king wanted to speak with you."

Tierney stood to face Keir. "He definitely delivered your message." She sent Gulliver a wink. "I've got your back."

"You know I can hear and see you two, right?" Keir's eyes flicked between them, like he couldn't quite understand anything they did or said.

"Why is he always in such a bad mood?" she asked Gulliver.

Gulliver shrugged. "Maybe they don't let him put honey in his morning porridge."

"Or maybe no one smiled at him yet today." As one, they both turned to Keir, giant grins on their faces.

He stared at them, his expression darkening, before turning on one heel and marching from the room.

Tierney held up a hand, and Gulliver slapped his against it, his tail coming up to hit it too. With another grin, she chased after Keir, falling in step beside him as he hurried down the corridor.

"You wished to speak with me?" she asked. "If it's about training the women, don't think you—"

"It's not about that."

"Then, what—"

"Not here." His eyes darted around the hall, his steps never faltering. With no warning, he grabbed her wrist and pulled her through a doorway, shutting the door.

They descended into darkness, and Tierney backed up, almost knocking over what she thought was a bucket. "Where are we?"

"This is where the maids keep many of their cleaning components."

The king had pulled her into a closet? She didn't know why that made her heart kick up a notch. "And why are we in here?"

"Because there are always fae listening to what I say in this palace, and I do not want us to be overheard."

As her eyes adjusted to the darkness, she realized they were close, too close. Stepping away, she cringed as a broom crashed to the ground. Her butt hit a cold stone wall, and she suddenly had nowhere else to go.

"I need you to be honest with me, Tierney."

"About what?" Her voice was embarrassingly breathy.

"Yvonne."

Tierney's chest seized. This was it, the moment he learned the truth of how they'd deceived him.

"She's not really your maid, is she?" He rubbed his forehead. "I should have known Grima wouldn't provide you with a maid for your return here. It made no sense, but I wanted to believe you."

Words clogged in Tierney's throat, and she tried to force them out. "Yvonne ... she's ..."

"Your guard," he finished. "It's so obvious. Her skill with the blade, the way she hovers near you whenever she can, how truly terrible she was performing the duties of a maid. Grima has female warriors, but we are not used to that in Vondur, and it blinded me."

Her guard? Breath rushed into Tierney's lungs. Keir deserved the truth, and he'd get it, but not yet. It wasn't her truth to tell, her life to put at risk. She nodded. "My guard. Yes, that's what she is."

He turned away from her, a frustrated huff expanding his cheeks. "You didn't have to lie to me, Tia. I know coming back here must not have felt safe for you. I wouldn't have respected you any less for bringing not only Veren but another guard as well."

"I know." *Think, Tia, think.* "It's just ..." Her next words burned like acid in her mouth. "I didn't think I could protect myself surrounded by those who wanted me dead not long ago. I am just one woman after all."

"If meeting you has taught me anything, Princess," he turned to look down at her, "it's that one woman can do anything. But even if you didn't believe that, I'd have protected you."

Tears built in her eyes, and this time, she wasn't playing up a lie. Only she knew the truth. No one could protect her. If they could, she wouldn't be here in Lenya at all.

Keir looked like he had more to say, but his words were cut off by a knock on the door. "Your Majesty? One of the guards said they saw you enter here. Are you in there?"

Tierney wiped her eyes. "It's okay. Go be the king."

He gave her one final look before opening the door. "Just having a meeting." He walked out of the dark closet like it was the most normal thing in the world.

The soldier was smart enough not to comment on it. "Sire, there's a situation."

"What sort of situation?" Keir asked impatiently.

Tierney followed behind them, not leaving unless she was asked. If there was an issue, she wanted to know of it.

"We have news of activity between our troops and the golden warriors."

"A battle?"

"Yes, sire."

No, this wasn't supposed to happen. Prince Donal promised to give Bronagh more time to turn Vondur into allies against the fire plains.

Keir's steps quickened. "Have we won?"

"That's just it, sire." The soldier's own steps faltered. "We do not know."

Chapter Twenty-Two
Keir

Anger ripped through Keir as he dug his heels into the sides of his horse, urging him to increase their pace. The moment he heard about the battle near the valley, where the largest part of the Vondurian army camped, he'd thought of little except getting there.

He didn't know if the fight was over, if there was a victor, nor how much of his army now lay dead at the feet of the golden warriors.

Tierney thundered up beside him on a giant gray stallion, having refused to remain at the palace. Behind them rode a contingent of guards along with Veren, Gulliver, and Yvonne. If they found themselves riding right into a battle, they'd need all the swords they could get.

Nothing else mattered anymore. None of the lies, nor the secrets he knew Tierney still kept. Not when his fae fought for their lives. And she'd come.

Branches lashed at his face as he barreled into the narrow part of the forest, knowing their destination was just on the other side. Pine needles stabbed his skin, but the scratches barely registered.

All he could hear was the horses, all he could see was the road ahead. Would Grima and Vondur ever see peace? Maybe none of that mattered either. Maybe the fire plains would destroy both kingdoms and wipe this land free of the blood and strife it had seen so much of.

By the time Keir reached the far end of this particular patch of forest, he was ready to fight. He led the riding party up over the crest of a hill, long-dead grass crunching under hooves. They stopped when they reached the top.

A field soaked in blood sat before them.

Bodies clad in red and gold armor were scattered about.

"Draw your weapons," he ordered, pulling his own sword free. The sound of scraping metal came from his right, and he turned.

Tierney's eyes narrowed in determination, as if this was her fight as much as his.

She met his gaze and nodded. He returned the gesture, glad they were on the same side for once.

"On my command." He drew in a long breath. As soon as they dipped into the valley, they would see whatever remained of the army camp. Smoke curled toward the sky, the only sign visible from their vantage point.

After a few beats, he lifted his sword. "Charge." Kicking his horse, he leaned forward. They plummeted down the far side of the hill. Fire. Churning black smoke. The acrid smell of burning flesh.

He didn't slow as he caught sight of the camp that had gone up in flames. A handful of soldiers lay dead among the ruins of tents, sleeping rolls, and cookery. Vondurians.

Beyond the camp, soldiers still struggled against each other, but this was not the kind of fierce battle Keir had expected.

He pulled up on the reins as he made it past the smoldering camp. Groups of men and women were stripped down to their underclothes. They huddled together, ropes securing their wrists and ankles.

Other soldiers patrolled the grounds. One slid his sword through a struggling man, like he was made of nothing but butter and oil. It took a moment for Keir to realize the soldiers rounding up prisoners wore Vondurian colors.

At the far side of the battlefield, fire licked at a pile of golden armor. Vondur had won.

Keir held up a hand to keep his men behind him.

Yvonne rode up next to Tierney and leaned in to speak, loud enough for Keir to hear. "This was not supposed to happen."

He didn't know what she meant, but there was no time to decipher her words because someone screamed, a man. He was one of the prisoners, and he lunged forward as a Vondurian soldier dragged another prisoner away.

The woman didn't fight him, didn't reach back for the man who had reached for her. Instead, there was hopelessness in her eyes. That was when Keir saw it.

A handful of bodies had been meticulously piled rather than scattered like the others. Those soldiers did not die in battle.

He leapt from his horse and opened his mouth to order every one of his soldiers to stand down, but before he could, the tip of a sword pierced the woman's chest. Red bloomed against her white underclothes like a thorny rose. A deadly rose.

No one caught her as she collapsed, her body going still.

The soldier pulled his blade free and gestured for two comrades to put her body with the others.

"Keir." Tierney's voice shook. "They're executing those who surrendered."

This couldn't happen. Not in his kingdom. Not in the Vondur he wanted to create. Storming through the remains of the battle, he sidestepped a dead Vondurian whose eyes were still open to the sky. "Lieutenant," he barked.

The officer turned, looking like he was ready to chastise anyone who addressed him in such a tone. Then, recognition showed on his face. "Your Majesty?"

Keir's jaw clenched as he stopped in front of the man. Tiny drops of blood spotted his cheeks, his uniform. "Report. What happened here?"

The lieutenant looked unsure of himself for only a moment before recovering. "Our camp was attacked by the golden warriors of Grima in broad daylight. Those vermin thought they could take us by surprise."

"Why would Grima attack now?" Yvonne asked. Keir hadn't realized she'd followed him.

The man acted as if he hadn't heard her. "What they didn't know was that our scouts spotted them first. We were lying in wait when they arrived."

Yvonne walked past them to view the prisoners. "I don't understand."

She was from Grima, so Keir tried not to speak ill of her people. "It seems your queen is just as power-hungry as her mother was before her."

Yvonne had her back to him, but he saw her stiffen. She didn't respond.

"How much warning did you have?" Tierney asked.

The lieutenant scowled. "Your Majesty, perhaps I should

report to you somewhere more private." Somewhere without women present, he meant.

Tierney rolled her eyes, but Keir's expression didn't change. "What are your men doing with those bodies?" He pointed to the pile that had grown by one with the recently executed woman topping the heap. He already knew the answer, but he wanted to hear it from this soldier's mouth.

Nearby soldiers stood at attention in the presence of their king but did not speak.

"They are enemies of Vondur. The palace dungeons are not large enough to hold every soldier who surrenders, much less feed them."

"You could let them go." Tierney crossed her arms.

He gave her a pitying look. "There's a reason we do not allow women to strategize."

Tierney lunged for him, but Gulliver and Veren held her back.

Keir busied himself viewing the prisoners. Not all were upright; some were quite injured and needed tending. "You're executing them. Even the injured, the women."

The soldier didn't have the decency to look ashamed. "We do what we must."

A familiar face caught Keir's eye, and he walked around the lieutenant to get a closer look. Yvonne had already found him and crouched at his side. The prince of Grima lay on the ground, his head on another prisoner's lap, his skin white as Grima snow. The young man was on death's door.

Donal's eyes fluttered open and fixed on Keir. "We face each other again, Vondurian," he croaked.

Keir's brow creased. "I do not think you are in any shape for a fight."

Donal's laugh turned into a cough. "Are you going to kill me this time?"

Keir looked away, his eyes finding the other prisoners watching them, the same defeat on their faces. The longer he looked at them, the less he saw an enemy. He saw the men and boys of Vondur, pulled from their fields with little choice but to fight for the families they left behind.

When had the common soldier become little more than fodder in this war between crowns?

His eyes drifted back to Donal, a decision made. "No. I'm not going to kill you."

Yvonne's sob echoed in the silence. He wondered if his own people would shed a tear for him like she did for her prince.

Straightening, he looked to his soldiers. "I am proud of your victory today." He paused as they cheered. "But a victory cannot exist without honor. And an honorable kingdom does not execute those who surrender." His eyes scanned the ranks, and he raised his voice. "Vondur does not kill without cause. Our great army is the protector of this kingdom, nothing more.

"We will rebuild your camp and fortify our scouting parties, but these people who fight for the gold crests on their armor are not your enemy when the battle is won. They will be allowed to return home to their families."

He nodded toward the prisoners. "Provision them, and tend to the wounded as you would your own."

Muttering erupted among his men, but he ignored it and turned to Donal. "But not you. You, young prince, are staying with us. Lieutenant?"

The sour man snapped to attention, his face showing none of his true emotions. "Your Majesty?"

"I do not want the prince moved without a healer present. Do you have one among you?"

"Yes, sire."

"Fetch them. And then give the fallen a proper funeral pyre with honor. Both those of Vondur and of Grima."

"You want to ... honor fallen enemies, sire?"

"I think it's time we honor all life as precious in Lenya." His men didn't yet know the fire plains would become their greatest enemy, bonding the two foes in their fight for survival.

Once they depleted the crystal reserves, there would be nothing standing between Lenya and the fires that would consume them.

Keir gripped the totem at his neck, begging it to give him strength. He rarely used the power, but its presence bolstered him. After seeing his orders to completion, he climbed back onto his horse, exhaustion weighing him down.

The hairs on the back of his neck prickled like someone had their eyes trained on him. He turned in his saddle only to find Yvonne standing at the side of the stretcher where Donal rested. Her lips were pursed as she studied Keir, her eyes shrewd.

Tierney broke their stare-off as she rode up beside him. "We need to talk."

CHAPTER TWENTY-THREE

TIERNEY

Tierney absently handed off her horse to the stable boy, her mind still on the battlefield. She'd experienced battle more times than she could count. Even now, years after the war for Myrkur ended, Tierney would wake up in a cold sweat, haunted by dreams of those days. When she was so wrapped up in her magic, she couldn't focus on her surroundings. But she'd been aware of the war raging around her, trusting in those who fought with her to protect her from harm while she did what no one else could do.

She was ten years old then. And maybe her grandmother Enis, preoccupied as she was with protecting the sacred book of magic, had made sure Tierney never saw the real atrocities of war.

Her thoughts strayed to the battle in Radur City when King Egan claimed the palace for himself, keeping Toby at his side. Even then, when her magic wasn't as sorely needed, she'd never seen anything as ... vicious as what she'd witnessed today.

She could still see the Grima soldiers. Men and women who'd surrendered when the battle was lost. Wounded that could have easily survived with the attention of a healer. All murdered. Put down like animals slaughtered for a feast simply to rid the Vondurian officers of a problem they didn't want to deal with. It came down to logistics. They didn't have room for prisoners of war, so they killed them.

"Tia? Are you okay?" Gulliver's tail wrapped around her wrist, the flat end thumping against her forearm in a soothing gesture.

"I'm fine." She nodded, as if to convince herself.

"Let's go see if Ariella can find us some of that awful tea they drink around here." Gulliver guided her into the palace and toward the east wing where they were staying. Bronagh had gone with her brother. Keir had insisted on bringing Prince Donal back to see the palace healers.

"Where are we going?" Gulliver kept pace with her as she altered their course.

"I need something stronger than tea," Tierney muttered, picking up her pace as they neared the king's rooms. "Keir!" she called, running to catch up with him, dragging Gulliver behind her.

"Tia, you should seek your rooms to rest." He paused in the doorway to his suite, gesturing to his guards to let her pass. "It's been a difficult day."

She brushed past him into his room.

"Don't mind us; I think we're looking for wine." Gulliver, still clutching Tierney's arm, stumbled into the room.

Keir followed, closing the doors behind him.

"There it is." Tierney reached for a glass decanter and three tumblers from the small table under the window. "Wherever there is a king, there is good wine." She lifted the bottle as she moved to sit in a hard wooden chair in front of the cold fireplace. She wondered if there was ever a time the Vondurians needed the fireplaces that seemed to adorn every room in the palace.

"You do know you're a guest in my home? If you wanted wine, you need only ask your maid to fetch it from the cellar." Keir's tone was teasing, but his face said he felt as bad as she did about what they'd witnessed today. He likely felt worse since it happened under his watch.

"Sit." She pointed to the chairs opposite her. "Both of you." She set the glasses on the table and poured two hefty glasses of wine and one half glass, which she handed to Gulliver. Spirits went right to his head every time.

She took her glass and tipped it back, taking a long sip. Wincing, she set it on the table. If this was the wine the king drank, she didn't want to know what everyone else got. It was nothing like the sweet heady fae wines of the four kingdoms. Gelsi wine, in particular, was the finest. She hoped she would get to drink her fill of it someday.

"It has to end, Keir." She took another sip. "Your war is stupid."

"Tell me how you really feel." Keir tipped his glass back and drained it.

"Did he just make a joke?" Gulliver snorted into his glass.

"Probably not on purpose." Tierney wasn't in the mood for jokes. "Your kingdom is suffering. It's time to settle your reign by putting an end to this war before it destroys you all."

"That is easier said than done." He stared over her shoulder and through the window behind her. "It would be my greatest wish to bring an end to this war, but I honestly don't know if it can be done. Maybe it is too far gone."

"You are king." Tierney leaned forward, refilling her glass. It wasn't so bad once one had a warm belly full of it. "You can do anything you want."

"I can, can I?" He turned his focus back on her. "And tell me, Princess Tierney, if there was a finite reserve of power left in your kingdom, and you were down to the last of it, what would you do?"

"I wouldn't fight over scraps with Grima, that is for sure."

"Magic is so overrated." Gulliver's tail swished behind him. "Wine ... is not." He giggled to himself, and then he shot his hand in the air, pointing straight up. "Magic causes more problems than it solves." He hiccuped and reached for the wineskin.

Keir moved it out of his grasp, leaning forward to set his empty tumbler on the table.

"Aw, you're no fun." Gulliver's tail reached over Keir's shoulder to grab the wineskin where it hung on the back of his chair. "I have magic, did you know?" He turned to Keir to distract him while his tail was busy trying to steal the wine he couldn't handle.

"Defensive magic as I recall." Keir had been on the receiving end of Gulliver's brand of magic once before.

"Right you are. I can't use it like other fae use magic. It's just kind of there. Like a second skin that protects me against all you other jerks trying to destroy things with magic you don't understand."

"Is he going to be okay?" Keir watched Gulliver, a smile tugging the corners of his mouth.

"He'll be fine as long as he doesn't drink any more." Tierney snatched the wineskin before Gulliver could get hold of it. "But he is right. Magic is a wonderful tool, but it is not everything. I've recently learned that lesson myself. The hard way. Anyone can survive without magic."

"So, you think my people should give up on our magic? Our way of life?"

"I didn't say that." Tierney still wasn't certain she could trust him with everything she knew. Not yet. "But if it were me, I would look for more."

"More what?"

"Magic."

"And where might I find another source of magic lying around unused?" Keir shook his head irritably.

Tierney tried not to think about the fire opals back home. The ones scattered across the Eldurian deserts like any other rock. The ones big as boulders in Fargelsi. The opal mines in Myrkur, and the whole of Iskalt, where the enormous snow-covered mountains were filled with the kind of crystals that would mean everything to the Lenyans.

"There are other kinds of magic. One needs only to know where to look for it and how to appreciate it for what it is, as much as what it is not."

"Pretty words, Princess." Keir reached for the nearly empty wineskin. "But we've moved far beyond philosophical what-ifs. We need to take action. And soon, or there will be nothing left of Vondur for the fire plains to consume."

Tierney's fist slammed against the table, and Gulliver launched from his chair, ducking behind Keir.

"For fae's sake, Tia. Don't do that." He crept back into his chair. "You know how I get when I've been into my cups." His tail wrapped around his leg, the tip twitching with a nervous tick.

"Sorry." Tierney sat back. "But I need you to listen, Keir. Vondur makes up a small portion of Lenya. There are others to consider."

"I am thinking of all of Lenya. Don't imagine for a moment that what we witnessed today did not affect me. Nothing of the like will happen under my reign ever again."

"Won't it?" Gulliver turned to Keir. "What measures have you taken to see that it's not happening elsewhere as we speak? You threw me into the dungeon upon my arrival, and the only reason I'm sitting here right now is because you've got a thing for ... hic ... hic ... T-ia." His hiccups were getting worse.

"Gullie—"

"No." He pointed a finger at her. "It's my turn to talk." His cat eyes drooped with the effects of the wine, but he clearly had something to say. "Do you even know what prisoners occupy your dungeons, King?"

"It hasn't been a top priority, no."

"Your father filled those reeking cells with innocents. Grima prisoners of war and Vondurians as well. Mostly soldiers who tried to return to their homes when their mothers and sisters, wives and daughters were starving. What have you done about them? Nothing. You let them rot. Yet, you challenged your father to the King's Comhrac to save our necks—and my neck thanks you for it—but the crown fell to you. Be a king, Keir. Be. A. King."

"Gullie is right." Tierney gave her best friend—her completely smashed-on-a-half-glass-of-wine best friend—a rueful smile. "If you truly care for all of Lenya like you say, then it's time to make your peace with the Grima queen and declare to all what kind of king you intend to be."

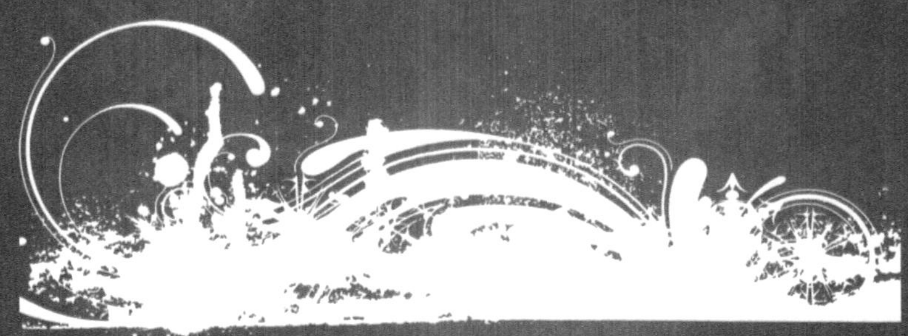

CHAPTER TWENTY-FOUR
KEIR

Keir left Tierney in his rooms so she could deal with a drunken Gulliver. He'd never met a fae who couldn't hold his drink, but he supposed there was a lot he didn't know about the Dark Fae of Myrkur.

There was a lot Keir didn't know about, period. He made his way down from the royal residence to the healer's quarters.

Tierney was right. This war was stupid.

"Your Majesty, a word." Lord Garnet quickened his pace to match Keir's long stride.

"Not now." Keir kept walking, ignoring the man's outrage.

"Your Majesty, I take issue with the crown's purchase of grain from my estates." The man had to run to keep pace with Keir. "The price per barrel has always been upwards of thirty coins. Last week's order yielded half that. I have a family to feed."

Keir stopped, turning on the much smaller man. The king towered over him. "You, a nobleman dripping in gold and jewels, have a family to feed? While half of Vondur starves? Take your sixteen coins per barrel and be happy it's not zero." Something about the look on Keir's face must have told the man he need not push the issue if he wanted to continue drawing breath.

Keir had bigger worries on his mind.

"Your Majesty." A young woman dropped her roll of bandages when he stepped into the infirmary. She was so flustered by his sudden appearance she forgot to bow—something his father would never have allowed.

"I must see the prince."

Stammering, she pointed through a set of double doors.

With a nod, he left her to her work.

"Donal." Keir was surprised to see the young prince sitting up in bed, looking far better than he had on the battlefield, though still quite pale.

"Keir." Donal gave him a curt nod.

"How are you faring?" He moved to sit in an empty chair.

"Better. I thank you for your hospitality ... and for not killing me. But why didn't you? I would have if it went the other way. That's twice now you've let me live."

"Let's just say I want something better for the future of my kingdom. And this war isn't it." Keir leaned forward.

"Your Majesty?" A gasp sounded at the door.

"Yvonne?" Keir frowned at Tierney's bodyguard-maid. "Shouldn't you be with your employer?"

Donal looked between the maid and the king, confusion on his face.

"I would dearly love to care for my prince." She dropped

into an awkward curtsy. "I've brought Prince Donal a tray from the kitchens."

Keir nodded, thinking she would set the tray on the side table and leave, but she pulled up a chair to sit with him while he ate.

Donal lifted a mug of broth to his mouth, taking a delicate sip of the steaming contents. "You were saying?" He urged the king to go on.

Keir glared at Yvonne. "It can wait."

Donal glanced at the maid. "Anything you have to say can be said in front of ... Yvonne. She is a loyal servant."

"Very well." Keir shifted in his seat. "What would it take to bring peace between our kingdoms? I am new to my reign, as your sister is to hers. I do not know yet what manner of queen she will be. But I would like to know if peace negotiations are something she would consider."

Donal nodded, sipping his broth. "My sister was never supposed to be queen. Our eldest sister was the heir. Yet, our kingdom has known nothing but war for more than a generation. My mother was a shrewd woman. After my father died, she ruled as regent, keeping a firm grasp on my sister's throne until she was of age.

"That did not happen. But Mother planned for every possible outcome. In her mind, we were all heirs to the throne. She trained each of her children to step into the role of monarch should we each fall. Bronagh might not have been born to rule like our sister, but she is no less ready for the task."

"Will she consider peace?" Keir grew weary of the prince's prattle.

"Bronagh will do what is best for Grima and her people. She will hear your peace talk—but only if Vondur is willing to compromise."

"I should like to meet this sister of yours." Keir rose from his chair. "I must speak with my council first."

"Let them know Grima will only give so much. Vondur will need to prove they are also willing to concede on the issues."

"I imagine the most successful peace treaties happen when neither side is particularly happy with the outcome." Keir gave the prince a rare smile. "I wish you a quick recovery."

"Keir we need to talk." The door to his bedroom slammed open. "I know it's late, but I've only just gotten away from your sadistic castellan." Yvonne twisted her hands together, pacing across his bed chamber.

Keir sat up against his headboard, setting the reports he'd just been reviewing on the bedside table. Staring at the young sort-of maid, he shook his head. "Have you lost your way to Tierney's rooms?"

"I'm here to see you."

"Did you just use my given name when you barged in here?" Keir slid out of his bed, reaching for the tunic he'd discarded earlier.

"Yes." She stood to her full height. "I am Bronagh, Queen of Grima." She lifted her chin. Her eyes narrowed to slits when Keir laughed in her face.

"I am deadly serious." She moved to sit in front of the fireplace, gesturing for Keir to take the seat opposite her. "Why do you think Donal allowed me to stay during your little chat earlier this evening? He is a prince of Grima; he would never allow a servant to be privy to such a discussion."

Keir wiped his eyes, still laughing as he sat in the leather chair, propping his feet up on the table.

"Queen Bronagh." He shook his head. He was going to murder Tierney. The daft woman brought his greatest enemy into his home. "Explain yourself."

"I do not like this war." She sat primly on the edge of her seat. Even dressed as a maid, now that she'd let go of the act, he could clearly see she was a queen in every way.

"You've been talking to Tierney." Keir ran a weary hand through his messy hair. Being king was harder than it looked. He hadn't had a decent night of rest since he challenged his father to the King's Comhrac.

"I've always thought this war was futile." She seemed to wilt before his eyes.

"Wine?" He stood to cross his room. Someone had already seen to refreshing his wineskin.

"Yes, please." She exhaled, sitting back against the smooth leather of her chair. "Your rooms are rather sparse for a king." She watched him return with fresh glasses and plenty of wine.

Keir groaned as he sat down, pouring them each a full glass. "It is different in Vondur. A prince isn't the king's heir. He's just a pawn. I never expected to be king. It isn't our way." Keir took a sip of wine, observing the Grima queen across from him. She was hardly more than a child, but she was better at this than he was.

"Yes, any man who wants the crown can take it." She took a big gulp from her glass. "As long as he can slaughter his predecessor."

He could hear the disgust in her voice. Staring down at the dark wine in his glass, he thought of the three innocent people with the hangman's noose around their necks that day. That moment haunted him. "I did it to save my best friend. And to save two other innocent lives. That is the only reason I am king now. And it is why I remain in the rooms of my youth. I do not feel like a king."

"I can relate to feeling like ... an imposter." Bronagh took another sip of her drink.

"Perhaps, it's time I move to my father's quarters."

"You are more of a king than those who have come before you. I have witnessed it for myself."

"Is that why you are here, masquerading as a maid—a terrible one—among my court?"

"I needed to know if there was any hope of our working together. Tierney said I could trust you, but I needed to see it for myself."

"And what have you decided?" Keir didn't want to think about the part where Tierney had stood up for him. He'd think about that later.

"You have honor. You care for your people, and you want to end this war as much as I do."

Keir lifted his glass. "I'll drink to that."

"I would love nothing more than for us to talk of peace." Bronagh sighed. "But—"

"We have much bigger problems than a war no one wants to fight anymore." Keir leaned back. This was going to be a long night.

"We have all of Lenya to think about." Bronagh reached to refill their glasses. "I'm afraid we will need more wine for this discussion."

"The fire plains are expanding into Vondur lands, as well as Grima."

"It started slow for us, but the expansion is happening faster. We are running out of time in Grima."

"We need stronger magic to slow the spread." Keir took his full glass from the queen and drank deeply, though he couldn't escape this new disaster in the bottom of a glass.

"My thoughts exactly."

"You propose we use the final reserves within the mines to fight the spread?"

"It won't be enough." Bronagh shook her head. "You know as well as I, what we've been mining for the last fifty years are murky stones not half as powerful as the pure crystals of our ancestors."

"What is your plan then?" For clearly, she had a plan.

"When you don't have enough magic to solve a problem, you find more magic."

"Tierney has been a good influence on you." Keir smiled.

"And on you. The crystals are plentiful in Iskalt. We will go there and propose a trade with King Lochlan."

"Excuse me?" Keir blinked rapidly. He must have misheard her.

"It will be a dangerous journey," Bronagh continued, not noticing his surprise at hearing such news. "But we can return with enough magic to push the fire plains back and contain them to their borders. We might even have enough to push them back farther."

They have crystals in Iskalt? Yet, Tierney had never trusted him with this knowledge.

"It is impossible." Keir forced himself to focus on Bronagh's chatter.

"We have built a ship. It was completed just before I arrived here in Vondur. It's the largest ship I have ever seen, but it is capable of crossing the raging seas to the northwest."

"You want to cross the maelstrom? Your ship will never make it." The seas around Lenya were dangerous. To the southwest, no one could pass through the rocky terrain lurking just under the surface. And to the northwest, the maelstrom waited to drag any ship foolish enough to approach to the bottom of the deep.

"The only other option is through the fire plains, and we don't have enough magic for such a journey." Bronagh's voice was firm and controlled. "The fastest route to Iskalt is across the maelstrom. We have nothing to lose and everything to gain."

"When will you send your men?"

"I mean to go with them as soon as we return to Grima."

"We?"

"Donal will stay behind to rule in my stead with my uncle, but Tierney and Gulliver will want to return to their home. Veren too." Though, the thought of his leaving seemed to sadden her.

"And what part will Vondur play in this adventure of yours?"

"Come with us. Let each monarch of Lenya approach the King of Iskalt as a united nation. We need his help. We are lost without it."

"How do I know you speak the truth?" Keir stared at the girl, wanting to trust her, but a lifetime of hate for Grima was a hard habit to break. "How can I trust this elaborate scheme of yours isn't just a ruse to seize power in Vondur?"

Bronagh leaned forward. "Ask Tierney."

CHAPTER TWENTY-FIVE
TIERNEY

All Tierney wanted to do was sleep. It was late, and the day wore on her, the images flashing through her mind like a never-ending reminder of the horror she'd seen.

By the time she'd managed to get Gulliver back to her rooms, it was too dark to see much. Someone had lit candles in her sitting room—probably Ariella, the angel—so the moment she stepped inside, the room came to life in the flickering flame.

Now, the candles were down to the nubs, and soon they'd peter out entirely. But she couldn't bring herself to extinguish them.

Gulliver lay sprawled across her bed diagonally, snoring

heavily in his drink-induced sleep. Which left her to curl up on the narrow settee, her head resting against the wooden arm.

Head aching, she closed her eyes and rubbed her finger along the totem she'd taken from Keir's rooms. She shouldn't have done it, but it sat there staring at her.

She should've known the only reason it wasn't around his neck was that all magic had left it. Or at least, none of it rose to the surface. She could still feel the burning ember of power at its core, like it would never truly be dead, never truly devoid of what gave it life.

The ache in her head slowly subsided, and she rubbed her temple, where wet hair dampened the skin of her forehead. After she'd washed the remnants of the battlefield from her skin in cold, leftover bathwater, she'd had no energy to do anything except let her body and mind both go still.

Bronagh was nowhere to be found, but Tierney hoped she too had found her bed and escaped into a few moments of blissful peace, free of worrying for her brother.

Tierney turned her mind inward, searching for her absent power. A spark of familiarity, a comforting twinge to tell her she wasn't alone in this body. She'd always seen her magic as its own entity, something most fae didn't agree with. Yes, she worked hard to control it, but the power chose whether or not to obey her. It twisted around her emotions, making it harder to keep them in check.

It was still there, deep inside. She could sense it, even if she couldn't physically feel it or call it forth. "Toby," she whispered into the dark. "I need you."

It took a heroic effort each day not to dwell on the distance between her and her twin, the dangerous path she'd soon embark on to get to him. Was it foolish? Probably. But that didn't mean it was the wrong thing to do.

She pictured the ship sitting in Grima waiting for them. If

Keir said no, they didn't have the time to wait for him to come around. They'd already been in Vondur for too long, and it was time to go. Time to try to get home.

Her eyes popped open when a soft tapping sounded at the door. She willed whoever it was to go away, to leave her to her silence.

They didn't listen to the thoughts she sent their way.

With a sigh, she pulled herself off the settee, her bare feet hitting the soft carpet. The floor turned from carpet to stone as she made her way to the door, and the soft slapping of her feet filled the air with its rhythm.

When she pulled the door open, she wasn't surprised to see Keir standing on the threshold, his chest heaving with exertion.

"I—" He sucked in a breath. "Need to speak with you."

Without an invitation, he pushed past her.

"Sure," she muttered, "come on in." Swinging the door shut, she turned to watch him pace the room, stopping when he caught sight of Gulliver in her bed.

"We should go somewhere private to speak." Each word came out as a bite of agitation. She knew he'd been through even more than her in the past hours as he'd watched what his army was capable of, but she wasn't feeling particularly charitable toward any Vondurians at the moment. They truly were the barbarians the Grimans claimed.

"Trust me, Gulliver isn't waking up tonight." When Keir didn't look like he believed her, Tierney walked to the bed. Leaning over, she shoved Gulliver's shoulder. "Wake up, you drunkard." She squeezed his arm and shook.

Nothing.

Turning back to Keir, she found him staring at her in the dim light, his eyes wide. It was then she realized she wore only a nightgown that was much too short for her long legs. Its lacy hem reached mid-way down her thigh. Wet hair hung in tangled ringlets around her face, dampening her shoulders.

Moving to the dressing table, she found a ribbon and secured her hair before pulling a robe off a peg in the armoire and swinging it around her shoulders. "You can stop looking at me like that now."

He cleared his throat. "Like what?"

She rolled her eyes, thankful the semi-darkness hid the action. "Like for once, you've stopped being angry with me."

"I'll never stop being angry with you."

A small smile came to her lips. "Good." She enjoyed arguing with him, enjoyed irritating him to the point his face went red. "Now, what did I do tonight that made you stomp in here like I'd stolen the last french fry?"

"The last what?"

She hid a smile behind her hand. "It's not important."

His scowl told her he didn't like her holding anything back, but they weren't here to discuss the political implications of human food. "I know."

Confusion flashed across her face. "You know?"

He heaved a deep sigh. "Everything."

"Oh."

"Yeah, oh."

One of the candles gave one last flicker before going out entirely. The final one was basically just a nub of a wick in a pool of wax. Tierney focused on it, knowing if she had her power, she could use the Fargelsian fire word and they'd have all the light they needed.

Being stuck in the dark with Keir and his new revelations was not an intriguing prospect. His expression was as dark as their surroundings, little light creeping in.

Tierney backed up until she bumped into the table behind

the settee. The nearly untouched tea tray rattled, and a single fragile cup tilted and fell.

Keir snatched it out of the air, reaching around Tierney to set it back on the tray. He was so close she could see the soft whiskers on his chin, where he hadn't shaved in a day or so. Many fae let their facial hair grow, but not Keir.

She wanted to feel the hairs, to touch the tiny bit of imperfection in his otherwise pristine appearance.

His jaw clenched, and she curled her fingers in, reminding herself she didn't get to reach out, to bring him closer.

Because she'd lied to him. About everything. And now, he knew.

The final flame died, throwing them into the black of night, where nothing existed save the tragic shadows haunting their dreams, the nightmares that didn't release them when they opened their eyes.

Silence stretched between them, the only sound their heaving breath.

A curse fell from Keir's lips, and Tierney felt his absence the moment he stepped away, her entire body wilting, as if she'd been trapped against the table and was now free.

Except, this wasn't what freedom felt like. Gnawing guilt wound through her. "Keir," she whispered.

"Quiet."

"But—"

"For once in your life, Tierney, let me think."

She felt a surge of power that didn't come from her, and flames erupted in the unused hearth over the ash-covered logs. Keir stood with his back to her, his fingers clutching a totem that now glowed in a rainbow of colors melding together to look like tiny flaming cracks.

The fae here used their magic so rarely she hadn't examined an activated crystal up close. With magic surging through it, it looked more like the fire opals she was used to. Stepping closer, she peered at it, unable to take her eyes from the fading colors.

"It's beautiful," she whispered, reaching out. "And familiar."

Keir stood still, his statuesque posture a manifestation of his anger. Yet, Tierney didn't stop. She took the totem from his hand, running her fingers over the smooth form. Its power tried to slither into her, but something blocked it, some part of her own magic.

"So, it's true." Keir's voice was low. "You have seen these crystals before coming to Lenya."

Tierney dropped the totem back into his hand and stepped closer to the fire, its heat an uncomfortable companion to the sanity-saving light it provided. "We call them fire opals."

"Yes, I've been told."

"By who?" She stared into the flickering flames, unable to face him as he revealed all her lies. She already knew the answer.

"Bronagh, Queen of Grima."

Her eyes slid shut for a brief moment before she asked, "Have you put Bron in the dungeons?"

When he didn't answer, she dared a look his way.

He stared at her with thinly veiled hurt. "I know the opinion you and your friends have of me, Tia. I know that what I do for my people isn't enough, it will never be enough. But I am not a monster."

"I know that."

"Do you?"

"I told her she could trust you, that you would do what was right, but Bron had to see that for herself."

Some of the tension drained from his shoulders. "Yes, she said as much. And yet, you ask me if I locked her up."

Tierney didn't want to ask again, but she still didn't have an answer.

"For fae's sake, Tierney, she's with her brother." He paused, studying her face. "With the healer ... not in the dungeons."

Relief flooded her, followed quickly by shame. She'd told Bronagh to trust him, and yet it seemed like advice she needed herself.

"We have a way to get to Iskalt." Rubbing a hand across her face, she lowered herself to the settee.

"The ship."

Her eyes snapped to him. "Wow, she really has decided to trust you."

He sat beside her, keeping a small distance between them. "Now, I need you to do the same."

Words clogged in Tierney's throat, and she swallowed. "You're right." She pushed out a breath. "No more lies. No more hidden truths or trickery."

"About time."

"Bronagh was right. Iskalt and the kingdoms surrounding it have an abundance of fire opals. They are useless for us, except in Myrkur, where they have a monetary value. In Iskalt, we sometimes use them to adorn furniture, for decoration."

He shook his head in disbelief. "All that power."

"That's the thing; they don't hold power for us." She thought of the way her dormant magic blocked the power from Keir's glowing totem. "Mostly. But for you, they could be everything. There's more than enough of the opals to bring back and keep the fire plains from destroying your kingdoms."

"But to get them, we need to brave the seas."

She nodded. "The Grimians have mastered the art of fishing in the rough waters, but their fishing vessels can't make it far from the coast. Veren—"

A dark look crossed his face.

Tierney sighed. "I know you don't like Veren, most of the time I don't either, but you might want to try, considering he's the reason they even built the ship. It's magnificent. I saw it with my own eyes. Giant sails with pulley systems to bring them in quickly to avoid losing them in a storm.

"A solid hull, impenetrable. We won't sink if we hit the rocks in shallow waters. The ship is built to take on water and shed it quickly. The shipbuilders and Veren have prepared for every possibility. The crossing will be dangerous, but, Keir, I truly think we're going to make it."

"But you might not."

"Well, yes. It is the maelstrom, after all. No one has attempted the crossing and returned to tell the tale. But that doesn't mean we shouldn't try. I'm not sure you understand. I have to do this. Even if the fire plains weren't expanding, Iskalt is my home. My parents and siblings are there. My duty is there. And Toby ..." She swallowed a sob. "I just really want to get home. If I die trying to do that, it's still better than sitting here across the fire plains."

She didn't realize his arm was around her until she pressed up against his side, inhaling the sweet oak scent of his soap. Tears stung her eyes, but she brushed them away.

After a few minutes of neither of them saying anything, Tierney whispered, "Keir?"

"Hm?"

"Do you forgive me? You have to forgive me. For the lies, the subterfuge. I promise, I meant no harm to Vondur, but I can't leave with the thought that I've betrayed you, that you hate me. We're never going to see each other again, and if this is our last moment alone together, I want you to know I forgive you for everything you did when I arrived."

He was quiet for a moment. "I do forgive you. But, Tia, we're going to see each other again."

She started to say something, but he shook his head. "Two choices lay before me. I can die here fighting for my kingdom as the fire plains sweep across the land, or I can possibly die trying to save Lenya."

"What are you saying?" She met his dark gaze.

"I'm going with you."

CHAPTER TWENTY-SIX
TIERNEY

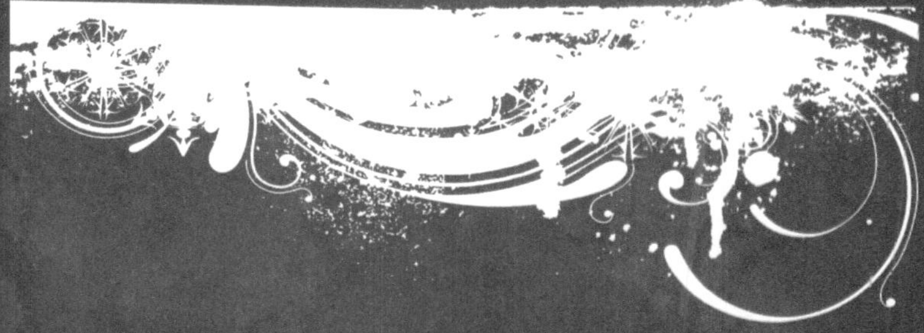

Tension gripped Tierney's neck and shoulders, and her head throbbed as she focused on her plans for the coming journey back to Grima. There was so much to do. She couldn't focus in the quiet corner of the dining hall, where she sat alone, poring over lists. Most everyone had come and gone for the afternoon meal, but Tierney didn't have anywhere to be.

She'd grown restless here in Vondur. Anxious to be on her way and finally taking action against the fire plains and to get herself and her friends back home. After all these months away, both in Vondur and Grima, she'd seen and heard nothing of Siobhan. She could only hope her friend never arrived in Lenya and was safely back home in Iskalt.

"What are you writing?" Gulliver came to sit on the bench beside her. He had an entire pie he'd likely pilfered from the kitchens.

"You have pie." Tierney took the big plate and inhaled the glorious scent of sugared berries. Desserts were rare in Vondur. They seemed to prefer spicy foods and savory snacks over anything sweet.

"Hey, I begged and bribed a kitchen maid to make that for me." Gulliver tried to snatch it back. "I even picked the berries myself. See!" He thrust out a skinny arm covered in scratches.

"But it's dessert, Gullie." She gave him her best broken-hearted look. "It's even got a crunchy, sugary, flakey, buttery crust on top."

"Fine, you get one piece," Gulliver relented.

"It smells divine." Tierney cut a gigantic piece for herself and slipped it onto the plate from her lunch. "I don't even want to know what you had to do to get her to make this." She shoved a bite into her mouth, savoring the tangy sweetness. "What I wouldn't give for some sweet cream to go on top."

"Who's your best friend?" Gulliver grinned and produced a small clay pitcher of cream from under his shirt.

"Gullie, you're a genius!" She glanced over her shoulder. "I know you stole that, and I don't even care." She drizzled the cream onto her pie. Dairy was in short supply in Vondur, and if they were caught, the castellan would take the cost of it out of their hides.

"When we get back to Iskalt, I'm heading straight to the kitchens, and I'm not coming out till I've had all my favorites. Smoked ham and fluffy white bread."

"With loads of butter and jam." Tierney groaned.

"And cheese. I miss real cheese. The yellow kind, not the white stringy stuff they have here." Gulliver sighed, a look of pure bliss on his face as he ate right from the pie plate.

"I'm sorry, Gullie." Tierney scooped up another bite, swirling it in the sweet cream. "I'm sorry I dragged you here and took you away from your family. And your favorite foods," she teased, elbowing him in the side.

"I'm not." Gulliver's tail draped over her shoulder, patting the side of her face. "If you were here and I was back home, I'd be a wreck. I'm glad to be here with you, Tia. And we're going to get home. Together."

Tierney leaned her head on his shoulder. "Thanks for the pie. It's the best thing I've eaten since we got here."

"Lenya is an interesting place, but they don't know what good food is." Gulliver ran a hand over his flat belly. "I swear I'm wasting away here."

Tierney laughed. "I love you, Gullie."

"I love you too." Gulliver shoveled more pie in his mouth. "I made you something." He leaned back to pull whatever it was from his bag. "I don't know if you've noticed, but the Lenyans have a lot of used-up crystals just lying around. The stones are quite nice for carving."

Gulliver could carve anything if he had a chisel and a good-sized rock, along with some extra time on his hands. Back in Myrkur, he ran a profitable business, taking orders for anything from elaborate knife handles, game pieces, and jewelry to sculptures and priceless works of art.

"To remind you of Lenya." He set a figure on the table between them. A Queen of the Night blossom. The beautiful flower grew near the fire plains.

"Gullie, it's beautiful." She lifted the intricate flower, knowing she would never look at it and not think of Keir.

"Just don't let anyone mistake it for a totem. These people are crazed for more power."

"It's strange how accustomed a fae can become to magic. And then, when it's gone ..." She stared at the delicate petals of the flower. "When it's gone, you find you don't miss it as much as you thought you would."

An unholy screech echoed across the dining hall and Tierney covered her ears.

"What is that awful noise?" Gulliver peered over her shoulder into the courtyard below. "It's ruining pie time."

"It's certainly not helping my headache." Tierney finished her last bite, vowing the next dessert she ate would be at home with her family by her side.

"Tia, come look." Gulliver waved her over to the windows. "You're not going to believe this."

Tierney went to have a look. "Is that Keir?"

"Training a bunch of villagers in the courtyard." Gulliver shook his head.

"Female villagers." Tierney laughed. Grabbing her lists, she ran for the stairs down to the courtyard.

Smiling, she approached the group of women. All commoners from the nearby villages. Each woman held a sword or dagger, watching their king as he taught them how to protect themselves.

"What's this?" Tierney caught Keir's gaze. "Did I miss class?"

"Keep practicing ladies; you're doing great." Keir helped one woman adjust her grip on her sword, ignoring the way they laughed when he called them all ladies.

"If I am leaving soon, I want to make sure all Vondurians can protect themselves and their homes. Bronagh and I will be signing a peace treaty this afternoon, but we don't know how our countrymen will react. Anything could happen in my absence. I worry about my people."

"You're a good king, Keir." Tierney watched him as he went around to each sparring pair, helping them correct their stance or the grip on their weapon.

"I sent word to the villages that we would be giving lessons at the palace and all were welcome. Men and women. The villagers aren't comfortable working with the ladies of the court, but they seem comfortable enough with me." He turned, smiling. "Tia, what do you have on your face?" He reached up to rub his thumb over the corner of her mouth.

"Oops." She laughed. "Gulliver talked a maid into baking us a pie." She wiped her mouth with the back of her hand.

"We have pies every night in the dining hall."

"You have meat pies. This was a berry pie. Sweet and juicy and delicious."

"We don't typically have sweets here in Vondur."

"You're going to love the food in Iskalt. And the wine." She gave a little excited hop. "I can't wait to show you my home."

"It's going to be a dangerous journey, but I'm looking forward to seeing your land of ice and snow."

"When will you be ready to leave?" Tierney was dying to get this journey started.

"Soon. Come with me to the peace treaty signing today?"

"Does your council even know about it yet?"

"They do. They aren't happy about trusting Grima, but they are happy to see the end of this war. Most of them anyway."

"Who doesn't want the end of war?"

"There are some who have profited immensely from the war with Grima. But it's time to look to the future. I have no patience for those who insist on keeping the hatred alive. We have bigger problems to worry about now."

Keir returned to his ladies and congratulated them on their progress. "One of my officers will see to your training while I am away. I look forward to seeing your progress when I return." He waved to the women, who all looked like they were thinking they'd be happy to leave their husbands if the king turned an appreciative eye their way.

She followed Keir back into the palace and to the council chamber where they would be making history in just a short time. On their way there, Bronagh and her brother joined them. Donal was still healing but looked better each time Tierney saw him. He would be strong enough for the journey back to Grima, where he would stay and rule in his sister's absence.

Tierney found herself wondering who would care for Vondur while Keir was away risking his life to save them all.

"Are you certain about this, sire?" Lord Robert handed a quill to the king.

"I've never been more certain of anything in my life." Keir took the quill, surveying the treaty that would put an immediate end to the war with Grima. Each sovereign would recall their troops once the treaty was signed.

The treaty also stated that whatever foreign aid they received would be split equally between the kingdoms and their people. Any trade they might negotiate with Iskalt, or the other kingdoms of Tierney's land, would benefit all of Lenya while each kingdom would take equal responsibility to fulfill any trade agreement or debt to the foreign monarchs.

He and Bronagh had worked tirelessly to iron out the details so that neither kingdom had to give up more than they were willing. It had taken some time with his council, but eventually, they reached an agreement.

"All that is left to do now is sign." Queen Bronagh's smile lit up the room. She was a good queen. Strong. And her people loved her. Keir never set out to become king of his people, but he could only hope they would respect him for what he did here today.

The door crashed open, banging against the wall, and several councilmen leaped to their feet.

"It's all true!" Eavha, looking travel-worn and weary, marched across the room to his side. "Everything Princess Tierney said is true. The fire plains are expanding. I've seen it with my own eyes."

"Your Highness, I think we've interrupted something here," Declan murmured behind her. "Perhaps we should come back later?"

"This is too important." She turned to Keir. "The fire plains will sweep across all of Lenya. I fear we do not have enough magic left to stop it."

Her eyes were wild with fright and too little sleep. Once again, he regretted sending Declan on the journey to Grima to confirm what he already knew. Had he known then that his sister would follow his best friend, he wouldn't have sent him.

"We are aware of the grave threat the fire plains pose to us. I thank you and Lord Declan for traveling with such haste, but the burning lands have already expanded into Vondur."

"What can we do, Keir?" She searched his face for answers, but he didn't have the words to say that would make her feel better.

"You're just in time to witness the peace treaty between the Grima queen and King Keir." Tierney, bless her, stepped in to steer Eavha to her side so they could continue.

"Okay. What did I miss?" Eavha whispered, following Tierney to stand behind Bronagh and Keir.

"A lot. I'll catch you up to speed after."

"Shall we continue?" Keir took up the quill and bent over the official treaty document. Taking a breath, he thought of his father, and the burn of the King's Comhrac magic seared his chest. He still owed his father a united Lenya. This treaty was not what the former king meant, but it was a step closer to the kind of future Lenya deserved. Keir didn't hesitate to sign his name for Vondur.

Handing the quill to Bronagh, she stepped forward.

"It gives me hope that we can all be in this room together today, taking great strides toward peace." She gave a nod to Keir and his council before she bent to sign her name with a flourish. "It is a happy coincidence that my brother, Prince Donal, is also here for this historic occasion. I will ask him to sign as a witness for Grima." She turned, handing the quill to Donal.

"It will be my honor." Donal moved to sign under her name.

"I would like to ask my sister to sign as witness as well." Keir reached for Eavha's hand. "No one loves Vondur and its people more than Princess Eavha. As my next of kin, I would ask that she offer her support to this treaty."

"Keir, I ..." She turned to the council with a stern look on her face. "No woman has ever been asked to participate in the governing of Vondur. It would be my honor to sign, but I would like to know what I'm signing." She gave a hesitant smile. "It is a momentous step for women in Vondur. I would do them proud."

"Of course." Keir pulled her to stand at the podium where the treaty sat. He ran through the highlights of the agreement, outlining the terms of their peace to end the war and the terms they negotiated to keep this war from ever happening again.

A tear ran down his sister's face as she bent to sign her name below his. "I never thought I would see the day when this war would end. I miss my father every day. He was a hard man, but he loved me. And in his own way, he loved Vondur.

But I believe King Keir is the best thing to happen to our people in many generations. I am so proud of you, brother." She smiled shyly and stepped back from the podium.

Pride swelled within Keir's chest as the council chamber broke into a round of applause. It was finished. The war was finally over.

CHAPTER TWENTY-SEVEN
TIERNEY

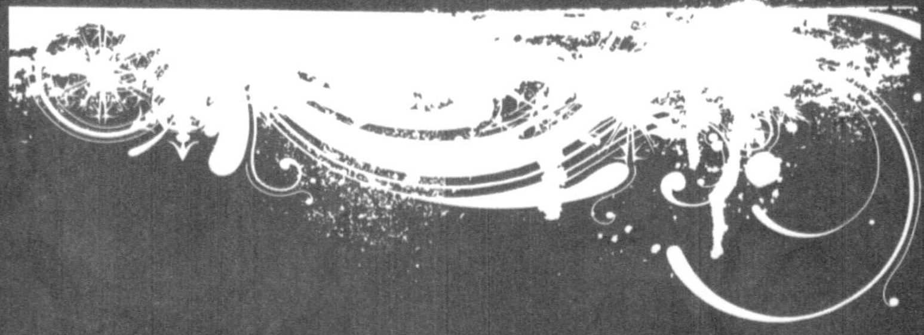

"Tia!" Eavha jogged to catch up with her in the courtyard. "Where are you going?"

Tierney lifted one shoulder in a shrug. "I'm not really sure. I just needed to clear my head."

After the council meeting, she needed to think. Time was running out for Lenya, and they had to get to Grima, to the ship, as quickly as they could. When she first arrived in Vondur, it had been as a prisoner with no hope of finding her friends, no hope of returning to Iskalt.

Now, she got to stand at the king's side during the most important council meeting he'd probably ever have. Gulliver and Veren were with her once again. And Keir ... the man who'd brought her here with ropes tied around her wrists ... he was different.

But something was still missing.

"Slow down." Eavha reached for her arm. "Talk to me."

Tierney wasn't one to brood, to keep her feelings to herself. It was why she'd gained a reputation for her bluntness, her ever-present honesty that attached itself to her rebellious ways.

Turning to Eavha, she took her in. The princess hadn't washed or rested since returning home. Her black riding pants, something she'd never have worn all those months ago, were caked with dust from the road. There were dark circles under her eyes, and her hair had a particular dullness that spoke of a long time without a decent bath. "You look tired."

"Thanks for that." Eavha pursed her lips. "You don't look much better yourself."

The two women stared at each other with scrutinizing gazes before the corners of Tierney's lips twitched. Eavha chuckled and wrapped an arm around Tierney's shoulders. "I think we need some tea."

"Or something much stronger."

"Come on." Eavha led her into the palace. The quiet palace. Most servants had tucked in for the night. It wasn't until they'd almost reached their destination that Tierney realized where they were headed.

"Wait." She pulled away. "We can't go in there."

"Relax. He is dead." She said it with cold finality and little emotion in her voice. "He always kept a good supply of wine, and unless the servants have raided it, it should still be there." She pushed open the door to her father's quarters, the king's quarters.

Tierney followed her in, feeling like an intruder in a place she hadn't dared enter. King Turlach had liked fine things.

While his fae suffered, he'd adorned his rooms in jewels and crystals that still contained traces of power.

Totems hung on twine behind the dressing table. No one had dared take any since he perished in the Comhrac.

Eavha opened a cherry wood cabinet. "Found it." She pulled out a bottle of wine unlike the others Tierney had seen in Vondur. "It's Grimian wine. The rest of Vondur wasn't allowed to trade with our enemy, but that didn't stop him from doing whatever he liked." She uncorked the wine and took a long pull before passing it to Tierney. "Oh, and I asked all your friends to meet us."

Tierney took a sip, cringing at the intense sweetness. It was better than Vondurian wine but still held no comparison to the reds in Iskalt.

The door pushed open, and Veren sauntered in, looking much less uncomfortable than she had in the old king's rooms. "Wow. Why isn't Keir living here?"

Gulliver shoved past him. "Maybe because his evil dead father did." He shot Eavha a look. "Sorry."

She shrugged. "He made poor choices, and he paid for it with his life. Sometimes, the truth hurts; doesn't mean we can't say it."

Bronagh was the last one to enter.

Eavha's eyes widened, and she dipped into a graceful curtsy. "Your Majesty."

Tierney took a pillow off the settee and threw it at her. "Please don't."

A smile tugged at Bronagh's lips. "Yes, right now, I am just another concerned fae whose life is at risk." She curtsied lower than Eavha had. "Thank you for risking so much to prove the truth of my words to your king."

Eavha blushed furiously. "Oh, it was actually fun. Getting away from the palace with Declan ..." She froze. "I mean, um, we were performing our task for the king, nothing else."

Bronagh turned to Tierney. "She babbles like you."

Tierney shot her a playful scowl. "No one can babble as well as me."

Eavha recovered. "Okay, everyone sit. We need to discuss what's wrong with Tierney."

"Many things," Veren said.

Gulliver raised his hand. "How much time do we have?"

"She speaks too many words," Bronagh put in.

Eavha stared at them. "Not what I meant, but okay. Did anyone else notice she left right after the council meeting? She didn't even stick around to gloat about being right."

Tierney took a seat and bent forward, head in her hands. Eavha was right. Something was very wrong.

Gulliver squeezed in beside her, dropping his voice. "Is she right?"

A sigh rattled out of her, and she lifted her eyes to his. "We're leaving Lenya."

"But that's what you want. To return home."

"Of course it is, but don't you realize what it means?" She looked from Gulliver to Veren. Only they would understand. Neither answered, but she saw the realization in their eyes.

"Anyone going to tell us what is going on?" Eavha crossed her arms.

Veren closed his eyes, shame washing over his face. "Siobhan."

"Who is Siobhan?"

"Our friend." Gulliver looked like he wanted to cry. "How could we not think of her?"

Tierney shook her head. "We've been so focused on saving Lenya, on returning to Iskalt." She met Veren's eyes. "Are you positive she isn't in Grima?"

He nodded. "When I first arrived and got to know Donal, he sent messengers to every village searching for all of you."

"We can't leave without her."

"But she isn't here. She isn't anywhere. What if she didn't make it?"

That was a possibility Tierney had tried not to think about. "We can't leave without her."

Gulliver's hand slid into hers. "We have to. Tia, it isn't just us at risk anymore. There's an entire kingdom that could be wiped away."

"Gullie." Tears danced in her eyes. "How am I supposed to return home and say I lost the best of us, that I'm the reason she's gone?"

"We'll come back. Once we get to Toby, he can help you portal back here to look for her."

She rested her head on his shoulder. "Promise?"

"Always." He squeezed her hand.

A tense moment passed, where each fae was scared to speak until Bronagh stepped forward. "I am sorry for your friend."

Tierney took another sip of wine. Gulliver tried to take the bottle, but she hit his hand away. She wasn't making that mistake tonight. "I am too."

"But Gulliver is right. We have bigger issues to face. This peace, for one. I do not know if I can make it hold when my council was not involved in the decision."

"But you're the queen." Tierney didn't understand. In Iskalt, the council advised, but the monarch had the final say.

"Yes, but I am beholden to my people."

"Just say your uncle." Veren met her gaze. "He's the only fae in Grima who might take issue with an end to the war."

Her chest heaved with a sigh. "Yes, my uncle is ... difficult. And if I am to sail on this ship, he will be left behind to rule along with Donal, and he must be in agreement. I must have my council finalize the treaty before I can leave."

"We can be your council," Gulliver said, his lips stretching into a smile.

Bronagh's expression softened. "And that is kind of you, but a council must consist of only the Grima born. Even now, my uncle sends my warriors into battles I would not support. He is not easily overcome."

An idea came to Tierney. "Bronagh, does the queen get to decide on a temporary regent in her absence?"

"Of course."

"Then, who says your uncle has to be granted that power?"

"It has always fallen to my uncle to rule in the absence of the queen."

Tierney set the wine bottle on the table and stood. "But there is someone resting in the healer's ward who can stand in your stead, yes?"

Understanding dawned in Bronagh's eyes. "Donal."

The young prince looked much better than he had after the treaty signing. Color had returned to his eager face. He lifted his head when he saw his sister, his eyes lighting up. "Bron."

She matched his grin. "You look like you're doing better. I worried the council meeting might have taxed you too much."

"The healers here have treated me well."

She set her hand on the bed, and he gripped it. "I need to talk to you."

His eyes shot to the others in confusion. "Sure."

Tierney watched the two of them, a longing burning in her chest. Not only for Toby but for all her siblings. Kayleigh and her need to be right, their youngest sister and her endless joy. Her little brothers always getting in trouble with the maids. The way her mom chased them around the palace as they all howled like wolves, scaring the guards and giggling when they jumped.

Her father's half-scowl, half-smile every time they tried that on him.

"You are my fiercest general, Donal." Bronagh smiled down at him. "But what if I told you it was time to lay down your sword?"

"I would thank you for preventing more deaths at my hands." His voice had grown soft, sad.

Bronagh's shoulders dropped, and she hiccupped back a sob. "I never ... Every time I sent you to battle, I didn't think ..."

"We were avenging our family. But we cannot claim vengeance forever. It is a sword that cannot be wielded, only fallen upon."

She dropped into the chair at his side. "Lenya needs peace."

"And the treaty will go a long way in bringing that peace."

"It will." She drew in a breath. "But I must go away for a while, across the sea to find the one thing that can save us all."

By his lack of surprise, Tierney knew she'd already told him of her intentions.

"Some might think you will not succeed across the sea, sister, but I know you will. I know it in my bones."

"Uncle will not agree with us."

Donal shook his head, and his eyelids fluttered shut. "So you would have me rule in his stead while you are gone?"

"Yes."

"I never wanted to lead the kingdom."

"I know."

None of them got what they wanted. Not Bronagh and

Donal, with their lost family. Not Tierney, with her missing friend. Nor Keir, defying everything his kingdom stood for. Yet, they were all willing to fight for a better future.

They had to.

Tierney turned away from the Grimian royal siblings, realizing what they needed now was a few moments to themselves. Gulliver looked at her expectantly, waiting for her to tell him what happened next. Veren made no move to leave Bronagh's side.

Movement in the door caught her eye, and she found Keir watching them. Watching the moment the siblings decided to work together for the peace he'd fought for, risked his standing with his council for.

His eyes met hers, and Tierney's skin heated in a way that had nothing to do with her power and every bit to do with a lack of it. Because it was time to admit she was powerless to save Siobhan, powerless to find a way home that didn't include a high chance of death.

And powerless to resist the feelings swirling inside her chest, clouding everything she thought she knew.

In an instant, she crossed the room. One moment she stood on her own two feet, strong in the face of the destruction this man had wrought on her life, the disaster awaiting her if she gave in.

And the next, she'd stepped onto a dangerous path, one riskier than any maelstrom in the ocean, any height of thrashing waves.

This was Keir, King of Vondur. Her captor. Her liberator.

When his intense dark eyes locked on hers, she couldn't help wanting him, even if just for this single moment.

Tierney's chest collided with his, and she rose up on her toes as he dipped his head. Their lips crashed in a torrent of pain and coming regret. They danced together in a movement of hope and relief.

Keir's hands tangled in her hair, pulling her head back as he dragged her into the hall, away from the eyes of her friends.

Tierney fought him for supremacy, for control, dragging her fingers up his chest until they wrapped around the base of his neck, holding him in place. Pain lanced through her lip as he bit it. She opened for him, allowing him deeper inside her mouth, her soul.

Keir pushed her up against the rough stone of the wall, pressing into her, melding their bodies together with a growl. They were feral animals, whimpering wantons.

When Keir finally pulled away, he rested his forehead against hers, their heaving chests fighting against each other.

"I've wanted to do that for so long." His breath whispered across her lips.

"Then, why didn't you?"

"Because you didn't want it, not yet. I had to wait until I knew you did."

"I'm leaving, Keir. I know you'll be with me at first, but—"

His eyes darkened as he pressed a quick kiss to her lips, quieting her. "For once, there is no future, no tomorrow. This moment is all that exists until the next. A thousand tiny parts of the whole, each one as important as any other."

"No future," she said, knowing how true it could be with the journey they faced.

He shook his head. "No tomorrow."

"Okay," she whispered, drawing him toward her again. "Okay."

CHAPTER TWENTY-EIGHT

KEIR

Keir didn't know what he was doing, only that he'd wanted this for too long. He'd wanted to look sideways at Tierney and not have to hide it when she met his gaze. He'd wanted to taste the curve of her lips, feel the softness of her skin as he traced a hand along the dip of her neck.

So few things about this woman were soft, fragile. Her strength intrigued him, excited him. But for the first time, she let a small vulnerability shine out of her, and it was beautiful.

Every day of his life was spent acting like an unbothered and aloof king, the man the kingdom could count on to protect them from the ravages of war. Here, now, he was just Keir Dagnan, just a man who knew whatever this feeling for

Tierney was, it couldn't last. Their paths would diverge once they saved Lenya—if they survived the journey.

Tierney turned to him, a smile stretching all the way to her eyes. "You know, I might actually miss Vondur."

Keir found his lips tilting into a half-smile. "Lies." He pressed a kiss to the corner of her mouth and backed her into the one room he'd never be comfortable in. "All lies."

"Maybe." She turned away from him to cross his father's quarters and push her way into the tunnels. There was one place she'd said she wanted to visit before leaving.

Their footsteps echoed off the stone floor, the sparkling walls. When they reached the cavern, it hummed with the energy of magic traces, just enough to lend power to the water.

Tierney lifted her eyes to the ceiling, illuminated by torches hanging along the walls. This cavern meant so many things. A place of healing, both of body and spirit. A place of training those who were not supposed to train.

"You know," Tierney said, her voice barely above a whisper, "when Eavha and Declan brought me here, it was the first time I felt any kind of wonder at being in a kingdom most people in Iskalt had never even heard of." A contented sigh parted her lips. "Before that, all I felt was fear and anger."

Fear and anger. Because of him.

"Tia." He stepped up to her side. "I—"

"If you apologize to me right now, Keir Dagnan, I'm going to stomp on your foot."

"Stomp on my foot?" His laugh echoed through the cavern. "You're supposed to be a fierce warrior, and the best you can do is stomp on my foot?"

She bit back a smile. "I never said it was all I'd do, but it would be the first thing. Stomp on your foot so you can't get away, and—"

"How hard are you planning to stomp? It wouldn't exactly hinder me."

She continued without missing a beat, "And then, I'd do something to distract you."

"Oh?" He liked the lightness she infused into him. "Like what?"

Tierney stepped close, and his breath stuttered. She pressed herself flush against him, rising on her toes. Her words vibrated against his lips. "This distracting enough?"

When he didn't respond, she grinned, pulled a dagger from a sheathe in his belt, and whirled around to press the tip into his back.

"I'm at your mercy now, Princess. What would you have me do?"

"I am a lady, your Majesty. I do not appreciate the lurid tone."

"I'm lurid?"

"Yes, it is very ... lurid."

"Why, my Lady, you do have a way with words." He wasn't sure what had gotten into him. Flirting was a new action, but it was a lot more fun than brooding.

"Shut up."

"Has anyone ever told you how irritating you are when you use your human phrases?"

"Has anyone ever told you how irritating you are all the time?" There was more laughter than bite to her words. She pulled the knife away, and he turned to face her, taking the knife and sliding it into its sheath.

They stared at each other for a long moment before he stepped forward. She backed up until she hit the stone wall and lifted innocent eyes to his. Except, they were anything but innocent. She knew exactly what she did to him.

"We might die on this journey." He pressed closer.

"I thought we were pretending the future didn't exist."

His lips hovered inches from hers. "We were wrong. Tomorrow always lies in wait, preparing to take everything from us. It is why we must hold on to today."

They collided in a heat of kisses, soft touches, and ragged breath. If this was all they had, he'd make it count, memorizing every gasp, the way her fingers curled into the collar of his shirt before sliding into his hair.

Keir hadn't forgotten what awaited Tierney in Iskalt. Pressure to marry a nobleman, a life that didn't involve the king of a far-off kingdom. And he knew she hadn't forgotten either.

But all of that seemed like a distant moment, one that didn't yet exist.

Tomorrow, he would prepare to leave his kingdom in the hands of his sister, someone who'd struggle and fight for every bit of power she could take simply because she'd been born a woman.

He would prepare to travel into the kingdom of a new ally, one that didn't yet know of the peace treaty their queen signed, the piece of parchment that transformed them from generational enemy to ally, foe to friend, with the single stroke of a pen.

Keir leaned away from Tierney, breaking their kiss. Tonight, they both needed peace to face the storm raging on the horizon. He threaded their fingers together and tugged. "Come on."

They crossed the cavern to where the healing waters stretched to the far wall. To the simple observer, they looked like nothing out of the ordinary—a simple, yet expansive, bath, but to touch the water was to know differently.

Lowering himself to the stone, he pulled Tierney down at his side and dipped his feet into the water. Just underneath the surface, it swirled and bubbled around his ankles, reacting to his presence.

Tierney followed his lead and sighed. "I would never leave this cavern if I had a choice."

Keir leaned back on his elbows. "Do you have healing magic in Iskalt?" He still knew so little of their power.

Tierney was quiet for a moment. "There are stories, rumors, that my mother once used her magic to heal my father. But it is not commonly done. Our healers can speed up the process in a way, but we believe a body must have time to heal itself."

"And the mind? Does your power give it peace?" When he sat at the healing pools with steam filtering through the air, he was able to ignore what ailed him, let his thoughts rest.

Tierney smiled, and she looked down at her hands. "We carry the power within us at all times. Sometimes, it can make me feel out of control, like I can't grasp my emotions, can't control my actions. And other times, it is like a constant companion and I am never alone."

She sounded sad, lost, and he wanted to reach out to her, but all he could do was watch her expressions shift. "Except here."

She hesitated a moment before nodding. "Here, I have been very much alone." A breath quivered coming out of her. "It is not only the power. My brother and I ... we're connected. He's a part of my magic. When I use it, I can feel him with me. Even after all this time in Vondur apart from him, I'm not sure I know who I am without that tie."

"You're a future queen."

A harsh laugh burst out of her. "Whether I want to be or not."

"You're a warrior."

That made her smile. "I've been trained to be nothing else."

"You kiss like the world is ending."

She looked down at him, a smirk flashing across her face. "It just might be."

Keir pushed off his elbows to sit up and bumped her shoulder with his. "Are you afraid?"

"Yes," she said, not hesitating.

"Of the journey?"

She nodded. "But more than that, I'm afraid we're leaving Siobhan behind in a foreign kingdom. I'm afraid kissing you was a mistake." She turned, her eyes meeting his. "I'm afraid we will fail, and I'll let everyone down."

He had no answers for her. Her final two fears were also his. So, instead of words, he pulled her into a hug, reluctant king to future queen. What he didn't do was promise they'd succeed, because it would have been a false vow. But they would try, they'd give everything they had to their kingdoms, risk their lives.

He only hoped it would be enough.

Keir left Tierney at the door to her rooms with a long look. When he turned away, he slid his mask back into place and became the king again. It was late, but he knew where Declan would be.

Since they were boys, Declan's sleep was troubled upon returning from a journey. No matter how exhausted and road-weary he was, sleep eluded him. And he'd never been one to sit in his rooms when he could be out under the open sky.

Keir nodded to the night guards as he entered the courtyard. Above, a full moon lit the sky, casting a silver glow over the palace walls. The crystal-infused walls reflected it back, sparkling.

Stars sprinkled the clear sky, creating a beauty only found in the heavens above Vondur. Maybe, once this war with the fire plains was finished and his people truly had peace, they could bring some of that beauty back to Lenya, rebuilding long defeated cities, villages that had lost too much.

He found Declan atop the walls staring out over the barren land between the castle and the forest.

"I shouldn't be surprised you knew I'd be here." Declan didn't turn to look at him.

Keir stepped up beside him. "You never did enjoy being confined by the palace walls."

"Some of us didn't grow up here." Declan had been raised in a nearby village, but he'd joined the army when he was not even ten, and the only boy young enough and green enough to spar with him was Keir in the years before his father became king. He hadn't been a prince then, but his father's status as a noble meant he'd spent his formative years at the palace.

"Did you fare well on the journey?"

Declan snorted. "You forget, Keir, I know you as well as you know me. I gave my report already, you did not come here to ask about my journey."

He was right. "Eavha would not like me speaking with you."

"I'm not sure I like it either."

Keir shook his head. "I must leave. There is no way around it. It is not guaranteed I will return, but even if I do, my sister will rule in my stead."

"A wise decision."

"But she will need protection."

Declan turned his head slightly to look at Keir out of the corner of his eye. "Do you really think you need to ask?"

"I know she is learning to fight, but that will not help her with those who do not wish to listen to a woman. Having my commander in her corner will convince a lot of fae."

"Again, Keir, I do not have a choice but to stand with her."

"There's always a choice."

A look crossed his face that Keir couldn't quite decipher. "Not when it comes to her. If anything should happen to Eavha, I ..." He rubbed the back of his neck and looked away.

Keir studied him for a long moment before clapping a hand on his shoulder. "You're a good man. The status of your birth cannot change that. Do not let it stand in the way of what you truly want."

Declan cleared his throat uncomfortably. "Sometimes, Keir, I think you were not made for the kingdom of Vondur."

"Sometimes, I agree with you." When his father was king, he'd always felt so out of place being made to do things he knew weren't right. "There's one other thing."

"I won't let your castle burn to the ground. Anything you ask of me is something I would do without hesitation."

Keir drew in a breath. "There is a woman called Siobhan who will most likely claim to be from Iskalt. Tierney thinks she must be in Vondur or Grima. I need you to send men to find her. Bring her to the palace and keep her safe. If we survive the journey, we will return and she can go home to her fae."

"Anything you ask of me, Keir, I will do."

Leaving Vondur in his sister's hands took no thought at all. His kingdom would be safe. But saying goodbye to Eavha, to Declan, the only two fae he'd ever truly loved, would be the most difficult thing of all.

CHAPTER TWENTY-NINE
TIERNEY

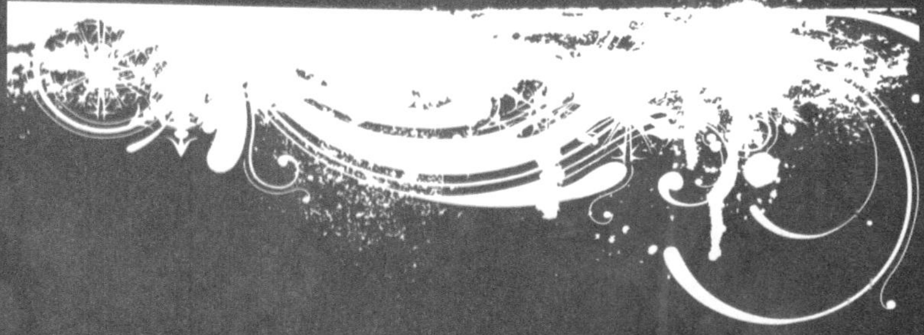

Tierney paced the length of her room, searching for the last of her things. During her time in Lenya, she'd managed to amass a hodgepodge of possessions she didn't want to leave behind. Keir had given her several histories on Lenya that would be great additions to the Aghadoon library. And she planned to give him a set of volumes on the histories of the four kingdoms in return.

Securing the lid on a jar of dried Queen of the Night blossoms, she tucked them into her bag. She would share them with her mother and sisters. Tierney had no doubt all the ladies at court would be eager to purchase their own once they heard about the lovely scented flowers.

Thoughts of trade between the kingdoms filled her mind as

she packed. She could see a bright future for the six kingdoms. Once they traveled the impenetrable seas, found their way into Iskalt over the mountains, and crossed the frozen tundra of eastern Iskalt. And then, dealt with the issue of the expanding fire plains. Easy stuff.

But later, when all of their problems were solved, she was confident Toby's O'Shea magic would allow him to portal to Lenya. He would have to help her create a portal here since one could only portal to a place they had visited before. But Toby was more than capable of helping her do it right. And then, he could travel here himself, bringing all the Lenyans home.

The thought made her sad. But they would see each other often as the four kingdoms brought Grima and Vondur into the fold.

It would be a whole new world for everyone.

The portrait on the wall rattled, but Tierney was used to Eavha coming and going whenever she wanted.

"Don't you know you can use the actual door to my rooms now?" Tierney folded her jeans and the t-shirt she wore upon her arrival in Lenya. It felt like a lifetime ago now. So much had happened.

"The tunnels are faster." Eavha pushed through the hidden door. "You have to talk to Keir," she blurted, looking agitated.

"What's he done this time?" Tierney turned to retrieve Gulliver's Queen of the Night blossom carving from the bedside table. Wrapping it in her spare travel tunic, she bundled it into their bag, hoping it would survive the long journey home in one piece. She hoped they all made it there in one piece.

"He's refusing to let me go to Iskalt."

Tierney sighed, turning to face her dearest friend in this

kingdom. "He's right, Eavha." She sat on the edge of her bed, patting the space beside her.

"I can make the journey. I am strong. You have to tell him it's not too dangerous for me."

"Oh, Eavha. You're one of the strongest women I've ever met. That's why you need to stay here." Tierney cupped the girl's cheek. "You remind me so much of my sisters. Strong-willed and spirited. Don't ever change."

Eavha moved back, pushing Tierney's hand away. "Don't you dare say goodbye, Tierney O'Shea. I am coming with you."

"Don't you realize how much Keir needs you here? Not to keep you safe but to keep Vondur safe in his absence."

Eavha's lower lip trembled. "I don't want to say goodbye."

"Neither do I. But I know—right here," she placed a hand over her heart, "I will see you again."

"What am I going to do without you?" Eavha took her hand, moving closer to her side.

"Declan is going to need you. He is a good leader, but he commands Keir's army. The council needs a royal to guide them. Not because those of us born to play the roles of kings, queens, and princesses are somehow better than others but because it's our duty to serve our people. You represent Keir's interests. His vision for Vondur. The council will follow your lead."

"They don't respect me. That Keir let me sign the peace treaty was a huge step forward for Vondurian women, but the council won't allow me to rule while the king is absent."

"Don't give them a choice." Tierney took both of the young princess' hands in hers. "You walk into that chamber like you own it and don't take no for an answer. They will respect you."

"It's a big job." She sighed, her shoulders drooping.

"Your brother knows you can do this. Otherwise, he would have put someone else in charge."

"You sound like Keir." Eavha's nose wrinkled. "I don't think I like it when you two are on the same side."

Tierney laughed, pulling Eavha into a hug. "I am going to miss you so much."

Eavha leaned her head on Tierney's shoulder. "Me too."

"I look forward to the day when my brother opens the first portal into Vondur and I get to bring you to Iskalt to meet my family. My sisters are going to love you. I have a brother just a year younger than you, and he's going to fall hopelessly in love with you."

Eavha blushed. "I think I'm spoken for already."

"I should hope so. All that time you traveled with Declan, just the two of you. I shudder to think he didn't get it through his thick head that he's in love with you."

"He thinks he isn't good enough for a princess."

"Men are idiots, Eavha." Tierney shook her head. "It takes them far too long to listen to us and realize we've been right all along. He will come around."

"Sometimes, I wish I wasn't a princess. It would make life a lot easier."

"Tell me about it. Wishing I wasn't a princess is what landed me here in the first place."

"Well, I am glad you hated being a princess because you've changed our lives, Tia. I don't know where we would be without you."

"Can the girl power meeting be over now?" Gulliver stuck his head into the room. "I've lost my good boots, and I'm pretty sure they're in here."

"Come in, Gullie." Tierney rolled her eyes. "You better be finished packing by now. We leave at first light, and we're supposed to be in the great hall right now. Tonight's dinner is a celebration, and we don't want to be late."

"Keir's had the cooks making all sorts of special dishes just for you two." Eavha wiped her eyes and fixed her dress. "It's going to be a feast of all your favorites. They even managed to find a few pigs to roast since Lord Gulliver has been lamenting our lack of ham since his arrival."

"Ham? There's ham?" Gulliver snatched his boots from the settee, where he'd left them, and shoved them onto his bare feet. "Let's not keep them waiting."

"The court?" Eavha frowned. "They wouldn't dare begin without the guests of honor."

"He means the hams." Tierney laughed as they moved into the hall and she closed the door behind her.

It was a feast. The cooks had outdone themselves with dishes that were somewhat similar to the foods they missed from home. The ham was delicious. And the desserts were even better. Someone made Gulliver his own cake with buttercream frosting. He was in heaven.

Tierney sat at the high table with all her friends and the king. Even Bronagh was given a seat of honor at the king's left. She and Veren were carrying on a private discussion, but Keir was quiet.

"Nervous about crossing the border, your Majesty?" She turned to get his attention.

"What?" He shook his head, as if he wasn't aware of his surroundings.

"You looked like you were a million miles away just then."

"I was." He smiled. "I'm not so worried about traveling to Grima. It's the sea voyage I'm not looking forward to. I've never been on a ship before."

"Really?"

"Vondur borders the fire plains. We have very little coastline where Grima is almost all coastline. We do have a port city on the far side of the kingdom, for small fishing vessels. They don't go far out. I've been there many times, but never on a ship."

"I hope you don't get seasick."

"Seasick. Is that a thing?" Keir frowned.

"It's definitely a thing," Gulliver interjected. "I used to get seasick a lot when I was a kid, but I grew out of it the more I traveled with Griff. He's my adoptive father—a Prince of Iskalt."

"Wait. King Lochlan's brother is your father?" Keir asked Gulliver.

"Yes. But Griff is super low key compared to Loch"

"Everything makes so much more sense now. You two really are like siblings." Keir looked from Tierney to Gulliver.

"Haven't we said that like a hundred times?" Gulliver shook his head, returning to his third plate of ham and roasted potatoes.

"We've been best friends since we were ten years old." Tierney smiled at the memory of her first meeting with the Dark Fae. She and Toby were ice skating on the lake just down from the castle when Uncle Griffin and Aunt Riona arrived from Myrkur with a skinny little boy with half a tail and a big appetite. His tail grew back. His appetite hadn't changed at all.

That was the day when Tierney decided they would be friends.

"No, Eavha. Don't ask me again." Keir took a long sip from his wine glass, as if fortifying himself for another argument with his sister. "You're not going."

"Keir I—" Eavha tried to interject, leaning across the table to get his attention.

"I'm serious." Keir spoke softly. "I need you here to keep

the council in line. Keeping you safe is just a secondary advantage."

Eavha smiled, shaking her head. "I can see right through that reasoning, Keir Dagnan, but fine. I will stay. That wasn't what I was going to ask though."

"Oh, what do you need then?" His tone said he would give her anything her heart desired if she would just stay home and stop arguing with him about it.

Eavha cupped her hands around her mouth. "A crystal," she whispered. "I know they're in short supply, but I've been practicing, and I think it would be helpful to have the extra power just in case."

"Yes, of course. Didn't I give you one from the king's reserve?"

"I gave it to Declan while we were traveling. We ran into some issues ..." Her voice trailed off, and she dropped her gaze to her plate

"I will have one delivered to your rooms this evening. If you have need of anything else, Eavha, you only have to ask. Even when I am gone, Lord Robert will be available to assist you with whatever you need. I trust him above all others on my council, second only to you."

"Just return home in one piece." She reached for his hand across the table, turning her gaze on Tierney. "Watch out for this one for me?"

"It would be my honor to protect your king, Princess Eavha." Tierney gave her a formal nod of agreement.

"You two think you're so funny." Keir's face flushed, and he gave them a crooked grin. "I can take care of myself. I am a master swordsman, after all."

"But you tend not to make the best first impression." Tierney arched a brow at him.

"And you're kind of growly and mean when you're uncertain of your surroundings," Eavha added. "You need to be on your best behavior when you meet King Lochlan and Queen Brea."

"Okay, you two, enough teaming up on me. We have an early morning tomorrow, and I have a last-minute meeting with my council before we leave at first light. I think it's time we all retire. Gulliver is going to fall into a deep food sleep soon, so we should probably get him upstairs. He didn't have any wine, did he?"

"Look at that." Gulliver grinned. "Keir's developed a sense of humor. Who would have thought?"

Keir was the first to laugh, and the others couldn't resist joining him. Tierney's cheeks hurt from smiling. She was going to miss this so much. As heir to the Iskalt throne, she'd spent most of her life believing others wanted to be her friend only because she was a princess. That was why she and Gulliver had remained such close friends all these years. She trusted in his genuine friendship and that he wanted nothing else from her. She could only say that about a few other people in her life. Most of them royals as well. Now, she could add a few more names to that short list of friends. She just hoped they would remain friends always. Even from a distance.

CHAPTER THIRTY

TIERNEY

Tierney barely slept her last night in the Vondur palace. Thoughts of home filled her mind with hope for the long journey ahead. It would be dangerous, but if sheer willpower alone was enough to get them through it, they would arrive in Iskalt in no time at all.

But thoughts of home weren't the only reason Tierney couldn't sleep. It was also the long road to Grima. The nights she would sleep under the stars. The long voyage across the seas, with nothing to do but spend time with Keir. Uninterrupted, idle time with the handsome king.

The king she should not fall for. She would rule Iskalt one day. She must marry someone who could be at her side, a nobleman or woman who did not have their own kingdom to rule. But that did not mean she couldn't enjoy kissing him while she had the chance.

"What has you smiling like Kayleigh in love with the latest pretty courtier?" Gulliver stuffed his saddlebags with extra food he'd pilfered from the kitchens after a bit of flirting. The kitchen maids here would be sad to see Gulliver go.

"Oh, hush." Tierney tightened her saddle and draped her bag over the horse's flanks. "I'm just excited to be going home, Gullie. It's finally happening."

Gulliver pulled himself up into the saddle and munched on a piece of fruit. Shaking his head, he scowled at her. "I will not be sad to leave this place and never see it again for the rest of my days."

"Won't you miss the people we've met here, though? We could come for visits once Toby creates a portal here."

"Portals go both ways." Gulliver waved his fruit in the air, pointing to the dusty road that led toward the fire plains. "They can come visit me in Myrkur."

Tierney laughed. She supposed if she'd spent their first weeks in Vondur in the dungeons the way he had, she probably wouldn't want to come back here either. She pulled herself up into her own saddle, smoothing a hand over her mount's soft black mane to soothe the nervous mare.

"I'm anxious to see my little sisters. Just don't ever tell them I said that." Gulliver tossed the remnants of his fruit into the bushes surrounding the stables. Gulliver's little sisters idolized their big brother. They also liked pulling his tail and pelting him with pebbles as they flew over his head. The girls were only six and eight years old, but it was no secret to anyone that Gulliver adored them.

"What are we waiting for?" He glanced around at the growing party of soldiers accompanying his Majesty to Grima. Veren and Bronagh were helping Donal onto a litter that would transport him home to Lenya. The prince was well on the mend, but still not up to sitting in a saddle for hours at a time. Tierney couldn't imagine any form of transportation would be comfortable for the young prince.

"I think we're just waiting on Keir." Tierney looked around for the man who stood head and shoulders above his soldiers. "And I expect Eavha will show up to say a last goodbye at some point."

"It's going to be hard for her to let you go, Tia," Gulliver said, leading his horse beside hers as they joined the gathering line of travelers ready to depart. "You're her hero."

"I'm no one's hero." Tierney sighed, thinking of all her mistakes that had led them here.

"You've given her confidence she probably never would have exerted without your influence. You've shown the women here how to stand tall. You've shown the men here that they need to let them."

Tierney laughed. "A select few of them, I suppose." Movement at the rear of the palace caught her gaze. Keir, Declan, and Eavha headed toward the stables, where their mounts waited.

"Is she coming with us after all?" Bronagh asked as she and Veren joined the queue, with Donal resting in the litter hitched to Veren's horse.

"Tia!" Eavha scrambled onto her horse and trotted across the stable yard to join them. "Declan and I thought we would ride out with you this morning just for a little way."

It would just prolong their goodbyes, but Tierney was happy to have a few last moments with the princess.

"How was your council meeting this morning, Keir?" Tierney asked as the king joined them and gave the order to move out.

"Good, good." He nodded, not meeting her gaze. "They

wanted me to send a delegate in my place, believing the journey too dangerous for their king, but I convinced them otherwise."

There was something he wasn't saying, but Tierney knew she couldn't be privy to all the king's conversations with his council. As long as he was coming with her to Iskalt, that was all that mattered.

"It will be a quick ride to the east road," Keir turned his attention to his sister, giving her a stern look. "Declan and I will ride ahead with the soldiers and leave you two to enjoy your remaining time together." Sitting tall in his saddle, Keir urged his horse into a trot and moved to the front of the line, without a word, Declan followed.

"He is worried." Eavha watched him go. "So much rides on the success of your journey."

"We will make it to Iskalt in time to stop the spread of the fire plains. I can feel it in my bones." She would risk it all to see her family again, but it wasn't just Tierney on this journey. She had others to think about too.

"I was serious when I asked you to protect him." Eavha turned in her saddle. "My brother will sacrifice his life to reach Iskalt. Not only for Lenya but for you as well. I hope you find your way home, Tia, but please keep him safe. I need my brother to return whole."

Tierney reached for Eavha's hand. "I promise I will do all in my power to send your brother home safely." As much as it would hurt to see him leave, his place was with his people. They needed their reluctant king because he was the best thing to happen to Vondur in generations.

As they neared the road that would take them toward the Grima border, Tierney grew sad. She didn't want to say goodbye to the girl who'd become as close as a sister to her throughout her time in Lenya.

"I'm going to miss you." Eavha sniffed her own tears back. "All of you." She turned to Gulliver and Bronagh.

Keir and Declan brought the short line of travelers to a halt and dismounted to say their last goodbyes. Tierney took Eavha into her arms, hugging her tight and resting her chin on the princess' head.

"The council has their instructions." Keir spoke softly to Declan as they walked to the rear of the line. "I leave it to you and Eavha to keep them on course."

"We will handle everything while you're gone, your Majesty." Declan gave a formal bow before he stood tall and held out his hand to Keir. "Be safe, brother."

Keir pulled him into a hug, slapping him on the back. "Take care of my sister."

"I'm pretty sure that's going to go the other way." Declan laughed, moving to stand with Eavha.

Tierney gave Eavha one last squeeze and pulled her to arm's length. "Stay strong. You've got fire in your blood. Use it."

"I will." Eavha flung her arms around Tierney one last time, tears rolling down her cheeks. She buried her head against Declan's chest. He held her close, murmuring comforting words to her as Tierney mounted her horse and prepared to ride away.

Keir guided his mount beside hers and gave the signal to march on. Tierney couldn't see through the veil of tears clouding her eyes, but she followed.

"We're doing the right thing, Tia." Keir reached for her hand, and she grasped hold of it like a lifeline.

"Why does the right thing always hurt a little too much?" She sniffed, refusing to look back because she'd just left a piece of herself behind in Vondur forever. She would miss Eavha like she'd missed her own sisters.

Just before sunset, they reached a forest of the massive trees Tierney had seen on her first trip to the Vondur palace. Back then, she hadn't dared ask questions about their surroundings.

"What makes your trees grow so huge?" Tierney asked, admiring the deep red tones of the tree bark.

"Don't you have ancient forests like this in Iskalt?" Keir asked. They'd ridden side by side through most of the day, talking like neither would have dared the first time they made this journey together.

"In Iskalt, we have snow, ice, and fir trees covered in snow and ice. They grow tall, yes, but nothing as large as these."

"Our history is veiled in shadows. Lenyans have been in these lands since the beginning of time itself. In ages past, when magic was in abundance, I imagine these forests grew tall and strong because it was in the very soil. I've read accounts of a time when our crystals littered the grounds and one had only to pick them up to have all the magic they needed. I can't fathom such a world."

"It is like that in Eldur and Fargelsi. Your crystals can be found anywhere. In Iskalt, they lie in abundance under the snow and within the mountains. And in Myrkur, there are many fire opal mines already."

"Will there be enough to share?" Keir frowned, seeming unable to comprehend just how many crystals she would be able to give him upon their arrival to her homelands.

"Plenty for all of Lenya, and still more for Myrkurians. They use the opals for trade. The other kingdoms use them because they are pretty. We won't miss what isn't much use to us and so vital for our new friends and allies."

Keir shook his head with a smile. "I still find it hard to believe such a place exists."

"You will see it for yourself soon."

"But first we must travel to the Grima palace. A place that will not likely welcome me with open arms."

Tierney and Keir followed the soldiers leading them along the dusty roads through the forests they began to leave behind. Smoky skies opened up before them across a wide-open terrain of stunted shrubs and yellowed grasslands.

"You will arrive at the palace with their queen as your ally." Tierney pulled a scarf over her face to shield her from the smoke. "They will accept you." Tierney frowned as they left the road, crossing the dry grasslands to higher ground. "Are we stopping already? There is still daylight left."

"The sun has set, Tia." Keir smiled. "You are seeing the lights of the burning plains. We could travel for another hour or two by the light of the plains, but that would put us closer to wolfhound territory at their peak hunting hours."

"Looks like a lovely place for a camp." She grinned, nudging her horse up the incline to the flat-topped butte, where they could better see their surroundings.

"There is a campsite here we frequent when traveling this way. It won't take long before we have a fire and hot food."

"And the first of many hard beds on the ground." Tierney rubbed her lower back, eager to get out of the saddle and walk around, stretching her legs.

In no time at all, Tierney sat beside Gulliver on an aged log that had seen many a campfire, stuffing her face with the roasted game and hard bread. On the trip to Vondur, she'd lamented the bland food they had on the trail. Now, after months of spicy foods, it was heaven.

"Hungry?" Keir laughed as he sat on the ground beside her.

Tierney wiped meat juice off her chin and went back for her last bite. "Starving."

"I'm going back for seconds." Gulliver left them by the low burning fire to join the soldiers still carving up the pair of fianna they'd hunted before they made camp. They were smoking a portion of the meat to bring with them. The rest, they would have for breakfast.

"No surprise there." Keir stirred the dying embers with a charred branch, coaxing the coals back to life.

Tierney slipped from her seat on the log to sit beside him on the ground.

"We made good progress today." Keir sat back, leaning against the log and draping his arm around her.

She scooted closer to his side, happy the others had made themselves scarce. Donal was exhausted from the trek and was already asleep. Bronagh had gone with Gulliver and was now making her own bed under the stars. The young queen had come a long way since she left the comfort of her palace.

"How long until we arrive at the border?" Tierney stared up at the stars shining bright overhead. She wondered if they were the same stars that shone down on Iskalt.

"If we ride hard tomorrow, we should reach the border by nightfall." Keir ran a hand over her hair, and his touch sent a shiver through her. "And another few days to reach the palace."

"And then, we set sail." She sighed, smiling to herself. For at least a few days, she could snuggle next to Keir under the stars and dream about home.

CHAPTER THIRTY-ONE

TIERNEY

"Do we even know if we're on the right road at this point?" Tierney squinted, trying to see through the haze of smoke. But the acrid air just made her eyes water and burn.

"We're nearing the palace." Bronagh adjusted the scrap of fabric she'd torn from her dress to cover her face. Sooty tears leaked from her red rimmed eyes. "We should reach the village soon. The fresh sea breezes should clear away this smoke and we'll be able to breathe easier."

Tierney shared a worried look with Keir. If the smoke from the fire plains had reached the main road to the Grima palace, what might they find when they arrived?

Far to the east, churning black smoke billowed along the horizon above the intense flames of the encroaching fire plains. Tierney didn't want to know what homes and villages once occupied the lands along the road they now followed. The thought of what those poor people were going through was just too much. Her palms itched with the faint stirrings of magic inside her. Magic that still lay dormant.

"You can't dwell on what-ifs, Tia." Gulliver rode quietly beside her.

"I don't know what you mean." She tore her gaze away from the fires and focused on what little of the road she could spot. It was like traveling through the worst blizzard she could remember back home. They couldn't see beyond their horses' next steps. And given the rapid expansion of the vatlands, it left her on high alert for dangers they couldn't sense.

"Yes, you do." He pulled his hood low over his eyes to protect them from the sting of the smoke. "You're thinking if you had your magic, you could do something to protect these people. But you don't have your magic, so it isn't healthy to think of things that might have been."

"If you tell me to focus on the solution and not the problem, I'm going to scream."

"I didn't say it."

"You were thinking it."

"So were you, or you wouldn't have said it."

"You two bicker like an old married couple." Keir shook his head at them.

"You take that back, Keir Dagnan!" Tierney growled at him.

"That was so rude, even for you." Gulliver gave him a disgusted look.

"I've found it best to just ignore their odd little relationship." Veren's voice was muffled through the many layers of his face coverings. He'd claimed the smoke would do untold damage to his skin if he wasn't extremely careful.

"Is that ..." Bronagh pointed ahead. "What's burning?" She turned to her brother riding along in his litter beside her.

Donal propped himself up to get a better look. "It looks like the stairway from the palace to the village is burning."

"The stairs are cut right into the mountain. It's all stone." Bronagh squinted to get a better look.

"Can stone burn?" Gulliver asked.

"It's ... glowing," Keir said. "Like metal under a blacksmith's hammer."

"Have the plains reached this far already?" Bronagh sucked in a breath as she dug her heels into her horse's sides.

Tierney urged her mount to follow as they rushed headlong down the road through the thick churning smoke.

"Tia, wait!" Keir called behind her, but she wouldn't leave Bronagh to this discovery all on her own.

As they neared the village, the smoke thinned and the fresh sea air filled Tierney's lungs. The charred smell of recently dead things still stung her nose, but the unmistakable ocean air cleared her mind.

"It's gone." Bronagh pulled her horse to a stop at the edge of the village. At least, what was left of it. "Where is everyone?"

Tierney's gaze followed the orange glow of the stairway that led up to the queen's palace among the mountains above.

"It's burning!" Veren shouted in alarm.

"No." Tierney frowned up at the palace and the mountain it sat on. "It's ... melting." The rambling roof of the mountain fortress oozed toward the ground, the walls collapsing in on themselves. The mountain itself, once whitecapped with snow,

now seemed to slump in defeat. "I didn't know stone *could* melt." She turned, catching Veren's horrified expression.

"The docks!" Veren kicked his mare into a gallop, circling the heat radiating from the ruined village. Tierney and the others followed.

The foul ruins belched sulfurous clouds of putrid smoke, and Tierney clutched her face covering against her nose. Dead and rotting gulls lay scattered along the rocky shores, where they fell from the skies in their retreat. Dead fish and charred seaweed churned in the shallows, steam billowing up from the boiling surf.

They made their way across the rocky shoals around the village and down to the docks. Tierney came to a dead halt beside Veren. She let out a strangled sob, her hand covering her mouth. Soul shattering fear shot through her, piercing her heart and stealing her breath.

Veren sat silently atop his horse, his face gone white with shock. "We've lost, Tia."

"No." She stubbornly shook her head, refusing to accept the defeat staring her in the face. "We will find another way. We will see our home again."

Keir guided his horse to stand beside hers, his shoulders slumped and his eyes smoldering like the fires they had no chance against.

"We will die along with every single Lenyan before that happens." Veren turned toward her. "We don't have time to build another ship."

Tierney watched the white smoke billowing into the air above the ship that should have saved them all. The fire still smoldered in places, long after it had consumed the massive vessel and reduced it to nothing more than a mountain of charred wood and ash sitting atop the water.

The warmth of Keir's hand closing around hers surprised

her, but it gave her strength too. Gripping his hand, she took a deep breath. "I will never stop fighting for Lenya and the hope of returning to my home someday. And neither will you." Tierney released Keir's hand and guided her horse back toward the village, determined to have enough hope for them all.

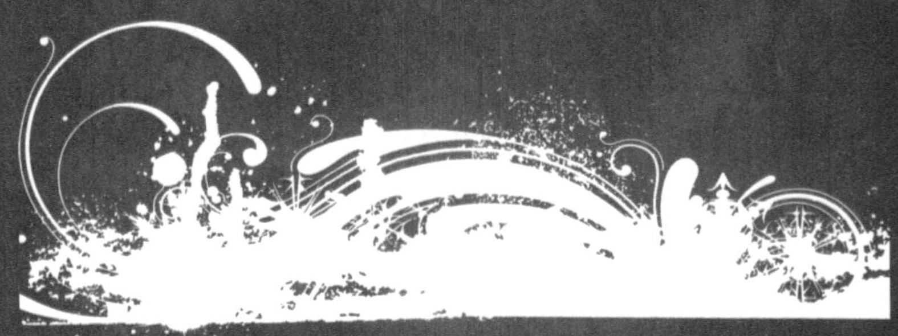

EPILOGUE
TOBY

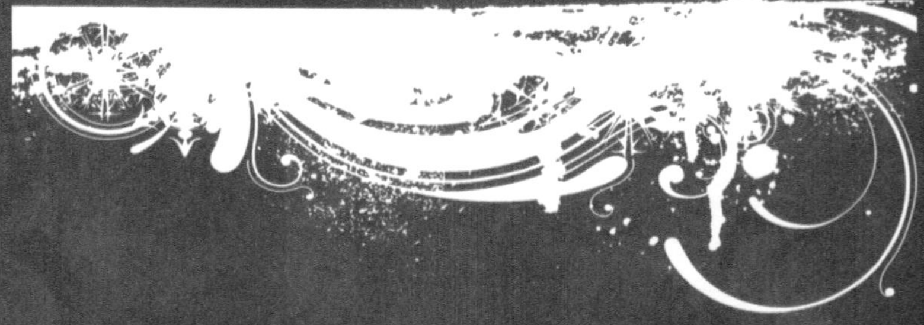

"Toby, what's wrong?" Logan reached across the library table for his hand. "You've gone white as the Iskalt snow."

Coughing, Toby gripped his intended's hand. He couldn't catch his breath. "Something's wrong." He launched from his chair and out the front door of the library just in time to lose his breakfast over the porch railing.

"Are you sick?" Logan came up behind him, checking his forehead for a fever. "You've been working too hard, and this desert heat isn't helping."

"It's not me." Toby shook his head, sucking in a deep breath and wrinkling his nose. "Can't you smell that? Ugh, it's awful." He waved a hand in front of his face. "It's like dead fish ... and sulfur."

"I don't smell anything. Are you sure you're not having an apoplexy?"

"No, I'm not having a stroke." Toby took the steps down to the street and turned toward the exit of Aghadoon. He needed to see the fire plains.

"What's happening?" His mom stood from her rocking chair on the porch of the house the king and queen were staying in.

"Have you found something, Toby?" His dad came to join them, his mom following close behind.

Toby shook his head, still trying to rid himself of that putrid smell.

Logan murmured behind him with Toby's mother as he darted through the ancient pillars and into the desert sands of Eldur.

For weeks, they had studied everything the library had revealed to them concerning the kingdom of Lenya and the birth of the vatlands. And still, they had no way of reaching his sister across the burning lands. Nothing they tried seemed to work. Magic was failing them.

"She's scared." Toby stopped when the intense heat of the fire plains became too much for him to bear.

"Come back away from the edge, Toby," his mother begged. "It's too hot."

"Tia needs me." He took another step toward his twin. "She's scared." He turned toward his parents, surprised to see Logan standing beside him, clutching his hand.

Sweat beaded Logan's brow, but it evaporated before he could wipe it away. His sun-browned face blistered in the shimmering heat of his homeland. Prince of Eldur and raised among the desert sands, the fire plains were even too much for him.

"Go, it's too dangerous." Toby squeezed his hand.

Logan shook his head. "I go where you go."

Turning back toward his sister, Toby sighed. "She's running out of time."

Will Tia manage to get to Iskalt in time to save Lenya? Find out in the conclusion to her story, Fae's Return. Coming June, 2021!

About Melissa

Melissa A. Craven is an Amazon bestselling author of Young Adult Contemporary Fiction and YA Fantasy (her Contemporary fans will know her as Ann Maree Craven). Her books focus on strong female protagonists who aren't always perfect, but they find their inner strength along the way. Melissa's novels appeal to audiences of all ages and fans of almost any genre. She believes in stories that make you think and she loves playing with foreshadowing, leaving clues and hints for the careful reader.

Melissa draws inspiration from her background in architecture and interior design to help her with the small details in world building and scene settings. (Her degree in fine art also comes in handy.) She is a diehard introvert with a wicked sense of humor and a tendency for hermit-like behavior. (Seriously, she gets cranky if she has to put on anything other than yoga pants and t-shirts!)

Melissa enjoys editing almost as much as she enjoys writing, which makes her an absolute weirdo among her peers. Her favorite pastime is sitting on her porch when the weather is nice with her two dogs, Fynlee and Nahla, reading from her massive TBR pile and dreaming up new stories.

Visit Melissa at Melissaacraven.com for more information about her newest series and discover exclusive content.

Join Melissa and Michelle's Facebook Group: Search for Melissa and Michelle's Fantasy Book Warriors

Follow Michelle and Melissa on TikTok at
@ATaleOfTwoAuthors

About M. Lynn

Michelle MacQueen is a USA Today bestselling author of love. Yes, love. Whether it be YA romance, NA romance, or fantasy romance (Under M. Lynn), she loves to make readers swoon.

The great loves of her life to this point are two tiny blond creatures who call her "aunt" and proclaim her books to be "boring books" for their lack of pictures. Yet, somehow, she still manages to love them more than chocolate.

When she's not sharing her inexhaustible wisdom with her niece and nephew, Michelle is usually lounging in her ridiculously large bean bag chair creating worlds and characters that remind her to smile every day - even when a feisty five-year-old is telling her just how much she doesn't know.

See more from M. Lynn and sign up
to receive updates and deals!
michellelynnauthor.com

Join Melissa and Michelle's Facebook Group:
Search for Melissa and Michelle's Fantasy Book Warriors

Follow Michelle and Melissa on TikTok
@ATaleOfTwoAuthors

www.ingramcontent.com/pod-product-compliance
Lightning Source LLC
Chambersburg PA
CBHW030528310726
48979CB00010B/1840/J
9781970052879